DR. S. K. BURKMAN

Wings and Wounds

The Dragon Doc Tales: Book 1

First published by Snapdragon Publishing Company, LLC 2022

First edition

ISBN: 979-8-9870590-7-4

Editing by Stacey Goitia
Illustration by J. M. Burkman

This book was professionally typeset on Reedsy.
Find out more at reedsy.com

The Dragon Doc Tales Series is dedicated to veterinarians the world over. To my colleagues who struggle to persevere in a profession that is often as overwhelming and heartbreaking as it is uplifting and gratifying, I see you. Your patients are grateful to you, and so am I.

Contents

1

The Mountain

When I graduated from veterinary school with much celebration and relief, I expected to be an ordinary veterinarian. Of course I would practice at a typical clinic, and I'd see normal patients like dogs and cats; maybe even ferrets, rabbits, or rodents if I felt especially brave. In hindsight, I suppose "ordinary" is overrated. After all, extraordinary things happen when one is willing to let go of the ordinary, and my career has certainly been extraordinary. So, what changed? Well, it all started when I almost died on a mountain.

The story is lengthy, but let me explain. Many years ago, on a much-needed day off from work, I climbed Humphreys Peak, Arizona's highest mountain. By mountaineering standards, Humphreys was not terribly tall; the peak stood just over 12,600 feet in elevation. This imposing, broad uplift of rock and soil was flanked with robes of pine, fir, spruce, and aspen, often crowned with snow despite occupying a state known for heat and cacti. Prior to that excursion, I summited several other mountains, including some at much higher elevations,

1

but I was not properly acclimated for this climb.

"Jordyn, are you okay?" my husband inquired as we rested, seated on a log about three miles up the trail. Thoughtfully, he looked over my pallid face. "You look a little off."

"Mmmm," I answered vaguely, tracing my fingertips over the peeling tendrils of bark next to my knee, absently holding the remains of a half-eaten granola bar in my other hand. "I'm fine. Just a bit of a headache."

"Why, because you got up at four this morning and went to bed at, what, eleven last night?" Jon asked, his voice laced with judgment.

Actually, I'd fallen asleep considerably after midnight, but Jon didn't need to know that. "Oh, probably. I don't think it's a migraine; it's not that bad. Don't worry. I'll be okay," I insisted. My stomach was growing increasingly queasy from the headache, and though I should have been hungry from the exertion, I didn't feel like eating. Folding the granola bar packaging over onto itself, I stuffed it back into my pack.

If I'd been honest with myself and Jon, I knew better. Acute Mountain Sickness (AMS) or "altitude sickness" classically began with a headache and nausea, and I failed to recognize or acknowledge that my symptoms matched this exactly. Instead of descending, I stupidly kept climbing, which was exactly what a person with AMS was NOT supposed to do. I supposed one could more kindly call it stubbornness rather than stupidity, but regardless, I made a grave mistake. Determined to reach the summit, I insisted that we continue on.

"Are you sure you're okay?" Jon repeated at the summit, suspiciously eyeing my sickly, greenish face.

"No, I'm not," I admitted. "This has turned into one of the

worst headaches I've ever had. Makes it hard to enjoy the view."

That time, I was honest. On that rare, clear, and cloudless day, the vista stretched for many miles in all directions. Seated next to a giant, squarish boulder, fruitlessly trying to avoid the harsh sun overhead, I squinted miserably at the Hopi Mesas and Grand Canyon to the north. Oak Creek Canyon carved a fissure in the edge of the Mogollan rim directly behind me. Home was beyond that spectacular gorge, too far away to be of any comfort.

Small, white-throated birds swooped low overhead. *"Screeeee! Screeeee!"* they shrieked. My head thrummed in objection to each harsh cry and my mood deteriorated. Closing my eyes, I leaned forward and rested my face in my hands, pressing firmly over my eyes, and willing the pain to go away. I didn't want to see any more of the magnificent view. I wanted to get off the mountain. "I'm really not feeling great. Let's go."

As we later learned, I was rapidly developing the more complicated and dangerous form of altitude sickness called High Altitude Cerebral Edema (HACE). My brain tissue swelled and started to short-circuit. My feet kept going, but I began to slow down as my sense of balance faltered. My head throbbed ferociously with each step, as though a hatchet were hitting my skull.

Just below timberline, I ventured away from the trail and Jon to answer the call of nature. A gentle rain began to fall. I sat down on a log, facing a huge expanse of the roots of a fallen tree that stretched tortuously over twelve feet in diameter. Most of the dirt and rocks had washed away, exposing twisted brown roots that had not yet weathered to grey. The tree had toppled recently enough that lingering plant oils glistened softly in the rain, giving the gnarled roots an iridescent sheen in the dim, dappled light.

My head pounded relentlessly, but the muffled quiet and peaceful rainfall beneath the trees soothed the pain somewhat. I lifted my eyes to watch the low, grey clouds scudding rapidly eastward through a gap in the leafy canopy, but soon the branches began to spin sickeningly around the swirling clouds, as though I were staring into a tornado's eye. Swaying and gripping the log tightly to keep from falling, I returned my gaze to the fallen tree in front of me until the dizziness subsided, ironically finding stability in the chaotic tangle of roots. *Whoa. Let's not do that again.* I was staring absently at the root ball, my eyes adjusting to the half-light, when I realized they weren't only roots. Something moved. My swollen and aching brain took a minute to really see it… a dragon lay coiled beneath and between the roots. She was gorgeous.

The dragon's diamond-shaped scales and leathery wings, folded snugly against her sides, shone with an iridescent brown that was nearly indistinguishable from the roots that twisted chaotically around her. Brown spikes crowned her head, spine, and tail, which was curled tightly against her wing. A single pair of horns curled gracefully backward from the crown of her head and disappeared into the snarl of roots overhead. The creature was so thoroughly intertwined that I could barely discern where the tree roots stopped and the dragon began. Her camouflage skills were amazing. *No wonder we humans never see these creatures.* Only her spiked wing tip, shifting slightly in position, had attracted my attention.

I sat there for a moment, frozen in awe. The sensible, rational part of my brain blared alarm bells, trying to tell me that clearly, something was terribly wrong. *WOOP WOOP WOOP! YOU ARE REALLY MESSED UP IF YOU'RE SEEING A DRAGON! WOOP WOOP WOOP!*

The same bit of my brain warned me not to go anywhere near the creature because surely, she was dangerous. *But if she doesn't exist, how could she possibly be dangerous?* The logical part of my brain insisted that nothing was right or safe about the situation, but I wasn't listening to logic or reason. That's what happens when your brain swells: things that don't make any sense start to make sense. So I kept staring at the dragon, who warily returned my stare with one emerald-green eye through a gap in the roots. I shifted to my left to see better, revealing more of her head, a glimpse of her other eye, and one wing. The dragon seemed feminine, though I didn't know what gave me that impression, nor if it was correct. An ugly, red patch caught my eye, and I scrutinized the small portion of wing I could see. Despite my impaired state, I quickly recognized the problem: the dragon was wounded.

For a veterinarian, nothing is more gratifying than treating a sick or injured animal and making them healthy again. That's what we live for. That's why we take critically ill patients home to watch them overnight when there's no twenty-four hour hospital available, or bottle raise a sick, orphaned kitten, or spend a Sunday off the clock amputating a pup's fractured leg so she can be adopted instead of euthanized. That's how we find ourselves trying to help injured stray dogs or cats, even when we're at high risk for injury ourselves. And that's why I couldn't walk away from the dragon. *I can't just leave. I have to help her.*

The creature tensed and drew her wings tighter to her sides, surprised to see a human approaching. Crouching, I squeezed my shoulders into the fallen tree's labyrinth and crawled toward the dragon, bending and breaking some of the smaller roots with a soft *snap* to make room. My backpack scraped and caught, and more roots broke as I pulled it free. A pungent, musky scent filled my nostrils as I neared the dragon, who apprehensively watched me advance through the maze of roots but made no attempt to flee or fight. She was tense and guarded but didn't protest when I handled her wing, gently touching the scaly hide and thick membrane surrounding the wound. Her hide felt rugged and rough under my fingers, like boot leather crossed with sandpaper. A nasty laceration, about nine or ten inches long, marred her beautiful wing, exposing a portion of the bone deep within. The exposed flesh and surrounding membrane were swollen, desiccated, and an angry, dark red. The wound smelled foul, and my nose wrinkled. *So awful! She has to have been wounded for days for the tissue to look and smell this bad.*

Drops of rainwater dripped coldly onto to the back of my neck as I contemplated the dragon's injury. The sound of the breeze and patter of raindrops were muted beneath the thick tangle of roots, and the dragon made no sound other than the quiet sigh of inhalation and exhalation as her wing softly rose and fell beneath my hands. Several small scars blemished other parts of her wing, and a long-healed hole gaped through the wing membrane not far from the wound, suggesting that this was far from her first injury. The scars gave her a tattered, battle-worn appearance. Obviously, she'd managed to heal multiple old wounds on her own, but this injury appeared to be much more severe and at risk of disabling her ability to fly. *A dragon that can't fly... That's not good at all. This could easily kill her.* The creature must have been extraordinarily rare

— after all, I'd never seen or heard of one outside of fantasy stories — so her death would have been a tragedy.

My short-circuiting, swollen brain defaulted to work mode, and I shrugged out of my pack, twisting and struggling as I yanked it forward, snapping more roots in the process. My head throbbed worse with the effort, but I obstinately ignored it. *No. Go away. I have work to do.* The pack finally yielded, and I retrieved my first aid kit from its pocket. Carefully, I unzipped the kit and propped it open across the roots to my right. *There, I even have an instrument stand.* I scrubbed the laceration with chlorhexidine, an antiseptic. Even though chlorhexidine stings, the dragon didn't flinch. But she didn't extend her wing any closer to me, either. She didn't seem to know quite what to make of this, but she evidently did not perceive me as a threat. I dried the wound with gauze and liberally applied the contents of four or five packets of antibiotic ointment.

"I hope that does the trick, but the infection could get worse," I said to the dragon as I closed the first aid kit over the wads of gauze and torn packets. "I hope not. If you were at my clinic, I'd prescribe oral antibiotics. But I don't carry those around in my pack." The dragon gazed at me intently with a captivating, emerald-green eye neatly framed between roots angled in a diamond shape. *A diamond to match her scales. That's cool. And what beautiful eyes.* "I'll call you Emerald. For your eyes. You're magnificent, Emerald, and I hope you heal quickly."

Another wave of dizziness washed over me, and the dragon's eye wavered within its diamond-shaped frame that shifted amorphously, as if underwater. At last, both the eye and its frame settled back to their original positions. The dragon peered at me with a less guarded expression, and instead perhaps… amusement? My forehead pressed painfully into a root, and I realized I'd slumped forward while my vision swam. Nausea rose mercilessly as my head pounded with renewed ferocity, and I swallowed repeatedly as I willed my churning stomach to abate. It reluctantly obeyed to some extent, and settled into a low but steady queasiness.

Shaky and slow, I put away the first aid supplies and crawled in reverse out of the snarled maze, dragging my pack with me and fighting pain and nausea all the way. As I struggled to my feet and slid my arms through the straps of my pack, I think I mumbled a goodbye, but I'm not sure. I also don't recall seeing the dragon as I unsteadily walked away, nor do I remember hearing Jon calling for me with increasing annoyance. The whole memory is fuzzy thanks to the state of my brain, which was worsening by the minute. I do remember feeling a sense of urgency to get back to the trail and Jon, who was no doubt wondering why the hell I was taking so long to pee in the forest.

Navigating the terrain back to the trail took me a minute or two or five, I don't know, more so with everything slick from the rain. Initially, I was excited to tell my husband what happened. A person doesn't get to see a dragon in the wild every day, much less do some wound care for one. But as I scrambled over logs and small boulders, concentrating extra hard to keep my footing since my brain didn't quite know where my limbs were, my mind pushed the memory of the dragon somewhere into a side compartment to focus on staying conscious. And alive.

"That took forever," my husband chided as I emerged from the trees. His impatience turned to fear as I wobbled toward him with vacant eyes. "What's wrong?" he demanded in a panicked voice. "Why are you walking like that?"

"My head just really hurts. I'm okay," I insisted unconvincingly. "We just need to get down the mountain."

Quite reasonably, Jon did not believe that I was "okay." But he agreed that we needed to get off the mountain, and fast. He had no idea what was going on, only that I was walking like a drunken toddler, definitely not in my right mind, and kept insisting on stopping to take a "nap" every hundred feet or so. Had I been on my own, I would have curled up for a "nap" in a nice pine needle bed under a tree, would have fallen unconscious, and would likely have never awoken.

Thanks to Jon's tenacity (for which he deserved an award), I did get off the mountain almost entirely on my own two feet. We encountered a handful of hikers during our descent, none of which I remembered later. Jon asked each one if they were a doctor, or nurse, or paramedic, or possessed any medical training whatsoever. No one did. So, Jon did the only things he could do: he urged me on, pleading and chastising in turns when I resisted. He pulled me to my feet whenever I stopped for a "nap," and he forced me to keep going as I became increasingly incoherent and weak. And when I collapsed, unconscious, fifty feet from the parking lot, he carried me.

My recollection of the descent is a vague haze of pain and confusion. Remembering that day, my mind delivers tangled, disordered vignettes of memories: bewildered, I stared at the hospital ID band and mass of tape over the intravenous catheter in my arm; I faded in and out of consciousness in the car; I snapped awake and realized I was inside the claustrophobic CT machine; a nurse expertly slid a trash receptacle in front of me barely in time as I vomited uncontrollably; a physician calmly recited medications, morphine, and furosemide, a diuretic… and eventually, like the sun dawning to a new day, I was back in my right mind.

I remembered nothing of the dragon until Jon drove me home from the hospital at four in the morning, both of us completely spent from the ordeal. Now that we understood what had happened to me, we were discussing altitude sickness, and my husband brought up Jon Krakauer's book *Into Thin Air*. The book described Acute Mountain Sickness, including a bit of information on HACE and its counterpart, High Altitude Pulmonary Edema (HAPE). Krakauer listed hallucinations as one of the effects of HACE, and my husband mentioned this.

The term 'hallucination' unlocked my memory of the dragon, and details came flooding back as though I'd suddenly recalled a long-forgotten fairy tale. Sitting bolt upright, I stared wide-eyed at Jon. "Oh!" I gasped. "The DRAGON!"

My poor husband screeched the car to a full stop and gaped at me with concern and bewilderment. "Jordyn… do you… do you need to go back to the ER?!" he stammered.

Laughing, I told him no, I just remembered a hallucination I had on the mountain. The roots of a fallen tree had morphed into a dragon. What a fantastic illusion! The memory delighted me, however Jon was too shaken to be amused.

Three frenetic days later, I finally cleaned out my backpack and found the stained gauze and empty ointment packets. *What on earth did I do with those?* Because the dragon was pure fiction, of course. Puzzled, I carried the spent first aid supplies toward the kitchen trash, looking for my husband along the way. I found him seated at the counter, eating tortilla chips with guacamole as he read a magazine.

"Jon, were either of us injured on Humphreys?"

"You mean besides your brain breaking down?" he asked

incredulously.

"Ha, ha, very funny," I replied. "No, I mean physically injured? You didn't cut yourself, did you?"

"No, why?" he asked through a mouthful of chips.

"Huh," I said, mystified. "I found some gauze and things in my pack that I used for something. See, look." I opened my hands to reveal their contents.

Jon recoiled from the wads of soiled gauze. "Gross!" he exclaimed, grimacing. "Not while I'm eating! That stinks, too. Don't throw it away in the kitchen! Take it outside."

"Okay, okay, fine," I retorted. "I'll put it in the trash cart. Do you know where I used this stuff though? It had to have been somewhere on Humphreys, but I don't remember where or why."

"No idea," Jon huffed. "Please get that stuff out of here."

Though I didn't want to believe it, I remembered exactly where I'd put the medical supplies to use. But for the time being, the first aid materials remained a mystery, and the dragon remained a figment of my imagination.

My colleagues, coworkers, and friends thought the tale of my hallucination was hilarious. Once I'd sufficiently recovered, I found humor in the story as well. My misadventure became the main source of entertainment at our next staff meeting, and everyone I knew recounted the story over and over. I happily repeated the tale numerous times myself. After my harsh lesson on the mountain, I was willing to indulge in self-deprecating humor and caution others about altitude sickness in the process. My audiences were invariably amused by the dragon, and so was I.

Amused, that is, until the very same dragon turned up at my veterinary clinic a week and a half later.

2

The Window

My absolute worst habit was staying late after work. I had been out of school for less than two years, and the skill of finishing records in a timely manner still eluded me (I've never completely mastered this). Also, complicated internal medicine cases intrigued me, but they sometimes perplexed me to the point of obsession. Therefore, long after everyone else had left the clinic, I'd typically be bent over my battle-worn desk, furiously writing charts or studying textbooks and journal articles, filling in the puzzle pieces to work out what was going on with a complicated case.

The week after "the incident" on Humphreys Peak, after the bruising on my arm from the intravenous catheter had faded, I sat at my desk late one evening, engrossed in writing records. In the middle of a sentence, the back of my neck tingled as I was overwhelmed by a distinctly unpleasant feeling. I sensed that someone or something was watching me, and my arms prickled into goose flesh. The sensation was accurate. I looked up to find a large, green eye surrounded by an array of brown scales staring at me through the tiny office window. It frightened the crap out of me.

My chair crashed over backward as I leapt to my feet, knocking stacks of records and books to the floor in my haste to get the hell away from the eye and whatever it belonged to, because it most certainly was not human (not that I would have been any more comfortable if it had been!). Fifteen seconds and dozens of heartbeats passed before I realized the eye was familiar. I moved to a larger window, yanking aside the dingy, blue curtain to get a better view, not believing what I knew I was going to see. The eye followed me to the other window too, but now it was part of a head, and the head was part of a body. With wings. A dragon head, body, and wings. *THE dragon, the one from Humphreys Peak. Emerald.* I was absolutely dumbfounded.

The dragon and I stared at each other through the window for a minute. She blinked languidly and continued to return my gaze as she briefly lifted her wings, then settled them decisively against her body, as if to indicate she wasn't going anywhere. I couldn't believe it. She was there intentionally, to… see me? Backing uncertainly away from the window, I crept to the front door and finally found the courage to crack it open, acknowledging that I was far braver with a swollen brain than when I was in my right mind. The dragon's head abruptly materialized mere feet from the door, startling me again. I slammed the door shut, heart pounding, then cautiously cracked it open again, peering through the tiny slit. We regarded each other. Her iridescent, deep brown scales shimmered in the glow of the streetlamp as the sun faded. She folded her wing in front of her. Opening the door a bit wider, I squinted in the dim light of dusk. *Oh. So that's why she's here.*

The laceration wasn't healing. It was badly infected, and part of the flesh had died and started to slough away.

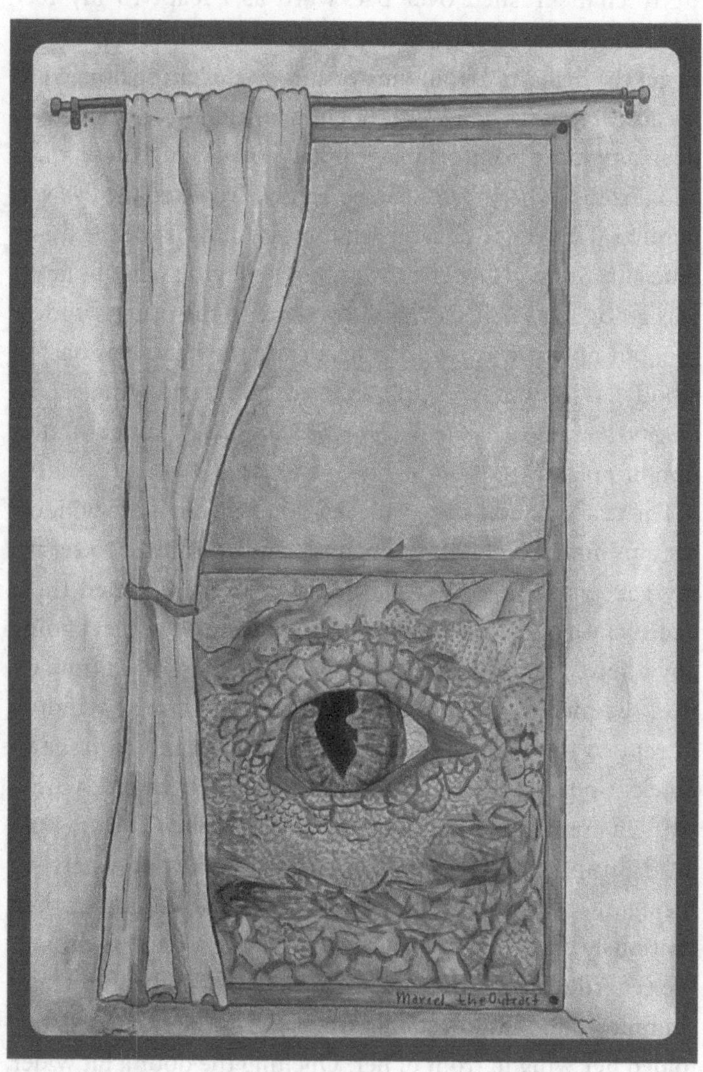

"You need help? That's why you found me? You want me to... treat you?" I asked. The dragon pushed her way through the door into the clinic lobby, her scales scratching grooves into the painted metal door frame as I hurriedly backpedaled in front of her. *I gather that's a yes.*

A maelstrom of thoughts swirled through my head, some along the lines of, *This can't possibly be real;* and *How am I having hallucinations more than a week after my brain swelled?* and *Do I have permanent brain damage?* but also *This is the craziest, coolest thing to ever happen to me, and no one will believe the story;* and also *How did she find me at my clinic over sixty miles from where I first saw her? And Wait, this means I really saw a dragon on the mountain? What is even happening?!*Despite my shock and disbelief, I had to confront the fact that the dragon was truly there, genuinely injured, and her wound looked and smelled terrible. Apparently she thought I could assist her, and I was determined to do so.

Veterinary textbooks didn't have sections on how to treat dragons, of course. But veterinarians were trained to manage multiple kinds of animals. We commonly extrapolated knowledge from one species to another, and the principles of wound care were the same, regardless of species. So I winged it. (No pun intended.)

I stammered something about getting some things from the treatment area, thinking she would stay in the lobby. The clinic was designed only for small animals, not large animals like livestock, and the dragon was bigger than any cow I'd ever met. (Looking back, I'm laughing to think how I would have reacted if a massive, fire-breathing dragon had shown up that night. I'd have been paralyzed in terror.) But she didn't stay in the lobby. She followed me, squeezing through the space behind the front desk and through the doorway into the treatment area, scratching and scraping the walls and desk as she went. A section of molding tore from the door frame and tumbled with a *clank* to the floor. *Oops.* At least she was closer to the supplies I needed.

My hands shook as I tried in vain not to drop things while I grabbed a tray, antiseptic solution, gauze, lidocaine, syringes, and instruments, all the while thinking frantically through a strategy for contending with this dragon and her wound. I threw frequent glances over my shoulder to see her watching curiously as I fumbled drawers and cupboards open and shut and rattled instruments into a tray. My palpable nervousness didn't seem to faze her.

The dying flesh needed debridement. In other words, I needed to rub, scrape, and cut the damaged tissue away to allow the underlying healthy tissue to heal. But debridement would be more painful than just cleaning the wound with antiseptic. *I did that, right? It really happened?* Administering a local anesthetic would sting, too.

How would she react to the discomfort? Would she understand and tolerate it? Or would she react and bite or claw me? *Or hold on, do dragons really breathe fire, and if so, does THIS dragon breathe fire? (Are there more dragons out there?!) Will she let me put a muzzle on? Seems unlikely... could I ask her nicely to wear a muzzle? That seems insulting... do dragons get insulted? Do dragons truly exist or am I out of my mind? Would a muzzle stop a dragon from breathing fire? Do we even HAVE a muzzle that big? Oh never mind, of course not.... And what about after debriding the wound, what then? She needs medications, but how do I prescribe medications for a creature that supposedly exists only in storybooks and movies?*

In the end I gathered what I thought was necessary, took a couple deep breaths, and told her what I needed to do. "Emerald... may I call you that?" I began hesitantly. She returned my gaze without moving. "Well... I don't know how you were injured, but this laceration is infected and necrotic. I need to debride the dead tissue away so it can heal." My voice became less tremulous as I went on, gaining some fortitude as I focused on the task at hand, strange as it was. "I'll administer an anesthetic, but it's going to sting much worse than when I cleaned your wound on the mountain." *Does she understand what I'm telling her? Do I need to explain in simpler, non-medicalese terms? What am I doing talking to a dragon?!*

In response, the dragon shifted her weight, stretching out her injured wing until the laceration was right in front of me. *Okay, then. We're doing this.*

Much later, I realized I inadvertently learned some important lessons that night. Always explain to a dragon what needs to be done to treat them. Even if they don't verbalize it, dragons understand. I'm not convinced they understand the medical terms, but they seem to understand the intent. Gain their confidence and permission to treat, and never try to force anything — well, for the adults anyway; hatchlings are a different story. Most importantly, don't even bother with a muzzle.

Ultimately, I treated the dragon's wound exactly like I would a large dog's, only not sedated, huge, with scales and wings, and possibly the ability to instantly barbecue me well-done if her mood changed. And no veterinary technician was there to assist, or to convince me this was really happening or not.

Eventually, I debrided the tissue to my satisfaction, although

I ruined two pairs of surgical scissors in the process, finding dragon flesh to be amazingly tough. Although, if I had ever contemplated it, that's exactly what I would have imagined dragon flesh to be like. She never flinched from the pain.

I thought about bandaging the wound and said as much to her, although I wasn't sure how I would bandage a dragon's wing securely enough to stay in place. The dragon pulled her wing away from me. *All right, I suppose that means no bandage.*

Healing the wound would require further intervention, however. She needed medication. Figuring this out was nearly as difficult as debriding the wound. I couldn't decide whether to prescribe as if she was a reptile, befitting her scaly hide, or birds, since her wing structure most resembled those creatures. In addition, her gait and limb conformation reminded me most of mammals. What if she were none of the above? Various types of medications were effective and tolerable for different species of animals, but which drugs would work for her? After deliberating, I chose an antibiotic that worked on a broad range of species, and I made a wild guess on the dose after estimating her weight. I also chose an anti-inflammatory pain medication that I simply hoped would help and not hurt.

A full 250 count bottle of enrofloxacin and a 180 count bottle of carprofen sat on the pharmacy shelf. I took both and held the bottles in front of her. "You need to take these for the wound to heal. Can you swallow twenty of these" — I shook a bottle — "every day, once a day, until the bottle is empty? This is for infection. They're even flavored… beef-flavored, I think. Do you eat cows?" The dragon stared at me with skepticism, I thought, and perhaps amusement.

Waving the other bottle, I forged on. "And this reduces

inflammation and pain. Even if your wing isn't that painful, reducing the inflammation helps the wound heal. Can you swallow twelve of these, twice a day? They're flavored, too, although I'm not sure what the flavor is, or if that even matters to you. Also I'm not sure how easily your stomach gets upset, but it's probably best if you eat something when you take the pills." Uncomfortable visions of her snacking on a human limb flashed through my mind, and I winced.

"Since it's not bandaged, keep the wound clean and dry. Don't… lick or chew at the wound? I'm not sure if that's something dragons do."

Emerald's bright, green eyes narrowed as she tilted her head. She regarded me for a moment, then clutched both bottles of pills in one massive claw, turned and squeezed back into the lobby (more molding from the doorway clattered to the floor) and out the front door, and was gone. I rushed to the door to watch her depart. The moon had not yet risen, and the night was quite dark, illuminated only by the single streetlamp near the parking lot. For a brief moment, I vaguely heard her vast wings flapping from the direction of a patch in the sky that was darker than night, then she was nowhere to be seen or heard.

Relieved and exhausted, I closed the clinic door and locked the deadbolt, then turned and slumped against the door, completely spent. An earthy but acrid, skunky scent hung in the air, all the more obvious after I'd had a breath of fresh air. I looked around, taking in the damage and disarray with a growing sense of dread. Claw marks blemished the lobby floor. Chunks of molding lay by the treatment room door, which stood at a slightly crooked angle. Rousing myself from my resting place, I made my way to the treatment area, noting with a twinge of panic that the bottom door hinge was bent. Not knowing what to do with the broken molding pieces, I nudged them out of the way with my shoe. An array of spattered blood across the floor accosted me as I entered the treatment room. More blood speckled the steel treatment table, and bloodied instruments were strewn haphazardly across the tabletop. The surgical trash bucket teemed with foul dragon flesh intermingled with broken instruments and soiled gauze. I nervously rubbed at the fresh blister on my thumb from struggling to debride the tough tissue. *How on earth will I explain what happened tonight?*

In a frenzy, I cleaned and tidied what I could. With shaking hands, I washed and dried the surgical instruments, hastily packaged them into autoclave pouches, haphazardly stacked them in the autoclave, and started the quickest sterilization cycle. Cupboard doors slammed with a *thunk* as I hurriedly put away supplies and dropped syringe needles into the sharps container with a *plink*. Scrubbing and mopping the blood spatters nearly sent me over the edge, since I noticed "one more spot" at least twenty times before I forced myself to quit. After fruitlessly scouring the lobby floor for ten minutes, I resigned myself to the fact that the claw marks were there to stay. The damaged door hinge and molding would also have to wait. Holding the fetid trash bag at arm's length and glancing around nervously as I dashed to the dumpster, I hurriedly disposed of the flesh and broken instruments.

After frantically debating what to do about the bottles of drugs, I decided to enter them into the computer under my own "first aid" account, supposedly to keep on hand at home. I would have a tough time explaining why I needed huge bottles of enrofloxacin and carprofen at home for my nowhere near dragon-sized cats, but that would be easier than trying to explain why vast quantities of drugs had mysteriously disappeared off the shelf, or worse yet, that I had dispensed them to a dragon. Feeling like I'd done my best to contain the mess, and yet couldn't possibly have done enough, I finally drove home.

My husband was accustomed to me staying late at work, but he questioned why I was later than usual. "What kept you so late— *Eww!* Jordyn, how the hell did you get so bloody and stinky? Did you wrestle a javelina or something?" He meant the wild peccaries that roamed the American Southwest, known for their foul odor as much as their ability to inflict serious injury.

"Well, I, uh… okay. Sit down, I need to tell you a story." I told him the truth. But here's the thing… for entertainment, I frequently told Jon tall tales (and still do). So whenever I told him a questionable (or at least odd) story, he never quite knew whether to believe me. It kept the mystery and romance alive, I suppose.

He didn't believe me.

The next morning, I drove to work with growing trepidation about the state of the dragon-damaged veterinary clinic. But my boss, the owner, was never much motivated to invest time and money repairing whatever fell apart around the old and somewhat dilapidated building. Clients sometimes complained about the appearance of the clinic, but ours was the only veterinary hospital in the entire valley. People could either bring their pets to us or drive half an hour to our nearest competitor. My boss counted on people avoiding the drive, and they frequently proved him right, often enough to keep us very busy. Consequently, he ignored most things that broke or fell apart. Staff grumbled about it, but there wasn't much they could do.

Early in my employment there, the monsoon rains began, and I discovered the roof leaked directly over my desk, and apparently had for years. When I realized that my boss was utterly disinterested in repairing it, I took my raincoat and rubber ducky to work and sat at my desk, singing bathtub songs as water dripped onto my raincoat hood while I wrote records. Tired of my antics, my boss finally fixed the roof. That's how obnoxious we had to be, as employees, to get anything repaired.

As a result, nothing much became of the dragon's mayhem. The moment I walked into the building that next morning, concentrating hard to conceal my apprehension, I noticed the lingering scent of the dragon. It smelled like moss, soil, and trees, and also burnt coal, musk, a bit of skunk, and…I wasn't even sure what else. Surely someone else would notice the odor, I thought, but no one mentioned anything if they did. I overheard the receptionist complaining as she tried in vain to scrub the black claw marks out of the lobby floor. She gave up, and I heard nothing more about it. The treatment room door was perpetually propped open, and no one noticed the bent hinge for months. The jagged chunks of molding languished in the corner where I'd optimistically propped them. Someone eventually discarded them. The inventory tech was puzzled by the rapid depletion of medications, but she reordered them without raising any suspicions. I seemed to be the only doctor who missed the broken Mayo scissors; one of them had been among my favorite instruments.

My sense of reality was the only thing that sustained serious harm. The dragon's visit made me question whether anything

I'd ever known or been taught was factual, and it left me truly shaken and disoriented. Eventually I would receive answers and solutions to my questions and doubts, and in time I would reconcile with this "new normal." Though the answers I sought came in the form of more dragons.

3

Revisited

Three months had passed since the dragon from the mountain visited me at the veterinary clinic. I hadn't said a word to anyone at work about what happened that night. Who would have believed me? I could barely accept that it happened myself, although there was plenty of evidence that it had.

The blister from debriding tough dragon flesh had healed, but I often rubbed that spot on my thumb in nervousness or contemplation. Sometimes I brought up my account in the computer to see the entries for the drugs the dragon had taken, and thought of her wrapping her giant claw around both bottles before she disappeared into the night. And of course, the molding around the treatment room door was still broken. At least the claw marks in the lobby floor had faded after plenty of foot traffic and countless rounds with a mop.

Thoughts about how the dragon had fared endlessly looped through my head while I simultaneously mused whether I had gone insane. *How is Emerald doing? Did the medications work? Did she experience any side effects? Did the wing heal okay?*

Did she die? Should I check myself into a psychiatric ward this afternoon?

In particular, I was worried about the anti-inflammatory pain medication I'd sent with her. Some species didn't tolerate NSAIDs well. What if the drug damaged her kidneys (if dragons had kidneys)? *I should have told her to stop taking it if her stomach got upset or she vomited... if dragons are even able to vomit.* The first and foremost part of the Veterinary Oath was "do no harm," and I fretted whether I might have crossed a line.

This whole dragon thing unnerved me, but I was fascinated nonetheless. I started consuming books and movies about dragons, devouring everything I could find on the legends of dragons, the beliefs that arose in various cultures about these winged creatures, how the fossils of dinosaurs ignited and fanned the flames of those stories. *Are dragons related to or descended from dinosaurs? Are we missing something in the fossil record? Could these creatures actually exist outside of legend and fantasy, and could they continue to exist in the present?* Well, of course they did. I had come face-to-face with an actual, live dragon not once, but TWICE. I had practiced veterinary medicine on that dragon. But I still could hardly believe it.

Life went on like this for those few months, with me working long and brutal hours at the clinic, immersed in dragon literature and movies at home, and ruminating over my questions and doubts, until things changed. One night, Emerald returned, and this time she brought a friend. *Or family? A mate?*

Long after closing, I sat entrenched at my desk in the clinic office, deeply focused on a journal article about feline diabetes. Gradually, I noticed a repetitive *tap...tap...tap...* near the window, at first so vague that I could barely hear it. Then it grew slightly louder. Since I had nearly wrecked the office trying to get away from the dragon's eye last time, perhaps she decided on a subtler approach this time around.

Leaving my desk, I went to the larger window and peered warily into the inky darkness, wondering if I'd see someone loitering in the parking lot or trying to break in. Our small town was plagued by methamphetamine addiction at the time, and more than once I'd had to call police to the clinic after hours to contend with vandals or aspiring burglars.

No people inhabited the parking lot. Just the dragon. And ANOTHER dragon. I blinked, then blinked again. Still two dragons standing on the asphalt, easily visible despite the feeble light from the street lamp. At least that time I didn't fling all my records to the floor in panicked flight across the office. But my heart rate still skyrocketed.

Guessing where this was headed, I cautiously opened the front door, trembling as much as I had the last time. Without preamble, both dragons pushed their way into the clinic, circling tightly and shifting their wings and tails to make room for each other as I backed across the room. Though our lobby seemed spacious for dogs and cats, the sudden surplus of dragons instantly made the room cramped and claustrophobic. One of their tails crashed over a row of chairs, and the stack of dog-eared magazines on an end table went skating across the floor. A wing bumped the flower vase on the front counter, and it smashed onto the reception desk behind, soaking stacks of records and notes. A formidably spiked tail tip sailed over my head and smacked the metal pet food shelves with a *clang* while I ducked and shrank into a corner. Six forty-pound bags of dog food slid to the floor, one of them torn and spilling kibbles that rolled in a dozen directions.

The maelstrom of scales, spikes, and appendages eventually settled into relative calm, and I finally got a decent look at dragon number two as my eyes adjusted to the dim light that filtered into the darkened lobby from the office. He (at least, I thought the dragon was male) stood taller than the first dragon but displayed shiny brown scales very similar to hers, though a bit paler shade, with indistinct striping on the wings. The array of brown spikes that coursed down his spine and festooned his tail closely matched those of his smaller companion, but four sets of horns adorned his head that loomed just below the ceiling in near total darkness. My nose wrinkled at his much stronger scent; though to be fair, perhaps the odor was more powerful because two dragons crowded the lobby instead of one. I couldn't decide whether to be pleased or terrified that they were there, that she was back, that this was happening again.

Just when the realization sunk in that she had lived, and I'd get to see the results of my efforts, she turned to position her wing near me. However, we were mostly in the dark. As excitement began to replace my fear, I headed for the switch to turn on the lobby lights. *Anyone on drugs loitering near the clinic is going to glimpse through the windows and think they are on a bad trip.*

No matter, the light shone brightly for only a moment, then the larger dragon turned his head, inadvertently smacking his prominent, pointed horns into the fluorescent fixture. The light buzzed angrily, flickered, sparked, and then went dark. *How badly will this building be wrecked if they bring their entire extended family next time?!* I didn't even want to think about it.

"Okay, please stay here," I told them exasperatedly. "Both

of you won't fit in the treatment area, and I can't have you breaking everything in the clinic. All right?" I backed slowly toward the doorway. Thankfully, the dragons stayed put while I exited the lobby and flicked on the lights in the treatment room, blinking in the bright glare. I fetched a transilluminator, an instrument with a powerful and highly focused light, and returned to the dark and odorous lobby.

"May I see your wing?"

Emerald extended her wing my direction, enough for me to shine the bright light over the site of her wound. A long, thick, bumpy scar covered what had previously been the nasty, deep laceration. The pale and dull scar lacked the iridescence of the surrounding skin and scales that glistened under the transilluminator. But it had mended, the infection resolved. *Note to self: enrofloxacin and carprofen are tolerated and effective in dragons.* Gently, I rubbed my fingertips over the scar tissue. It felt surprisingly firm, more what I would have expected from bone than from flesh.

To see a patient that's healed following surgery or wound care is rather fulfilling for a veterinarian, especially after the more harrowing or complicated procedures and questionable prognoses. Sometimes we see pets that were torn practically to shreds during a fight, a "big-dog-little-dog" conflict as we call it, or skirmish with a wild animal or car. It's long, hard work getting these pets patched together, comfortable, and well, but so worth it when they come bouncing into the clinic all healed, eager to take treats, head scratches, belly rubs, lick our faces, and drool on our shoes. Dragons are far too dignified to pant, drool, or accept belly rubs, so for me to simply see Emerald's healed wing was enough. I was delighted to have her back, cured, and knew that I had really, truly helped her. And apparently, she trusted me and had faith in my skills, because she had returned with yet another dragon. Genuinely elated, I grinned to myself.

Speaking of another dragon, why was this one here? Was dragon number two sick or injured? *Is this... a referral? From Emerald?* Ludicrous thoughts of offering her the "refer-a-friend" discount ran through my mind.

"Do you need my help? Are you hurt?" I asked, my enthusiasm growing about having another dragon to treat, especially considering my success with the first. He swiveled his head and neck toward me and positioned his right eye dizzyingly close to my face. My enthusiasm faltered, and I backed up a couple steps. The bigger dragon's movements were more abrupt than those of his female companion, and I found him rather unnerving. He froze and blinked at me. And blinked again. Ugly, mud-colored discharge crusted the corner of his eye.

"Okay, I'm sorry. Let me look closer." I shone the light from the transilluminator into the dragon's eye. The pupil constricted to a narrow slit, like a gigantic cat's eye, but with small scallops on either side; or somewhat like a horse's pupil but vertical. This dragon's green eyes were flecked with silver and grey, slightly different from the pure deep green of dragon number one. They must have been related, I concluded. *Siblings, maybe? Or just similar specimens of the same species?*

The eye was also red, and it shouldn't have been. Dilated vessels, inflamed and congested with blood, bulged from the surface of iris. The light subtly reflected from the front chamber of the eye, hinting that the fluid inside was slightly foggy. "May I compare to your other eye?" He rapidly swiveled his head to face the opposite direction, and I flinched, resisting the urge to step backward. I saw no vessel dilation in that eye, no flare from the front chamber. And the pupil did not constrict quite as much in the normal eye. "Okay, back to the other eye. May I touch your face and eyelids?" He drew back his head and hesitated for a moment. *I wonder how Emerald persuaded him to be here?* He didn't seem to be entirely comfortable with the situation.

I glanced at Emerald to see if she might be silently encouraging him. She stood quietly off to the side, not communicating with the male dragon in any obvious way. She merely lurked in her half of the room. That is, if an overlarge dragon could possibly "lurk" in a comically undersized veterinary clinic lobby. Her tongue flicked, and she unceremoniously spit out a handful of dog food kibbles. Shaking my head, I turned back to my patient.

The dragon's hesitancy lasted for only a few moments, then he presented the inflamed eye back to me. As he moved, I glimpsed a small defect in the edge of the cornea, the front surface of the eye. Without success, I tried to retract the eyelids to get a better look at the cornea and the sclera, the white of the eye. The eyelids were practically unmovable, and I couldn't expose the sclera at all. The scales of his eyelids felt firm and unyielding under my fingertips. I might as well have tried to move cobblestones set in cement.

"Please wait here. I need to stain your eye to see the injury in your cornea. I'll shine a blue light in your eye to fluoresce the stain. And then we'll decide how to treat this." He surveyed me with his inflamed eye as if he were scanning me. I suddenly felt uncomfortable and vulnerable, as though I were standing there in a ratty hospital gown that gapped in all the wrong places. *I'm going to call you Scary.*

From the treatment room I retrieved fluorescein strips, eye wash, gauze, and a cobalt blue filter. I grabbed a bottle of proparacaine drops, a topical anesthetic, from the refrigerator. The dragons did not attempt to follow me into the treatment area, for which I was certain the door molding was grateful. A few quiet huffs and snorts emanated from the lobby. *Are they communicating with each other? What are they saying?*

The snorts halted the moment I returned to the lobby with materials and instruments clutched in both hands. Scary stuck his head in front of my face before I was quite ready, and the supplies nearly tumbled out of my grip. Working with the dragon's head and eye rattled me far more than Emerald's wing. Catching the ophthalmoscope before it crashed to the floor, I shoved all I was holding onto the front counter before I dropped everything altogether. I exhaled in relief. While my boss didn't care much about the building, expensive equipment was a different story, and he would have been livid if I'd damaged the delicate eye scope.

"Umm… all right, first I'm going to put these drops in your eye," I explained. "This should numb the eye and reduce the pain." The dragon fluttered his eyelids after the drops, then shut his eye tightly and refused to open it.

"Well, if you're going to insist on keeping your eye closed, then let's work on cleaning up this discharge." Tackling the gooey crust in the corner of his eye using eye wash and gauze, I was awed and discomfited by how sticky it was.

Awe shifted to alarm as my fingers began to itch and tingle wherever my skin touched the eye discharge. *What's in dragons' body fluids, and what is this stuff going to do to my skin? What are dragons even made of?* As I silently swore and chastised myself for neglecting to wear exam gloves, I excused myself and quickly scrubbed my hands before donning bright blue nitrile gloves.

After about five minutes, with the crusted discharge reduced to a fraction of its original size, Scary shook his head, relaxed his jaw, and opened his eye. "That should feel better. Is your eye numb now?" The dragon blinked. I thought that must be an affirmative. Until then, I hadn't realized that he had been clenching his jaw tightly from pain, which made him seem even more intimidating. *Maybe I named you too quickly. You're not so scary now.*

"Okay, let's put this stain in your eye. It may feel a bit sticky, but it shouldn't hurt." I struggled with the fluorescein strip for half a minute, dripping orange stain everywhere but in the eye. Applying stain to a huge but nearly vertical eyeball turned out to be rather difficult. "Could you please tilt your head so your eye is facing up?" The dragon immediately complied, then blinked rapidly as several drops met their target. "Perfect, that's better. Okay, you can straighten your head now."

Honestly, my day job would have been much easier if dogs and cats were as cooperative as this. However, dogs and cats lacked the ability to eat me as an appetizer. Nor did they break overhead light fixtures with their heads.

"Here comes the blue light. Please look up so I can see the bottom of your eye better. No, not your whole head, just your eye. Yes, perfect." Then I saw it: a puncture in the dragon's cornea, fluorescing brightly under the blue light of the filter. The stain had seeped down into the wound to a seemingly impossible depth. The corneas of dragons' eyes must have been incredibly thick. Despite that, this wound nearly penetrated the cornea, deep enough to trigger uveitis, or severe inflammation in the iris and the front chamber of the eye. No wonder Scary had sought my help, or was persuaded to come by the first dragon. Uveitis was extremely painful, and if left untreated, it could have ruined his vision and the entire eye.

The dragon needed topical and oral medications to heal the puncture and resolve the pain and inflammation. But could he manage eye drops or ointments? The creatures in my lobby seemed rather intelligent, so I thought eye medications were worth trying.

Carprofen had apparently worked well for Emerald, so I grabbed a giant bottle of that off the shelf. Perusing the eye medication section of the pharmacy, I picked out a bottle of atropine drops, then pondered the antibiotic eye drops and ointments for a minute, uncertain about which one to choose. In the end, I selected the erythromycin ointment, not for any clear medical rationale, but because the dragons' pupils reminded me so much of cats' eyes. I prescribed erythromycin ointment for cats all the time.

Following my optimistic instructions on how to take the medications, Scary took the bottle of pills and the two tiny eye medications out of my hands. Or tried. He delicately grasped the dropper bottle between the points of two gigantic talons, and the bottle promptly pinged away and skittered across the lobby. "Uh, do you... well, let's get a sack for the meds, okay?" I searched for the stash of plastic bags behind the front desk. While back there, I cringed at the mess created by the spilled and smashed flower vase. *Oh no. This is not good.*

Grasping the plastic bag (imprinted with THANK YOU and smiley faces) of pills and eye medications, Scary disappeared into the night along with his companion. This time the moon shone brighter, and I could see them in the sky for a few seconds. *How did they fly into the middle of a populated area without being seen, except by me? Or did anyone else witness them? Will the local news contain some interesting headlines tomorrow?* I've since learned some of the techniques dragons use to conceal and camouflage themselves, and their abilities never fail to impress me.

More questionable drugs went on my account for "first aid" at home. After rearranging the chairs and magazines back into order in the lobby, I hopefully patched the torn dog food bag with packing tape and stacked the bags back onto their shelves. I couldn't do much to remedy the flower vase disaster. Carefully, I brushed the shards of glass and mangled flowers off the counter and mopped up as much water as I could using rags and towels. I left a sticky note on the front desk blaming one of the clinic cats for the mess (I'm so sorry, Rico, you didn't deserve that).

The itchy, red splotches on my fingers were beginning to fade. In time, I would learn that dragon saliva and eye or nasal discharge would create temporary redness and itching in most people's skin. The phenomenon was a bit uncomfortable, but short-lived and seemingly harmless.

When I arrived at work the next morning after far too little sleep, I encountered my boss perched on a ladder in the unlit lobby, frowning in confusion at the broken light. The bent and cracked fixture hung crookedly from the ceiling with electrical wires protruding from the base. A distinct scrape from the dragon's horn marred the adjacent drywall. "Good morning, Bill," I said as nonchalantly as I could. Bill scratched his head and mumbled something indistinct in reply as I hurriedly escaped to my desk.

Scary returned a week later, this time without his companion. The puncture had nearly healed, but the eye had developed an infection despite the preventive ophthalmic antibiotics I had dispensed. At first, I suspected he had failed to use the eye medications. But the pupil was dilated, so I knew he'd had success with the atropine, since I'd prescribed it specifically to dilate the eye. And now that I looked, a bit of eye ointment clung to the edges of his eyelids. He must have been using the erythromycin, too. It simply hadn't worked.

With fascination, I peered through the microscope at the glass slide that I'd swabbed with the dragon's eye discharge. Loads of rod-shaped bacteria crowded the slide, along with what I suspected were white blood cells, but unlike any I'd ever seen. Apparently, erythromycin ointment didn't work for dragons, at least in this instance. *Note to self: just because dragons' eyes look like cats' eyes doesn't mean that cat medications will work for them.*

The dragon left with a bottle of ofloxacin drops to use instead of erythromycin. Feeling emboldened, I even told him to return if the eye continued to bother him. Maybe, just maybe, I was beginning to enjoy this crazy, implausible, thoroughly unnerving, but exhilarating process of treating dragons.

Scary never turned up again. But other dragons came.

4

Secrets and a Surprise

That I had not only witnessed, but also treated actual living, breathing, flying dragons, and on multiple occasions at that, became a delicious secret that I carried with me constantly. Dragons fluttered on the margins of my thoughts during all my interactions at work and home, and they soared and dived and swooped through my dreams at night. Dragons warmly glowed deep in the recesses of my mind whenever I struggled with emergency patients in the middle of the night, fuzzy and dull with fatigue and lack of sleep.

Thoughts of dragons kept me going on the toughest, most discouraging, demoralizing days in the clinic. Sadly, those days were plenty.

The fact that the dragons were truly real, and not merely products of my imagination, took time for me to reconcile. Once I wrapped my brain around that, I felt incredibly fortunate to have stumbled onto their existence, and privileged to have practiced veterinary medicine on their kind. I was thrilled that they had sought me out, and astonished and humbled by their trust in me.

On the other hand, the dragons were intimidating and presumably dangerous. If nothing else, they had proven themselves detrimental to the clinic and its contents, although they hadn't intended any harm. Each time the dragons turned up, I was an anxious wreck, concerned for my safety, worried about the inevitable property damage, troubled by the unavoidable fallout if (or when?!) anyone discovered my unusual moonlighting "job."

A few new dragons accompanied Emerald to the veterinary clinic. She must have been bringing the dragons to me, I assumed, or convincing them to come. Then dragons started to appear on their own.

Eventually, after numerous clandestine visits from dragons, all of which left me unsettled but less so with time, I started compiling actual notes on my medical observations of them. My notes have grown and evolved over nearly twenty years of practice, and I now have a sizable compendium on the medical conditions of dragons, common injuries and illnesses and how to address them, how to perform various medical procedures in dragons, how to administer injections and anesthesia, and a formulary of drugs and dosages. At some point, I hope to publish these notes in a textbook. Although, as you might imagine, publishers won't exactly take my dragon textbook seriously.

Some dragons were similar in size to the first two I saw, and similarly crammed themselves into the clinic, resulting in continued minor property destruction (apologies to my boss). Then a considerably bigger wyrm, an aged and intimidatingly large dragon, arrived whose head would barely fit through the front door, and I treated him in the parking lot. Fortunately, I was more comfortable with dragons by that point, or I would have been petrified in fear (as it was, my nerves were absolutely shot after his visit). After the wyrm, I wised up and insisted that all the dragons stay in the parking lot — not the exposed front lot, but a secluded corner behind the building — and I gathered supplies into a tray or bag that I carried to them.

I began to recognize the likenesses and differences between dragons of the same species. Relatives of the first two dragons all shared a roughly similar body shape and the same elegant, chiseled head. They all possessed triangular tail tips and similar arrays of spikes and smooth, ivory-colored horns. Some of the dragons displayed striping or spots on their diamond-shaped scales, which came in an array of colors. The striped orange ones reminded me of tigers. Aside from variation in size, I could judge their relative ages based on the numbers and sizes of horns and the density of spikes on their tail tips.

Then dragons of other species came, or at least what I assumed were other species, displaying broad variations in colors, patterns, and conformation. Stockier, more barrel-shaped dragons arrived, as well as slender, lithe dragons with elongated faces that reminded me of alligators or crocodiles. Some possessed five toes on their claws, some four, and others only three. Rather than spiked triangles, some of their tail tips were pointed or flattened into ovals, and a few tails sported brutally spiked, bulbous tips that resembled medieval maces. Dark, shiny horns that twisted into graceful spirals adorned many of the dragons, while others lacked horns altogether. Some species flaunted frills of brightly colored hide around their heads, and others displayed rows of frills along their tails. I observed round, squarish, and sharply pointed scales arranged in uniform rows as well as amorphous scales arrayed in seemingly random patterns. A couple dragons turned up sporting feathers along with their scales, a characteristic that made me think more seriously about their connections to dinosaurs and their avian descendants. I started taking notes, not only on drugs and dosages, but on my observations of the creatures in general.

Whether exclusively scaled, or feathered and scaled, the dragons exhibited striking coloration. Even the more neutral-colored dragons, in grey, brown, or black hues, displayed mesmerizing iridescence or highlights. The brightly-colored dragons were stunning indeed, flaunting all colors of the rainbow and then some. I observed an endless array of patterns in dragons' scales, spikes, horns, and frills, with countless differences between individuals even among the same species. I began to wonder if the scale and spike patterns were wholly unique to each individual, like fingerprints in humans. Because of the endless variations, I sometimes found it difficult to determine whether a particular dragon was of a new species, or merely a variant of a species already known to me.

As for gender, I could sometimes easily tell the difference, and sometimes not so much. My initial impressions of the early dragons' genders, even though they were based on mere gut instinct, were somehow correct. The more of the creatures I met, the more I recognized the differing characteristics between them. The males were typically larger and spikier than their female counterparts, with broader skulls, wider-set eyes, longer horns, and considerably more scars. Females' heads appeared narrower, with more prominent and rounded bones around the eye orbits. Their pelvises were wider, presumably to allow eggs to pass through. Although, despite the males' smaller pelvises, a region in the lower groin looked — ahem — bulged compared to the females. Genders of adolescent and adult dragons were easier to discern than juveniles. Sometimes, regardless of age, I encountered dragons that resembled neither males nor females that I could tell. Maybe they were neither. Or both.

I wrote everything down, denoting my hypotheses with abundant question marks, hoping to eventually arrange the data into sensical order. Based on the dragons I'd treated, the dragon lore I'd consumed contained some grains of truth. But, as with all legends, exaggeration and fiction were rife. Most of the dragons I'd met fit the description of the proverbial "European" dragons, with four limbs, two wings, and scales. However, this was southwestern United States, not Europe. Had so-called "European" dragons originated in Europe, but migrated and populated North America? Or did the legends have it all wrong? Dragon lore described North American dragons as heavily feathered, with vestigial (or rudimentary) limbs. Feathered dragons occasionally came to me for help, but I wouldn't have described them as heavily feathered; they had plenty of scales too. Their conformation differed significantly from their classic "European" relatives, but I could hardly have called their limbs "vestigial." Comparatively small, yes, but still functional.

Dragons' elements of camouflage defied my attempts at description (and still do). Certainly, dragons must have possessed chromatophores similar to chameleons, but their disguise abilities went far beyond that. They could, to all but the most practiced eye, appear nearly transparent. Witnessing the transformation always amazed and exhilarated me: a clearly visible dragon would quickly fade into an unrecognizable, ephemeral shape that would appear simply as a vague distortion of the background (this description doesn't do justice for the phenomenon, but it's the best I can manage).

Luckily, the first dragons I treated were relatively small, with reasonably straightforward medical conditions. Therefore, I gained the confidence to practice medicine on dragons in general, before the more sizable and intimidating creatures and more complicated conditions found their way to me. Dragons arrived with various injuries, infections, parasites (fascinatingly disgusting), skin/scale problems, ocular conditions, gastrointestinal issues, and a myriad of other ailments.

Intervals of weeks or months went by between visits from dragons. Over the first couple years, my reactions to the creatures evolved between fascination, terror, and excitement to sometimes annoyance and anger. I was eager to learn more about entirely different species from what I'd learned in school, but dragon medicine was dangerous and dirty. And yet it was so gratifying.

But I couldn't tell a soul about the dragons. Well, I did tell my husband, but he thought I was kidding, and it became a running "joke" between us.

"Ha," he'd said on one occasion. "Great story. You ever think about writing these down?"

"I suppose I could, though I don't know if anyone would want to read them. But it's not just a story, Jon. This stuff is really happening."

"Sure, Jordyn, sure it is. Let me know when a unicorn comes in. I've always wanted to see one."

I'd sighed and rolled my eyes. "No, Jon—"

"Or, wait, unicorns would be large animal medicine. How

about a leprechaun? That would be small enough—"

"You think unicorns would be larger than dragons?!" I'd retorted, feeling indignant despite the fact he was joking. "Believe me, dragons are far too large to fit in—"

"Well, I suppose they can be as big as you want to make them. You're the one telling the tale, after all."

"Jon, no. I'm telling you the truth...."

Most of these conversations ended in an impasse with rolled eyes and frustrated sighs from both of us. At least I could talk to Jon about the dragons, which was better than having to remain completely mum, but I wanted him to believe me.

Spilling the story to my boss, colleagues, or coworkers was out of the question, as I surely would have lost my job and reputation. So, I kept the dragons a closely guarded secret.

Dragons would sometimes turn up on the worst possible nights, when I was already spent, irritable, sick of work, and desperately wanted to go home and go to bed. Frustration and resentment frequently got the best of me at those times. However, I could never bring myself to turn a dragon away. They completely enthralled me, even though I had to keep them to myself.

Nevertheless, even at the best of times, their visits were intrusive and exhausting. Practicing veterinary medicine involved long, hard hours and lack of sleep, and that was without treating "imaginary" creatures after-hours. Every night a dragon arrived meant "lost" time addressing their needs and then cleaning up the aftermath, piles of records delayed, and considerably less sleep. I'd drag into work the next morning, eyes bloodshot, desperately gripping a coffee mug, and someone would ask, "Hard night on call? Wait, were you on call last night?" I would mumble some excuse about insomnia or whatever else I thought up. Often, I looked pretty rough. And my colleagues noticed.

The dragons were getting expensive, too. Many veterinary drugs weren't cheap, even with an employee discount, especially when a dragon required twelve, twenty, forty, or however many tablets per dose. Of course, the clinic shouldn't have had to shoulder the cost since the dragons didn't generate any revenue for the business, nor would my conscience have sat well with chalking it up to clinic losses. So, I continued to put whatever medications and supplies I used onto my own personal account and paid for them out of my salary. Dragon medicine became a unique and costly hobby that periodically ate up a chunk of my paychecks.

The clinic manager brought up my personal "first aid" purchases only once, in such a way that I realized she thought I was diverting or "grey-marketing" veterinary products, e.g. selling the medications for profit to online pharmacies.

"So, Dr. Blackstone, how's the profit?" she demanded one day.

"The profit? What profit?" I replied, utterly bewildered.

"All this stuff on your account must be going somewhere besides your medicine cabinet. Where are you selling it?"

I found the idea so ludicrous, and I genuinely laughed so hard, that she dropped the subject and didn't raise it again. But I'm sure she continued to suspect something strange was going on. Maria, if you're reading this, you were right to be suspicious, just not in the way you thought!

Veterinary medicine didn't pay very well, especially relative to the cost of veterinary education, and Jon knew it. This clinic, the very first place I practiced as a veterinarian, calculated doctors' salary based on our production, so every paycheck was different. Since I had no previous salary to compare, Jon didn't know exactly what to expect, and he never questioned my earnings. And, since I handled all of our bills, taxes, and record-keeping, he never scrutinized my pay stubs closely enough to notice the unusual deductions.

Once almost five months passed without a visit from a dragon, and I was beginning to think they had lost interest in seeking my help, or perhaps decided they could get by without veterinary care. After all, they had made do without my assistance for possibly centuries, so why now? Or maybe they had lost their confidence in me, although I had no idea why. And I couldn't quite decide whether I was disappointed or relieved by the possibility.

However just at the point I resigned myself to the idea that I'd never see another dragon, and oscillated between sadness and gratitude as a result, two turned up only days apart. And that week, I saw dragons do things I'd never seen before.

A young, tannish-orange dragon listlessly sidled up next to my car as I was leaving the clinic late one summer evening. Thick nasal discharge crusted both nostrils, and congestion rattled and bubbled noisily as she breathed. Lethargic and dull, she morosely stood with her head drooping toward the pavement. I'd seen a small handful of dragons with respiratory infections before then, and every one had been juvenile. Their immune systems weren't yet mature enough to effectively ward off respiratory pathogens, I surmised. This dragon, starting to lose her adolescent appearance as she verged on adulthood, seemed relatively old for such an infection.

By this time I routinely treated the dragons in the most secluded corner of the parking lot behind the clinic, where they were less likely to attract an audience. That's where

I led the orange dragon, behind six short palm trees that stood in a row along the side street, obscuring the view of my unorthodox patients from the occasional passing car. She stood pathetically hunched on the pavement, nose still pointed toward the ground, unmoving as I examined her. Unmoving, that is, until she explosively sneezed, projecting two lines of smoldering black soot and snot across the asphalt as well as my shoe.

The incendiary blast took place just as I was removing the stethoscope from my ears, and I yanked one of the ear pieces across my face, leaving a red streak on my cheek. Frantically, my heart hammering, I lurched backward in graceless disarray with wisps of smoke trailing from my blackened shoe. Odors of burnt rubber and scorched asphalt wafted through the parking lot. Coming to my senses, I realized I was trying to flee from my smoldering footwear, but of course I wasn't gaining any lead.

Embarrassed, I discontinued my panicked flight and looked myself over. Nothing but my shoe appeared to be damaged. My toes felt uncomfortably warm, but not painful. A singed shoelace broke in my hand as I yanked the shoe off, wiggling my toes to inspect my sock and foot. Both were unscathed. Sighing, I nudged the charred shoe with my toe, turning it upright. It still smoked and reeked like burning tires. So much for my favorite work shoes.

Since I had never previously observed fire-breathing, I had dismissed it as a fanciful myth. I've been particularly cautious around dragons with respiratory infections ever since then, and I have witnessed dragons sneeze flames numerous times. It still often startles me after all these years.

Once I calmed my nerves for a few minutes, I returned my

attention to the dragon. "Okay, Sneezy, I did not expect that. Looks like I need to be more careful." Hobbling with one shoe, I finished examining her. Her lungs sounded great for as miserable as she looked. The poor thing sneezed flames twice more before I was done, leaving an array of black streaks on the pavement. But thankfully, she missed my feet, which I kept well away from her nose. The dragon didn't appear at all concerned about or troubled by the flame emissions, merely... well, sick of being sick. Fiery sneezes must not have been unusual for an ill dragon, I gathered.

Doxycycline had worked well for the few other dragons I'd treated for respiratory infections, so I gave Sneezy a one-hundred count bottle of the antibiotic capsules. The previous dragons hadn't been sneezing as much, however, and they certainly hadn't sneezed flames. I pondered whether I could do anything to alleviate her explosive sneezes.

Having asked the dragon to wait a moment longer, I hobbled into the clinic to take a bottle of diphenhydramine, an antihistamine. Perhaps that would reduce the sneezing. Returning to the parking lot, I mused about how often forest fires might be ignited by sneezing dragons. *What would Smokey Bear have said about that? Only YOU can prevent forest fires... by sneezing into your wing instead of trees and shrubs.*

The sniffling dragon lifted off into the night sky, and I lost sight of her within seconds. But moments later, twin streaks of flame flared in the darkness. *Gesundheit, little dragon.* Fireworks popped in the night sky mere seconds after Sneezy's last sneeze. Independence Day was approaching, and revelers were ramping up their nighttime incendiary displays. Convenient disguise, I supposed, for a dragon in flight with uncontrollable fiery sneezes.

5

The Odor

Merely three days after the sneezing dragon singed my shoe, I left the veterinary clinic relatively early for once, having suffered through a day of difficult cases, cranky staff, aggressive pets, and hostile pet owners. Not eager to deal with stacks of records as well, I decided to call it a day.

The staff had all left a short time before, so the clinic was quiet as I gathered my things. Arizona summers were murderously hot even well into the evenings, and that day had been the hottest yet. Slinging my backpack over my shoulder, I paused to collect the lunch I hadn't had time to eat from the break room refrigerator, cursing the broken handle for at least the hundredth time. Immediately accosted by the blistering heat upon my exit, I locked the side door, gingerly turning the hot doorknob through the fabric of my scrub top to check the lock. Wilting climate aside, leaving work before sunset for once was refreshing.

My Volkswagen sputtered to life as I turned the key. The car felt like a kiln after sitting behind the clinic all day, and

I burned my fingers on the seat belt — again. You'd think I'd learn, but I did that just about every day. With the belt eventually fastened, I fiddled with the AC and vents to get some air circulating before I drove away. Finally, I let out the clutch and tapped the accelerator, and the car began to move in reverse as I glanced in the rear view mirror and— *THAT'S A DRAGON BEHIND ME!* The engine shuddered and stalled as I stomped on the brake. *You've got to be kidding me. A dragon again, now?! So soon after the last one?*

I took a longer look in the rear view mirror and confirmed: a shimmery, cobalt-blue dragon stood directly behind my car. He lowered his head to peer at me through the rear window. Twisting in the driver's seat to meet his gaze, I scrutinized the handsome creature. Pale, milky-white scales embellished the dragon's chest and abdomen, glistening like mother-of-pearl in the bright sunlight. He loomed so close to my car that in my hurry to get home, I'd come within inches of hitting him. *Trying to explain that to the auto insurance claims people would have been entertaining.*

Turning away from the dragon, I rested my forehead on the steering wheel and sighed in irritation. I was SO tired and frustrated, not even sure I wanted to be a vet anymore, much less spend my "spare time" practicing medicine on supposedly "fantasy" dragons in secret. *Some fantasy,* I groused. Sighing again, I thumped my forehead on the steering wheel a couple of times, then slammed my fist on the wheel for good measure.

But my heart told me the dragon was in trouble and needed my help. *Okay fine, let's get this over with.* I yanked the seat belt off, burning my fingers again in the process, shoved the door open, and stood up in the sweltering parking lot. The dragons were getting bold; it was still broad daylight, after all. And this one, with his bright blue coloration, easily stood out from the surrounding desert tans and browns. That made me nervous, since I couldn't imagine anything good coming from the dragons being discovered. Apprehensively, I looked around for spectators, pulled over on the side of the street, mouths gaping, but the parking lot and adjacent street were deserted.

The dragon didn't appear at all perturbed after I'd nearly backed into him with my car. By then I knew that dragons, with their thick scales, horns, and tough flesh, were amazingly hardy creatures. But of course, they weren't infallible and impervious to injuries, otherwise they'd have had no need for my services. My car might have inflicted serious damage if I had hit him, and I was thankful I hadn't.

Despite my relief that I hadn't backed into him, I was still annoyed, and may have channeled some of the aggression directed at me by multiple patients and clients that day. I approached the dragon far too rapidly, my movements much too abrupt, my voice considerably too loud and harsh. "All right, what's your problem?" I demanded.

In less than two seconds, the dragon arched his neck, stiffened his forelimbs, flared his wings, opened his great mouth, and instantly convinced me that I was going to die. Fortunately, I was mistaken. He emitted a brief, sharp hiss, similar to that of a cat but shorter and more forceful, and expelled a burst of inconceivably foul breath.

Upon the dragon's abrupt warning, I reflexively blanched and ducked. I found myself crouched next to the back of my car, huddled uncomfortably close to the hot metal of the quarter panel, as if I'd expected the Volkswagen to save me. *Did my panicked brain plan to use the fender as a shield?* A long while had passed since I was so shaken by a dragon, and this time my discomfort was entirely my own fault. Shaking my head, I gasped a deep breath, then forcefully and regretfully exhaled, desperately trying not to breathe the horrid and inescapable odor.

"I'm sorry, okay? So sorry. Let's try this again." I coughed. "It's only… I'm in a very bad mood, but I can still help you. I'm going to stand up now." My legs wobbled as I timidly rose from the pavement, spying a fresh abrasion that peeked through a tear in one knee of my scrubs. A retch rose in my throat in response to the stench of the dragon's… hiss? Was that some kind of breath weapon? It smelled like skunk spray mixed with fertilizer and burning tires. Coughing again, I fought the gag reflex back down.

"What's wrong? Are you hurt? Or sick?" Keeping my voice quiet and gentle and trying to calm my nerves and roiling stomach, I slowly crept a few steps closer. For a dragon that was so brazen as to reveal himself in the daytime, he was easily spooked. But then, perhaps he hadn't intended to be bold; maybe he just urgently needed my help.

The blue dragon shifted with unease, unwilling to entirely trust me after I'd provoked his skunky breath weapon. Trying to be patient, I stood and waited, quietly seething that I wouldn't get home at a reasonable hour after all. At the very least, the dragon needed to hurry up and get himself hidden before someone else happened along.

Leveraging the interlude, I took a few moments to look myself over. *Is that... dragon snot on my scrub top?* My eyes watered from the stench, and I wiped my upper arm over my face, then grimaced as I realized my mistake. My arms smelled as putrid as everything else, and I'd just smeared more of the dragon's breath weapon over my face. I fought down another gag. The odor was so awful.

"You know, I was thinking of calling you Cobalt, or maybe Pearl, for your pretty scales." I paused to cough. "But I'm going to call you Pepé, for Pepé Le Pew. Although I don't suppose you watch cartoons." Pepé stared at me suspiciously as I continued to cough and sputter.

After a few minutes that felt like hours in the simmering heat, the dragon did something very strange. He lay down on his side in the parking lot. Perplexed, I frowned at the creature, inspecting him from head, to neck, then forelimbs, the one wing I could see well, his body, the right hip... *Ah, got it.* Blood coated the injured right rear foot. The dragon straightened his knee to extend the leg toward me, and my eyes widened as I watched him turn to sniff in the direction of his hind claw, or what was left of it. Not one, not two, but three toes were missing.

More than a few dragons are missing a toe or two. This contributes to the "battle-worn" appearance for which a great many dragons pride themselves, vain creatures as they are. But never before nor since have I encountered a dragon that managed to traumatically amputate three toes on the same foot all at once.

As I scrutinized the damage, I pondered how on earth he'd been injured. (That's something I commonly wonder about dragons, but I rarely hear a confession from them.) *Did another dragon inflict the trauma? Or another animal? A human? Or did the dragon somehow miscalculate or get into some kind of accident?* I would never find out.

The wounds appeared to be quite fresh. Two of the toes were amputated close to the last joint. But the third toe was amputated at the base, and still oozed sludgy, dark blood. Shredded remains of the digital nerves dangled from the jagged wounds. *No wonder he's in a rush to get help; those severed nerves must be so painful. That also explains why he was so quick to blast me with stink spray. If my foot looked like that, I'd be cranky too.* I regretted my annoyance and impatience.

This species of dragons had four toes on each hind claw. Fortunately, one toe was undamaged, and I'd be able to preserve parts of two toes. However the inside toe, the one that dragons relied on most for balance, was a total loss. The absent digits would impair his balance for a while. However, I'd found dragons to be incredibly resilient creatures, and I was confident that with time he would adjust and manage without those digits. Cleaning and suturing the wounds, however, was going to take some time. Inwardly groaning, I resigned myself to another late night at the clinic.

Nearly three hours later, I counted broken suture needles as they dropped from my fingers with a soft *clink* into the sharps container. Six. That sounded about right. Two needles broken on each toe thanks to ultra-tough dragon skin and scales. At least the old-fashioned, manually-threaded suture needles held up for a while suturing dragon flesh, although threading them was awkward and tedious. The first and only time I tried the conveniently pre-threaded and pre-packaged suture and needle on a dragon, the needle immediately bent and snapped. Nothing was easy in dragon medicine.

The surgical needle holders squeaked as I opened and closed them a few times. The hinge was loose, but the clamp still worked. Making a mental note to bring pliers and vice grips from home to trial during the next dragon suturing adventure, I ran the scrub sink full of water over the needle holders, forceps, mayo scissors, and the bone rongeurs and rasp I'd used to shape and smooth the phalangeal bones.

Trimming and filing the ends of the bones to enable closing the wounds had been nightmarish. Dragon bones bore a strong visual resemblance to the delicate, hollow bones of birds, but the similarity ended there. Their lightweight bones were perfect for flying, but appeared fragile enough to easily fracture and fragment. Despite their appearance, all my strength was needed to squeeze the bone rongeurs over the truncated ends of Pepé's relatively small toe bones. After treating numerous dragons, substantial calluses had formed on my fingers from surgical instruments, and by then I usually avoided blisters. But that night my hands ached, the calluses raw and angry.

Having scrubbed and sterilized the instruments and disposed of the soiled gauze and gloves, I turned my attention to myself and the horrible stench of the dragon's breath weapon. After focusing on Pepé's foot, I'd found that my olfactory sensors calmed down, or more likely became overwhelmed and simply quit firing from fatigue, so I could no longer easily smell the dragon's breath weapon. But even though my sense of smell had dulled, I was certain I still reeked.

A memory arose of my father, who years before thought he might have been sprayed by a skunk, but wasn't sure. So he walked through the entire house to locate my mother, wanting to ask if she could smell skunk spray on his clothes. Of course, he skunked the whole house on his quest to find her. Now I could empathize, and I grinned wryly at the recollection.

Those days, I habitually kept spare scrubs in my desk, for which I was extremely grateful that night. Debating whether to attempt washing my torn and soiled clothes or toss them in the dumpster, I changed in the employee restroom and shoved my stinking scrubs into a trash bag.

The can of air freshener on the back of the toilet was about to meet its greatest challenge. Carrying it through the clinic, I optimistically spritzed generous amounts in each room, but held no illusions that the stench would dissipate before the next morning.

Let's see, half a bottle of injectable bupivacaine, equal amount of sodium bicarbonate, four syringes (or was it five?), antiseptic, six suture needles, maybe one-eighth of a spool of Fluorofil suture — grinning, I thought of how the hot pink sutures coordinated so well with the pearly sheen of Pepé's scales — *a paper surgical drape, one bottle of pain medication, and one bottle of antibiotics.* Everything went onto my own "first aid" account. Apparently, the clinic manager had decided to ignore my unorthodox purchases since I always promptly paid off my account out of my paychecks.

Rarely did dragons return to have their sutures removed. Pepé flew off following my instructions to somehow remove the bright pink sutures after fourteen suns, and I emphasized to him that I'd have preferred to remove them myself (and use the opportunity to reexamine his toes and make sure they had properly healed). Whether he would actually come back, I doubted. Dragons were able to pull out the sutures with their teeth or claws, I suspected, or even burned them off by breathing fire over the healed wounds.

Eventually, I locked the clinic door behind me, had second thoughts, reopened the door, and fetched a bottle of skunk odor pet shampoo from the retail shelf in the lobby. It worked on freshly skunked dogs, so maybe it would work on the undeniably skunky odor of the dragon's breath weapon.

After that incredibly malodorous odyssey, I finally drove home in the fading light of sunset. The only thing more foul than the stench that permeated my skin and hair was my mood. It occurred to me how much my Volkswagen would reek as well, and I winced. The car was almost new, a celebratory splurge upon starting my first job as a doctor. Though I loved the car, I regretted the debt. A veterinarian's salary didn't stretch very far, especially after paying student loans (not to mention funding medications for dragons). And my car would undoubtedly still smell like dragon breath by the time I would eventually pay it off.

My husband softly snored as I crept into the bathroom to shower and scrub with the skunk odor shampoo. The results impressed me. As I slipped quietly into bed, I thought perhaps I'd successfully eliminated the smell at home… but I was wrong.

The next morning, entirely too early on my day off, I awakened to my husband complaining about the smell of my shoes. *Oops. I should have left those in the garage.*

"Holy hell, these stink! What happened? Did all of your patients get skunked or something?"

Squeezing my eyes shut tighter, I sighed. I had always been truthful with Jon about my exploits with dragons, but he still didn't believe me and was getting tired of the "joke." Sometimes, telling him a more plausible untruth was easier.

"Yeah, it was a skunked dog," I mumbled sleepily. "Sorry, I should have left them outside."

He didn't reply, and I could sense he was fixated on something. Cracking one eyelid open, I saw Jon frowning at the blackened toe of my shoe, the one that had been scorched by the dragon's sneeze a few days before. *Maybe I should have chucked those shoes in the trash instead of the garage.*

"Jordyn, how did you say you burned your shoe?" he asked.

I sighed again, too weary and sleepy to think of a credible story. "I told you. A dragon sneezed flames on it."

"Seriously, come on. The dragon stories are funny, but what really happened?" he demanded.

Now I was annoyed and really wanted to go back to sleep. "Fine, I was roasting marshmallows with my toes and I got too close to the fire," I retorted. "Happy?"

He shot an exasperated look my direction and carried my putrid shoes out the bedroom door. The only reason he didn't suspect me of cheating, I think, was because I routinely arrived home in a most unsexy array of gross, hairy, bloody scrubs, hair disheveled, occasionally with dried bits of blood on my face and clothes, regularly sporting the scent of anal glands or cat urine. And this time I had come home covered in skunky dragon breath. As I drifted back to sleep, I contemplated what other spectacular dragon messes I would inevitably get myself into.

6

The Tech

Dragons had the uncanny ability to determine what days I worked and when I was alone at the veterinary clinic. Or more likely, they hid nearby and watched the clinic, keeping track of who entered and left the building. But if dragons were hiding in the area, to my knowledge none of my colleagues or coworkers ever saw them, or believed their eyes if they did. I never heard anyone talk about seeing or hearing anything strange in the sky, either. Their stealth was truly remarkable. But regardless of how they accomplished it, the dragons invariably arrived when I was alone.

That is, until the night a dragon revealed himself to a veterinary technician. The tech, Diane, and I were on-call for emergencies, and we had just discharged a pit bull, still unsteady from sedation, after removing over 300 porcupine quills from her face and chest. We finished up close to midnight. My tech headed for the back door of the clinic while I collected my keys and jacket to leave as well. Instead of hearing the door slam, I heard a lengthy scream, then silence. Initially, I suspected she had encountered one of the local drug

57

addicts in the parking lot, and that concerned me far more than my scaly patients. So I ran to help her. But instead of a human, I found her confronted by a dragon.

Diane had backed into the side of a dog run, pressed hard into the chain link, immobilized in fear. Her eyes and mouth gaped wide. Car keys dangled from the white-knuckled fist that she clutched to her chest, and the jacket she'd been carrying lay splayed on the floor where she'd flung it. She stared through the open back door at an adolescent dragon who peered back at her with casual indifference, his nose barely within the door frame.

Careening across the slick concrete floor between Diane and the dragon, I wheeled around to grab the tech's shoulders.

"Diane, it's okay! He won't hurt you."

Keeping her terrified eyes on the dragon over one of my shoulders, then the other as I tried to block her view, she began to stammer at high volume.

"It's a… it's a… that's a… a…." Her voice was shrill and quavering with panic as she raised a shaking hand to point. Her car keys jangled in her grip.

"Yes, it's a dragon. Diane, I know them! I know the dragons. He won't hurt you." I glanced over my shoulder at the adolescent, who had stuck his head through the doorway to get closer to the excitement. He was starting to look agitated from my tech's panic, frills flared menacingly around the back of his head, and I hoped I wasn't mistaken by calling him harmless.

The tech was so fixated on the dragon, I might as well have been invisible. Shaking her by her shoulders, I tried to get her to focus on me.

"Diane! Look at me. Listen… I know it's terrifying. Yes,

dragons are real. They come here—they come to me—for veterinary care. I promise you will be okay."

No sound from her. She stared at me in shock and disbelief.

"Look—just—stay right here. Stay here! I'll find out what our dragon needs."

Backing slowly away from Diane, afraid that she might frighten our visitor by running or yelling, I coaxed the nervous creature to withdraw his frilled head from the doorway and follow me to the corner of the parking lot. His silver scales sparkled under the street lamp, and his frills relaxed into soft grey folds that draped languidly around his neck as he settled his wings around him. The squatty palm trees along the street stood taller than the diminutive adolescent.

As I evaluated him, talking softly to keep him calm, I kept one ear toward the clinic. Expecting any moment to hear Diane's pickup door slam and tires squeal hastily out of the parking lot, I realized with surprise that instead, she was slowly and tentatively walking toward me and the dragon.

She stopped about twenty feet away and remained there, silent and motionless, staring warily at me and the dragon in turns as I examined him. My exam hadn't yet yielded anything amiss. The young dragon fidgeted and jerked his head as I handled him, and he repeatedly swiveled his head to look at Diane, distracted by her presence. Evidently, he wasn't going to readily show me what was bothering him. But he kept subtly chewing and chomping his teeth, and I suspected something was wrong with his mouth.

Hesitating, I considered how best to proceed. Dragons' mouths and noses intimidated me, even more so after the creatures sneezed flames onto my foot and blasted me with a breath weapon, and I was leery of spending much time near the fiery parts. The physiology of fire breathing and other breath weapons mystified me, and I didn't know whether opening the mouth or handling anything in there might inadvertently trigger flames or a horrible burnt skunky smell. And to be honest, dragon teeth looked simply... scary. Imagine alligator teeth, but much larger, with fire spewing from between the jaws. Or skunk breath, and I wasn't sure which was worse.

Okay, let's figure this out. Taking a deep breath, I coaxed the dragon to face toward open pavement and away from me, Diane, and anything flammable. As the dragon tossed his head and snorted, ruffling his neck frills, I pressed on his lower jaw and pulled upward on his lip, trying to persuade him to open his mouth wide. Just as I was losing my patience, he finally complied.

Cautiously, I leaned closer and peeked at the dragon's formidable teeth, sniffing the foul odor that wafted from his mouth. A giant tongue depressor would have been nice. An idea popped into my head and I scanned around the dim parking lot, looking for a discarded pallet from the clinic or the adjacent warehouse. A pallet board would have made a perfect dragon-sized tongue depressor. But no pallet was to be found, and I would have to do without.

All the teeth and gums on the left side appeared healthy, as far as I could tell. I spent a few moments examining how the teeth were arranged, trying to distinguish between incisors, canines, premolars and molars. All the teeth were pointed, so telling the different types apart was difficult. The inside surfaces of all the teeth were darkened to grey, presumably because of their exposure to flames. Four of the teeth along the mandible had emerged only about halfway from the gum line. These teeth weren't quite so dark as the fully emerged ones.

Are the dragon's adult teeth just coming in? No, clearly mature teeth sat farther back in the jaw, some of them crusted with rings of brown tartar. *I wonder... do dragons grow multiple sets of teeth?* Vaguely, I remembered some bit of knowledge from veterinary school about alligators and crocodiles, and how a replacement tooth would emerge after the original tooth was damaged or diseased. "Polyphyodont" was the term, I thought. *Is that what's going on here? Are dragon teeth like crocodile teeth?* Considering alligators and crocodiles, and dragons too (I hypothesized), were all throwbacks to dinosaurs, similar dentition would make sense. I made a mental note to study polyphyodonts.

The young dragon's mouth remained open wide, and he bobbed his head with impatience. A diagnosis still eluded me. I honestly didn't know how a dragon's oral cavity should normally smell, but this one's mouth truly reeked. The odor of the dragon's breath weapon that had struck me in the past was absolutely horrid. *Maybe this degree of halitosis is normal for him. Then again, maybe not.*

Imploring the dragon to remain still, I carefully moved to the other side, taking a wide berth around what I imagined would be his "strike zone." No flames resulted. I exhaled in relief. Impressively, the dragon had kept his mouth open as I circled, and I slowly approached the other side of his teeth. Instantly, I discovered the problem. A tooth near the front of the mandible — the canine tooth, perhaps? — was fractured deep into the crown. Swollen, angry red gingiva, or gum tissue, surrounded the broken tooth. Tentatively, I retracted his bottom lip to observe the inflammation extending deep into the tissues and then, wincing, I cautiously pushed his tongue away from the inner side of the tooth. The tongue felt rough and sticky on my fingertips. My nose wrinkled at the stench that wafted from the pus nestled around the fractured tooth.

Dogs and cats both commonly developed periodontal disease and fractured teeth, and I frequently diagnosed tooth root abscesses in those species. For my typical patients I would have prescribed antibiotics and pain medications and planned to extract the affected tooth or teeth. But what to do for a tooth root abscess in a dragon? Medications I could handle. But I hadn't yet experimented with sedation or anesthesia in dragons, nor did the clinic have dental instruments large enough to extract a tooth of this size. Nor was I familiar with dragon dentition. *If a replacement tooth is emerging from below, would I damage that tooth by extracting the fractured one? Should I even try?*

As I continued my inner debate, I backed a few steps away from the dragon and told him he could close his mouth. He obeyed and immediately resumed chewing and chomping, flicking his tongue over the broken tooth. My fingers itched and tingled from touching the dragon's saliva. *Dammit, I really need to start carrying exam gloves in my pockets.*

Having decided on an action plan, I asked the dragon to wait as I turned to fetch medications from the clinic, then stopped short as I encountered Diane, still unmoving several feet away. I had been so focused on the dragon, I'd nearly forgotten she was there.

The tech's hollow and haunted eyes flicked briefly to meet mine, then she resumed staring at the dragon with her jaw slack and lips slightly gapped open. She looked horrible. Her entire reality had crashed down, much as mine had a few years before. *Did I look this terrible when I first saw a dragon?* Well, to be fair, I had altitude sickness when I FIRST saw a dragon, so I undoubtedly didn't look so great. But what about the second time, when a dragon first visited the clinic? Had I looked this awful then? I shuddered to think that indeed, I probably had.

"Diane," I said gently, empathizing with her panic and turmoil, "I'm going into the clinic to get meds for this guy. Want to come with me?"

Keeping her eyes on the dragon, she faintly shook her head.

My eyebrows raised in surprise. "So… that means you'll be alone with him for a few minutes. Are you comfortable with that?"

Moments passed. Diane subtly nodded, then again with more emphasis, eyes still on the dragon instead of me. *Well then. That's considerably brave of her.* The creature terrified her twenty minutes before, but then she was willing to stay with him alone.

"I'll be right back, okay? Just think, Diane, you have llamas at home that spit at you. You can handle this little guy." The corner of her mouth twitched. *Did she just almost smile?*

Stepping away, I watched to make sure both the dragon and Diane stayed put until I disappeared through the back door of the clinic. Worried about what might transpire in the parking lot in my absence, I practically sprinted to the pharmacy shelves. *Antibiotics— oh, how much does he weigh? Maybe 1000, 1200 lbs? Surely at least 1100... pain medications... maybe a local anesthetic? Sure, why not.* I grabbed a bottle of injectable bupivacaine and a syringe, then my lunch bag from the break room.

Drawing up the local anesthetic drug as I went, I hurried back to the parking lot, numbers swimming in my head as I mentally calculated drug dosages. About fifty feet away

I stopped, then walked slowly and deliberately toward the dragon and Diane, both of whom were in the same spot where I'd left them, suspiciously eyeing each other. Realizing I was panting, I paused to take some deep breaths. The last thing I needed was to spook the creature into further terrifying my technician.

Explaining to the dragon what I needed to do, I coaxed him to open his mouth again and carefully squirted the topical anesthetic onto the exposed angry tooth pulp. That would reduce the pain while the oral medications were taking effect. He shook his head and squelched his tongue back-and-forth past the tooth, grimaced as he tasted the bupivacaine, then closed his mouth and quietly chomped. He reminded me very much of a horse at that moment, and I laughed.

"See, Diane? Dragons are a lot like horses. Only with wings and claws and fire-breathing abilities."

The technician blanched and retreated several steps. *Oops, sorry.* Apparently, she hadn't considered the possibility of fire-breathing.

"We should call him a horsey name," I added, trying to distract her from thoughts of fire. "How about… Storm? What do you think?" Diane gaped at me as though I'd just spoken an alien language.

Turning back to the dragon, I convinced him to swallow a bunch of the antibiotic and pain medications right then and there, mashed into my leftover half sandwich from dinner. He was so young and flighty, and I wanted to make sure he could do what I asked. Satisfied that he was able, and hoping he would keep it up according to my directions, I sent Storm off into the night with the bottles of tablets.

Diane gazed wide-eyed at the bit of sky where the creature

had disappeared, scanning back and forth to catch another glimpse.

"You won't see him now, they're too talented at disappearing," I explained. "Magnificent, isn't he?"

She glared at me. "Dr. Blackstone... I don't... I don't understand what that— what just— happened."

Oh man, I've been there. And I didn't have anyone to talk to about it.

Agonizing how best to help Diane, I debated what to do. *Should I drive her home right away? Sit down in the clinic and talk? Call a therapist first thing tomorrow for an appointment?* At minimum, Diane looked like she needed a really stiff drink. I glanced at my watch. It was nearly one in the morning.

For the one and only time in my career, I offered to take a technician to the bar. And worse, we were both still on call. The moment I suggested it, anxiety took hold; we both could have gotten in so much trouble. But having gone through this exact crisis myself, I needed to support Diane through it, too. I wanted the opportunity to talk, and time for her to recover somewhat, I hoped, before I took her home.

Now, I was no longer the only person aware of the dragons' existence, which was completely new territory for me. And whatever Diane decided to do with her newfound knowledge remained to be seen.

7

The Quandary

Of course, meeting a dragon could be terrifying. Luckily, since I was not in my right mind during my first exposure to a dragon, I was fascinated rather than frightened. Although once my brain was back to normal, I was petrified when the same creature reappeared. But at the least my mind-altered state during the first introduction helped soften the impact, I think.

Diane wasn't so lucky. Being accosted by a dragon had absolutely horrified her. I hoped she'd come to appreciate the remarkable winged creatures as much as I did — of course, first she had to reconcile with the fact that the creatures were real, as I had — but in the meantime she was stunned and miserable. Diane really needed a drink, and I wanted to help her, so off to the bar we went.

I didn't expect the bar to be crowded this early in the week. But as I pulled open the heavy door, I was surprised to find a noisy, rowdy group of business casual-clad people occupying the front. Pausing a moment in the doorway, I braced myself for the commotion swirling within. The heavy odor of booze mixed with cigarette smoke wafted outward, despite the fact that the bar was supposed to be non-smoking. A *crash* and *tinkle* of breaking glass sounded from behind the bar. "PARTY FOUL!" half a dozen drunken voices shouted at once.

"Oh geez, Diane, I think we've inadvertently crashed a company party." Without reply, she followed me through the small throng. Rather conspicuous in our scrubs, we awkwardly threaded between bodies and found an out-of-the-way table in a back corner where no one could easily listen in. Classic rock thumped in the background, guitar wailing. The bar would remain open for just over an hour.

A frazzled server with dark circles under her eyes materialized next to our table. "Just iced tea for me, thanks," I told her. "And... whiskey for my friend?" I glanced at Diane, who nodded her head slightly as she gazed at the table top. "Yes, whiskey," I confirmed. I would have loved a stiff drink as well, but I needed to stay sober to drive and see other emergency patients if needed. The server left, then returned with our drinks so quickly that wisps of her grey hair floated in her wake.

Diane stared into her drink. Excusing myself, I exited to the parking lot, wincing as I called other veterinary technicians. Apologizing for the late hour, I implored anyone to please take over on-call since Diane "wasn't feeling well." By the second call I had a sleepy and reluctant taker, and returned inside to inform my traumatized technician that she was off duty for the night. "Thank you," she quietly murmured as she vacantly nodded her head.

Pink Floyd's *Comfortably Numb* flowed from the speakers. *Diane looks numb all right, but certainly not comfortable.* She didn't seem to know what to say. So I started telling stories about dragons and how I'd come to be a dragon veterinarian. Pool balls sharply cracked across the bar, shouts and cheers intruded, and I raised and lowered my voice to keep pace with the shifting background noise.

Diane already knew the tale of my "hallucination" from altitude sickness on the mountain. I told her the deeper truth, that the dragon was real, that she'd visited me at the veterinary clinic and later brought others. And then more and more came. By that time, I had treated a few dozen dragons.

In the beginning, I had been terror-struck, too, I assured her. But the creatures were such incredible beings, and to think that they existed was so crazy, so wild, so utterly unbelievable, and yet they were real. And the dragons really did get less intimidating with time, I promised. I felt so privileged to have been let into their world— Diane flicked her eyes at me. She didn't look like she felt so fortunate.

The tech downed the first whiskey, then another, absently pushing the glass in circles on the table while she listened to me, staring blankly at the table or into her glass. The bar was closing and we made our way out, avoiding the small but loud group of inebriated revelers in the parking lot. Some guy wolf-whistled in our direction, and I shot a poisoned glance his way as we got into my car, resisting the urge to raise a middle finger. Pausing in the driver's seat, I stared through the windshield and fantasized about "siccing" dragons on drunken morons, until my passenger pointedly looked at me. Guiltily, I started the car.

I tried to get some feedback from Diane while I drove to her farmhouse outside of town. She stared through the windshield at nothing, and I couldn't tell what her state of mind was. But she wasn't interested in talking, so I finally let her be, focusing on the road slipping quickly away past my headlights. My Volkswagen still smelled like burnt rubber and skunk spray thanks to the dragon's breath weapon months before, but I thought it best not to bring that up. She had undoubtedly noticed but hadn't mentioned it, and I suspected she wouldn't have appreciated the story.

The tech sat for a few moments after I pulled into her driveway. I turned off the engine and waited. The base of my skull began to ache, and I self-consciously pressed my knuckles into the back of my head, trying to massage the tension out before a migraine took hold. Eventually, she turned to me, eyes shadowed and haunted. "I really don't know what to think."

"Diane, that's okay. You don't have to know what to think," I reassured her. "At first, I didn't know, either. So take your time. And… call me anytime if you want to talk."

Without another word, she exited my car and walked up the steps to her porch. I waited until she was inside and the door was closed before backing out of her driveway to go home. Just as I reached my own driveway, my phone rang. Swearing, I picked up. My night had already been long and stressful, and I wasn't sure I had the reserves to see another emergency.

"Hello?"

"Yeah, I got a question."

"Okay?"

"Can I put antibiotic ointment on my cat?"

I glanced at my watch. Ten minutes past three a.m. People never ceased to amaze me.

"…Well yes, but—"

"Okay, thanks." *Click.*

I let loose with more profanity. Why someone felt compelled to call at three in the morning to ask about ointment was beyond me, but this kind of stuff happened on an infuriatingly regular basis. The poor cat possibly had a bite wound abscess and really needed to be seen, at least the following day if not that night, but they had ended the call before I could make any recommendations.

Fuming, I went inside, left my scrubs and shoes in a heap, and joined my husband in bed. My phone sat within arm's reach, ready to ring and wake me at any moment. The night's events, and all the fear, anxiety, and frustration to go with them, revolved in an endless loop through my mind. Not surprisingly, the tumult in my head kept me awake for at least an hour. Jon softly snored next to me. I couldn't help but envy his peaceful slumber.

Had I been awakened from a sound sleep by that phone call, I would have been even more irritated. People must have thought that a cadre of veterinarians spent their careers doing nothing but answering random questions during the night and sleeping all day. But that wasn't true. We regularly worked all day, answered the phone and saw patients all night, then worked the next day, too. And I had to be to work in — another glance at my watch — less than four hours. Diane was scheduled to work that day, too, I was pretty sure.

However, Diane called in sick to work that morning. And again the next, although by then her pickup truck had disappeared from the parking lot.

Those two days I spent constantly worrying about her and also about the dragons. *What will happen now that someone else knows they exist? What if Diane tells others? Would anyone believe her? I'll have to corroborate her story; my conscience won't let me do otherwise. What then? Will I lose my job? Will I be able to find another, or will my reputation precede me? Would Diane be fired, or will she quit? Should I call her? Or leave her alone?* The two of us were mired in a huge, complicated mess.

On the other hand, I hoped that Diane might become an ally in my crazy, complicated side job. Having someone to help would be such a relief. Even just someone to talk to about the dragons, to commiserate about the various challenges and dangers of dragon medicine. Someone who took the creatures seriously, unlike my husband who was convinced they were pure fiction.

Diane came back to work the following day. She looked pinched and pale, and she was quieter than usual, but otherwise acted her normal self. When I finally had a moment alone with her in an exam room, I broached the subject, eager to know where her mind was at.

"Hey, about the dragons, I—"

Diane reacted instantly and vehemently. "Not a WORD!" she hissed. "I don't want to hear anything, ever, about… dragons." She cringed at the term. "Not ever, Dr. Blackstone, understand me?!"

Diane's forceful response took me aback, but I could understand her sentiment. Sadly, she wouldn't be the ally I had hoped for, but at least she seemed to be doing okay (as far as I could tell), and the secret of the dragons appeared to be safe with her. Thoughtfully, I nodded. Certainly, I could respect her wishes. "Okay I get it, not a word."

Diane and I continued to work together at the same clinic for years, and we never discussed dragons again. To have a helper and confidant for my clandestine dragon medicine activities would have been great, but not to have lost my job, or Diane's job, or both, was good enough. With some chagrin, I noticed that Diane made every effort not to be on-call for emergencies the same nights I was. And on the occasion when she couldn't avoid working my on-call shift, and we saw a "normal" dog or cat emergency together, she would finish up as quickly as she could and practically dash out of the building, driving away as fast as possible. Ah well, I really couldn't blame her.

8

Riddles and Revelations

My eyes were closed, limbs slack. The soft comforter rested lightly over me as I slowly inhaled and exhaled, not asleep, but not entirely awake, either. I needed to get up and get ready for work, but not quite yet. A sick dragon had kept me up late the night before, and I was dreading the moment I'd have to get out of bed.

Early in the mornings, I often contemplated the first time I saw a dragon, just below timberline on a mountain, my head swimming and throbbing due to altitude sickness. The one I called Emerald. *Did she intend to reveal herself to me?* I'd concluded that she probably hadn't.

Perhaps my sputtering and misfiring synapses activated some long-dormant neurons that allowed me to see through her camouflage. The same parts of the brain that enabled children to see ghosts and monsters and "imaginary" friends, but went dim and quiet before the drudgery of adulthood set in. Or possibly the rational, logical, inhibitory components of my brain were shutting down to reboot. Therefore, I could

73

see the creature because my brain couldn't filter her out as "nonsense." *Regardless, why did she allow me to approach her, and even touch her wing and scrub her wound? Why not flee or fight?* Dragons had been successful at avoiding humans for so long, we'd ceased to believe they ever existed. *Why did Emerald make an exception for me?*

Years ago, I'd visited east Africa to climb Mt. Kenya and explore several of the game parks. At one of those game parks, I witnessed a very peculiar event. A large herd of zebras peacefully grazed near a lake, with a smaller herd of Thompson gazelles grazing to the side, everyone minding their own business, the sun a shimmering, scorched tangerine as it began its descent toward the horizon through a hazy but cloudless sky. Multiple clusters of acacia trees dotted the landscape to complete the rather peaceful, beautiful, yet ordinary scene.

Then a young male lion sauntered into view. He was on the verge of adulthood, but the faint striping on his limbs betrayed his immaturity. However, he was old enough to have been kicked out of his pride. No other lions were nearby. He was alone.

Some of the zebras and gazelles raised their heads, watched the lion for a short time, then casually returned to grazing. The lion tentatively ambled toward a stand of bushes and lay down in the grass not more than ten meters from the zebras. The seasoned Kikuyu guides were absolutely astounded. They had never seen anything like it. These two herds of prey animals had evaluated this apex predator and judged him to be no threat.

But even without the finely-honed instincts of zebras or gazelles, we humans could see it, too. The lion looked lost, and even afraid. He wasn't after a meal. What he needed couldn't be fulfilled by chasing down a zebra.

Honestly, I believe the dragon high on the mountain similarly sized me up, found me to be impaired, and judged me to be harmless. Also, she may have assumed I would never survive to tell the story. *If so, she was almost right.* I smiled but also shuddered at the idea. Whatever Emerald's thoughts on my impaired state, she apparently determined that I was no threat to her, and she allowed me to approach her.

Reluctantly pushing the sheets and comforter aside, I paused to brace myself for another long day of contending with pets and their people at the veterinary clinic. Whether or not I would need to diagnose and treat a dragon after work, I never knew until it happened. There was never any warning. A dragon would arrive on average every two or three weeks, but sometimes a month or more went by between visits. Or sometimes merely days.

Sometimes a colleague or coworker comments about how "every day is different" in veterinary medicine, which is true. Our days in practice are filled with a variety of patients, conditions, and complications; no two days are ever alike. Now, even after nearly two decades of practice, I still occasionally see things that I've never encountered before.

However, I always have to laugh when such comments come up. Try practicing veterinary medicine on fire-breathing creatures after hours, anywhere from cow-sized to bigger-than-elephant-sized, and you never know when they'll turn up or what might be wrong with them when they do. Oh, and the creatures are supposed to be imaginary. *Try THAT for random.*

Begrudgingly, I finally hauled myself out of bed to face the day. "Morning," I mumbled sleepily to Jon as I passed him on the way to the bathroom.

Already thoroughly caffeinated, he turned to me, ready to chatter about whatever was on his mind. He thought better of it when he saw my face, pale and drawn from fatigue. "Uh, good morning?" he replied hesitantly, then wisely let me be.

Reluctantly, I scrubbed as much of the sleepiness from my face as possible, dug a rumpled but clean set of scrubs out of a laundry basket, and managed to put them on right-side out. I poured myself a giant mug of coffee, turned down Jon's offer of eggs and toast, and left for work five minutes late, in a foul humor, and not looking forward to my day.

To my surprise, that particular day at the veterinary clinic was relatively easy. Several appointments didn't show up, so my schedule was light. No one tried to bite me (although one cranky cat undoubtedly considered it), and no one yelled at me. In a rare feat of efficiency, I finished my records before the front door was locked. The sun was still three hours from setting when I drove home in the desert heat, relieved and grateful for the respite from my usual demanding routine. If any dragons were lurking around the clinic and waiting to catch me under cover of darkness, they'd have to wait for another night.

For once I arrived home earlier than Jon, who was working late. The house felt not just quiet but soporific, and I yawned. Our orange tabby cat chirruped a sleepy greeting as I scratched his chin for a minute before fetching a beer from the refrigerator. Sitting peacefully outdoors felt like the ideal end to an easygoing day, so I slid a chair under a mesquite tree's shadow and sipped my beer, idly enjoying the view of the red cliffs in the distance as the sun slowly descended toward the horizon. I felt more relaxed than I could remember being in years.

The day, overall, was a unicorn, which left me with spare time to contemplate other "fantasy" creatures besides unicorns, like the ones that commonly disrupted my evenings and nights, leaving me sleep-deprived and irritable. *Life would be so much easier if the dragons made appointments.* But that sounded comically improbable. To think of a dragon calling from a pay phone to schedule, carefully pressing numbers with the points of her talons, made me laugh.

Phone calls and appointments aside, I had discovered that some of the dragons were capable of talking! Late on a winter night, just over three years since I met Emerald, an enormous and arrogant wyrm spoke to me. I was shocked speechless. For so long I had talked to the creatures without a word in return, I wasn't sure what to say once I could anticipate a reply.

Effectively communicating with dragons, however, proved difficult. First, dragons' voices were strained and gravelly, very similar in tone and timbre regardless of gender, their annunciation and word emphasis quite different from ours. Consequently, I struggled to make out what they were saying. And while dragons chose their words carefully and were not prone to endless rambling, their language was filled with nuances and riddles. They were poetic, perhaps, but not at all straightforward to interpret.

While in work mode, I routinely asked pet owners succinct questions, hoping for equally succinct answers, trying to obtain the salient points of history, nutrition, symptoms, contributing factors, etc. My goal was to determine a diagnosis and plan for treatment during the short time allotted for an appointment, or at least figure out which diagnostics were needed to get there.

This approach dismally failed on dragons. Even a question as simple as "How old are you?" elicited a cryptic response.

"I am younger than the mountain that feeds this river. I am older than the first dwelling of your kind in the valley," the wyrm had told me.

Okay, cool, I'll just run off to the library to study geology and the history of local human settlements to figure that one out.

Admittedly, he had answered my question closely enough. A nearby town had sprouted around a copper mine in the 1800s, perched so precariously on the steep mountainside that someone could step off their balcony and fall into their neighbor's chimney. And Native Americans had populated the valley long before the copper mine, evidenced by the ruins of their dwellings in the cliffs and pueblos near the river. The great wyrm was ancient, indeed.

I marveled at how much he must have seen, how dramatically the world had changed during his time on earth, what fantastic experiences he must have had. *And yet he's right here in front of me, alive and well, except for his tail. Amazing. Especially for a creature that isn't supposed to exist.*

"Please tell me when this injury occurred?"

"At the light of the quarter moon, when the brightest planet in the sky rose where I would next see the sun."

Fantastic. I'll add astronomy and lunar cycles to my study agenda.

Not that I would have expected the dragon to answer my questions like a person would. He had gone to the trouble to learn the English language (was he fluent in others, I wondered?), but why bother with the human construct of time? The cycles of the sun and moon, movements of the planets and stars, and geologic events would be far more meaningful to a dragon than minutes, hours, days, or years, especially considering the creatures apparently lived for centuries.

The hide beneath the dragon's palm-sized scales was so tough, I had given up trying to suture the beagle-sized three-cornered tear near his tail base. After cleaning debris from the wound and flushing it with antiseptic, I improvised gigantic "steri-strips" using five sections of duct tape across the laceration. I wasn't sure if it would work, but I found myself improvising treatment for these overlarge patients on a regular basis. The dragon must have collided heavily with something to create such a tear through his thick armor. Whatever had caused the wound, I had no idea, and he wouldn't tell me.

As I finished taping the wyrm's tail, I pondered whether I might ask him anything that he would answer, and better yet that I could understand, before sending him off into the night. I couldn't expect him to stick around long enough to teach me all I wanted to know about dragon anatomy and physiology. But perhaps I could learn something?

"Sir..."

The wyrm glared at me with contempt. I've since learned that dragons of advanced age prefer lofty titles like "Great One" or "Mighty One." They really are proud and arrogant creatures.

I pressed on. "If I may ask... I believe I know why the first dragon allowed me to treat her wing that day on the mountain. But— why do dragons continue to come here, to me, for veterinary care?" My plea was as old as humanity itself, as old as the history of human suffering: *Why me?*

"You are known," the wyrm replied simply. And with a whoosh of his huge wings, he was gone. A cold winter breeze, edged with hot and acrid air from the dragon's breath, blew in his wake. The nearby row of palm trees rustled and swayed, and my short hair fluttered against my face and ears as I squinted into the starlit sky where he'd vanished. A patch of stars quivered for a split second and then steadied, the palm leaves settled as the wind died down, and all returned to normal.

That was it. To be honest, I was puzzled and disappointed. Numerous times since that mysterious night, I had thought about the enigmatic wyrm that I'd named King. I pondered what he'd meant, just as I did while I rested under the shade of the mesquite tree all those months later. Sweat beaded on my face as I frowned, and I rolled the cold, damp beer bottle over my forehead and temples, reveling in the chill of the glass on my skin. The mesquite trees resembled acacia trees in Africa, and I thought again of the forlorn, bewildered lion I'd reminisced about early that morning.

King had said nothing about any confidence in my skills, nothing about why dragons were seeking veterinary care now, when they'd survived without my help for centuries. Judging by the look of the wyrm, he'd endured and recovered from far worse injuries than the laceration I addressed. *So why me? Why now? How do they find me?*

Definitive answers to those questions have never come. Although years later I can claim to have partial answers, having filled in the gaps with assumptions and suspicions. Initially, based on my experience with the wyrm, I thought that language skills were unique to very old dragons. I was wrong. Two more dragons spoke to me within the next few months, and neither of them were anywhere near elderly. I began to suspect that other dragons might have been able to speak but chose not to.

Gradually, I learned to decipher some of the dragons' cryptic sayings. "My sustenance rebelled" I interpreted as nausea and perhaps vomiting. "The plumpest deer lack appeal" indicated loss of appetite. "Constant whines of the cursed hell hounds ceaselessly haunt me" meant tinnitus, I think, although I've been unable to confirm that. Anyway, you get the idea.

Since you're reading my tales about dragons, chances are you've seen *The Hobbit: The Desolation of Smaug*. The scenes where Smaug conversed with Bilbo and the dwarves made me laugh every time, because his verbiage was so simple (Smaug's words as recited in Tolkien's book were somewhat more realistic, in my opinion). Also, the movie version of Smaug was absolutely humongous. I've never met a wyrm that large, and I'm not certain dragons of that size actually exist. Anything to make a movie more dramatic and appealing, I suppose. Although, who knew? If I had been asked years ago, I'd have said there were no such things as dragons.

On multiple occasions, I've questioned verbal dragons about the source of an injury. "Details matter not," or a similarly huffy dismissal, was the typical response I'd get. In other words, the dragon somehow seriously miscalculated, and with great intelligence came the capacity for great embarrassment. However sometimes they would admit what happened, although I had to listen between the lines to figure out what they were actually saying.

One impetuous adolescent male dragon confessed to his attempt to fly sideways through the uprights of a railroad trestle spanning a river gorge, a stunt that earned him the moniker Klutz. He described the trestle as a "path of the metal snake over the water," and it took me a few minutes to figure out what he meant. Apparently, he misjudged the opening beneath the trestle and smacked both wings into the uprights ("liquid that turns to stone" meant concrete, I think, and "metal nest" I suspect meant the steel framework), then tumbled into the gorge ("countless turns before water and stone"). The poor guy sustained some nasty wing lacerations, a concussion, a broken horn that refused to stop bleeding for quite some time, and two torn talons. And after all that, Klutz found his way to me. A fall from that height likely would have killed any other animal, but dragons were tough.

His concussion presumably dulled his inhibition to talk, I suspected. I could empathize, since my poor swollen brain had lost its inhibitions to see fantasy creatures. After treating the railroad trestle victim, I've always wondered whether dragons engaged in dares or bets with each other, or perhaps showed off for potential mates. Klutz reminded me of a teenage boy. In fact, he had the audacity to insist that the "metal nest" moved to ensnare him, rather than owning up to misjudging the span. Teenagers have always been crafty at shifting blame.

And speaking of teenagers, another talkative young dragon solved a mystery for me. Every year, usually sometime around mid-September, I'd start seeing adolescent dragons with indigestion. A rash of these would appear over three to five weeks, then none at all until the following year. The affected dragons usually responded well to antacid, anti-gas, and pro-motility medications to stimulate intestinal movement. Sometimes they required anti-nausea and pain medications too, and rarely IV fluids for severe cases. I had no idea what was causing this, but every year I would brace myself for the onslaught. The condition always occurred in adolescent dragons, never hatchlings, young juveniles, or adults.

Most of these dragons never said a word, but I could diagnose the problem easily enough based on the signs of belching (occasionally with flame emissions!), horrid flatulence, and a hunched posture that indicated abdominal pain. Straightforward enough, but what on earth was the cause, and why did it happen with such a distinct seasonal pattern? As a side note, flatulence in fire-breathing species was no joke. Not only was the odor intolerable to an eye-watering degree, the flammability was rather problematic as well.

At last, a young female spilled the beans, or corn, as it were. She informed me that adolescent dragons, typically in pairs or small groups, often frequented corn fields (which were grown in multiple parts of Arizona, despite the heat) once the corn had ripened. Their favorite pursuit there, I was told, was to find dried corn stalks left standing in the fields. The dragons would take a large mouthfuls of corn, then breathe fire, mouths closed, to make the corn pop.

And you thought cruising Main Street with your friends was an entertaining pastime in high school. Try popping popcorn in your own mouth. The trouble with this habit was that the dragons usually swallowed the popcorn they'd created (truthfully, who could blame them?). And dragons' gastrointestinal tracts, well-suited for fresh prey or even carrion, did not tolerate corn well. Thus the indigestion. Despite the sometimes significant discomfort, adolescent dragons found this quite amusing. Admittedly, I had to appreciate the appeal and admire their creativity. Once I understood what caused this seasonal spate of GI distress, which I informally dubbed "popcorn-itis," I started closely examining the sick dragons' mouths (a body part that still frightened me). Sure enough, I'd usually find popcorn kernels, scorched strands of corn silk, and the telltale odor of popped corn.

My disquieted mood from contemplating the wyrm lightened considerably while I thought about silly adolescent dragons and their cornfield shenanigans, and I chuckled to myself. The brown ale had warmed to its optimal temperature, and I savored the malty, caramel flavor as I drank it down, eager to finish it before it warmed too much.

The dragons, whether they were verbal or not, had taught me so much over the years I had known them. When I encountered the first dragon on the mountain I was a relatively new graduate, still gaining skills and confidence in practice. And I was miserably, inexorably shaken when these "imaginary" creatures started showing up ill or injured at my clinic. Years later, practically nothing rattled me.

Even the fiercest house cat (you may laugh, but just try taking a rectal temperature and vaccinating one) or most aggressive dog wouldn't raise my blood pressure. I was calm and collected through seizures, hemorrhage, heatstroke, and rattlesnake bites; and I prevailed over surgical complications without imploring colleagues for help. Meanwhile, I sleuthed pathways through complicated internal medicine and endocrinology cases, vaccinated and snuggled puppies and kittens, and at the other end of life, held paws and comforted owners as their beloved pets took their last breaths. The hours were routinely difficult, draining, and sometimes heartbreaking, but I had settled into my role. And finally loved it… most of the time, anyway.

Through all of this, I never knew when a sick or injured dragon would show up and require my time and skills. And the dragons required infinitely more courage and ingenuity than my small animal patients ever did. I simply learned to roll with this surreal, grueling "routine" filled with unpredictability, stealth, and risk. But my "routine" was about to undergo major upheaval. My husband and I were planning to move to Idaho.

Jon finally arrived home and joined me in the back yard to watch the sunset as we chatted about the logistics of relocating. We covered a few details of real estate listings, moving trucks, and transporting pets and houseplants while we drank beers; his first, and my second. After immersing my thoughts in dragons for much of the evening, conversing with my husband about moving felt rather mundane, even almost dull, though comforting. However, I was still troubled not only by the wyrm that raised more questions than answers, but by dragons in general.

Although Emerald had tracked me down over sixty miles from where I first encountered her, I was certain that the dragons would not have the ability nor the interest to follow me across three states. So while I said goodbye to the red rocks of the desert, to my dear colleagues and coworkers, and to a multitude of dedicated clients and beloved patients, I was convinced that I was saying farewell to my clandestine dragon patients as well.

Despite feeling somewhat sad about leaving, I truly looked forward to the move. I held similar mixed feelings about leaving the dragons. Surely they would be fine, having survived without veterinary care for millennia. As for the thrill and challenge of seeing them, that I would miss. But as for the danger, the mess, the stealth, and the stress of keeping them secret… the idea of leaving all that behind was honestly refreshing.

Once we were sure of the move, I informed every dragon I saw that I would be gone in several months' time. How dragons communicated to each other over long distances was something I've never entirely understood, but I was hoping that the word would get around. No use having dragons lurking around the veterinary clinic and risking discovery when I was no longer there.

However, I didn't tell them where I was going. No reason to, I surmised, since I was positively certain that once I left Arizona, I would never see another dragon again.

About that, I was mistaken.

9

Alarmed

Despite my few misgivings, we departed the Southwest in high spirits, equally excited and optimistic about the future. Our optimism quickly evolved to more complicated emotions when we met with reality. We moved in February, shortly after a sixty-five degree Christmas Day in Arizona, and I remained an icicle for weeks in the frigid Idaho winter. Keeping up with laundry became an unexpected challenge, as I churned through layers and layers and layers of socks, shirts, and leggings to stay warm.

Difficulty with acclimation aside, we felt refreshed to live somewhere with "real seasons" again. Jon and I had been daydreaming about buying land someday, and we agreed that the Arizona desert wasn't for us. We talked of mountains, trees, and water. While we couldn't yet buy a large property, it felt like we were one step closer by moving to our own modest house on the edge of town in Idaho.

Primarily, we relocated to buy a veterinary practice in a small city. I was excited to be a practice owner, relieved to have the freedom to manage it as I wished. Also, I was miserable as a practice owner. The clinic monopolized the entirety of my time and energy; and not only mine, but also my husband's, since he was our office manager. We were terribly stressed, and I spent most days feeling as though I were attempting to juggle eighteen different things and dropping sixteen of them.

Some days were fantastic, and I was confident we'd made the right decision. Other days were awful, and I survived on adrenaline, caffeine, and antacids, certain we'd made a terrible mistake. Working with my husband added another level of tension since we lacked anything to talk about other than the clinic, and discussing the business was nerve-wracking for both of us. We grew volatile from the pressure, and we frequently sniped at each other.

At times I missed the relative simplicity of being an associate veterinarian, although that came with its own significant stressors. As for the Arizona heat, ubiquitous prickly plants, and abundant rattlesnakes, I was glad to be rid of those. However, I missed the dragons. Even though they exhausted and regularly frustrated me nearly to tears, I missed the challenge, the exhilaration, and the novelty of seeing them. But considering how overwhelmed I was as a practice owner, I thought it was just as well that dragon veterinary medicine was behind me.

Months went by. Just when I felt we were beginning to take things in stride, and the clinic was ticking along somewhat closer to how I envisioned it should, we suffered a break-in. Someone smashed in the glass front door late one night, seeking drugs, but left empty-handed after prying in vain at the heavy cash safe that held our controlled substances. Thankfully, no one was hurt, but as owners we felt violated, outraged that someone so callously wrought damage to the small business into which we'd poured our hearts and souls.

As I bitterly swept up the million shards of tempered glass that had flown to every corner of the lobby, I resolved to have an alarm system installed as soon as possible. We'd been planning for this anyway, but it had never quite made it into the monthly budget. *Clearly, we have to find a way to pay for that. It can't wait any longer.*

Contractors visited, bids were made, and a short time later we were the proud owners of a security system, complete with motion alarms, entry alarms, panic buttons, and indoor security cameras. Any of the alarms or panic buttons triggered an alert to police dispatch, and the unfailingly efficient dispatchers would send officers within minutes.

Unfortunately, over the next few months we discovered how easily the alarm system could be triggered. Officers responded to alarms when our clinic cat escaped her cage, hospitalized patients rolled over in their kennels, and even a plant dropped a leaf near a motion sensor. We learned that the police would tolerate several false alarms, particularly from a business going through the learning curve of a new security system. However, the police department threatened to fine us if the false alarms continued. And if that didn't solve the problem, they would stop responding altogether. The alarms could have sounded for any reason, and the police would have ignored them.

Needless to say, we were eager to keep our good standing with the police. The security system would have been pointless without their cooperation whenever the alarms were tripped by anything more nefarious than the lobby plants. We apologized repeatedly and had the contractor out multiple times to make adjustments, posted signs reminding staff to securely lock up the clinic cat after hours, and carefully trimmed the plants to avoid criminal falling leaves. Finally, we succeeded in fine-tuning the system to our liking. Months passed by with no need to apologize to the police for a false alarm.

Until the entry alarm went off late Thanksgiving evening. The security company called us first, which gave us the option to decline dispatching police if the alarms were consistent with adventures of the clinic cat (again). But this alarm wasn't the cat's fault. Someone was most likely trying to break in. We told the security company we'd meet the police at the building.

We shook off our postprandial lethargy from Thanksgiving dinner and sped to the clinic. Three patrol cars were there, and officers were in the building, which should have been locked tight for the holiday. As we hurried inside, I was relieved to see that the glass doors were intact, but what was going on?

An officer explained that they had easily walked through the lobby side door, which was standing open. Suspecting an intruder to be inside, they'd drawn their guns and searched every corner of every room. They'd found no one. Five or six policemen were milling about the clinic, one of them distractingly tall.

We reviewed the security footage of the lobby with two officers watching over our shoulders. A shadowy shape appeared through the glass door just before it opened. The footage was fuzzy and indistinct, but something could be seen inside the door frame for a moment. Someone's gloved fingers, maybe?

My husband paused the video and zoomed in. *Are those... claws?* My stomach dropped as the realization ricocheted through my frontal lobes and then pinged to my amygdala, triggering my own personal alarm. *WOOP! WOOP! WOOP!*

THE DRAGONS ARE BACK! WOOP WOOP WOOP!

Squeezing my eyes shut, I fought against the revelation that I knew to be true. *No. No. No!* I was determined to wish the dragons away.

The officers continued chatting with my husband, confident that someone had managed to unlock the door, held it open for a moment with their gloved hand, then apparently had second thoughts and ran for the hills. How amazing that they'd been able to unlock the door without damaging it, and were we absolutely certain that it was locked to begin with? The officers glanced at my husband, then they all three looked at me. Jon's eyes narrowed when he saw my pale face, and the officers' serious expressions transformed to concern.

"Ma'am, are you feeling okay? Do you need to sit down?"

"I'm fine — it's just stressful, I guess." *Little do they know.* "The staff lock the doors and are supposed to verify that before the alarms are set. Usually I check the doors, too, but I don't remember checking last night, so it's possible one was missed. I'm sorry for the oversight." I had lied. I was absolutely certain I had checked the door and found it locked.

The scrutiny rapidly became uncomfortable, and I excused myself to the restroom. I would have preferred a soundproof room to shout profanity at high volume, but the bathroom would have to do. *This CANNOT be happening.* I'd loved my years of treating dragons (well mostly, anyway), but those days were over. Owning and managing the clinic demanded far too much of my time and energy, and I could not fathom fitting dragons into my chaotic routine. Not to mention, I dreaded the stress of keeping them secret and safe from discovery.

Also, I had always been honest about the dragons with Jon, but he'd thought it to be an elaborate story, something creative and fun I had devised so I could avoid dwelling on the raw heartbreak and frustrations of "real" practice. *What now? Will he be forced to believe me?* I spent a moment bracing myself for my husband's probable upcoming existential crisis. Then I moved on to worrying about everything else all at once. The base of my skull began to throb, and I sighed. *Of course, I'm getting a headache.*

Splashing water onto my face from the faucet, I began to convince myself that I was mistaken. Perhaps that was someone's hand after all, and the alarm scared off the intruder. Ironic that I would have preferred a real break-in over what I suspected was the truth. *But maybe it's NOT the truth.* Maybe I was seeing memories of dragons, shadows of creatures that lurked in my past.

Exiting my cramped refuge, I found my husband bidding goodbye to the last two officers at the back door, including the really tall guy. Jon retreated inside while I thanked the police and apologized for the inconvenience on Thanksgiving, no less. I shivered in the cold breeze, hugging myself over my insufficient jacket, though the freezing air felt great on my aching head. The pain abated but the back of my skull remained stretched tight, as though it were squeezed by a rubber band.

The officers required no apology, they insisted. This was no false alarm; they'd even had occasion to draw their guns, after all. This was much more interesting than the clinic cat.

"You know," the shorter officer remarked, "the cameras inside are great, but you really should install security cams out here, too. One over every door, and at least one pointed at the parking lot...."

Nodding in agreement at the policemen facing me on the sidewalk, I idly wondered how tall the one must be, six-feet-five or six-feet-six at least. Then I nearly lost every last shred of composure I possessed when the nose of a dragon, followed by the rest of the dragon's head, poked out from between the branches of a scraggly lilac bush right behind the officers. Her nostrils were at the same height as the tall cop's ear, not even three feet away from his head.

".... if there'd been a camera over that door," the officer continued. "Would be nice to catch the perp, not just scare him off...."

Ignore the dragon, focus on the cops, don't look at the dragon, focus.... The dragon's nostrils flared as she exhaled, though the sound was lost in the wind. The tall cop's hair fluttered from the dragon's breath.

"Ma'am, are you sure you're okay?" the officer asked, abandoning his tutorial on security systems. Both officers gazed at me intently, brows furrowed.

The dragon's head withdrew into the depths of the lilac bush. Her horns dislodged a dozen dried leaves that noiselessly flew away in the breeze. How on earth she hadn't caught her head in the dense tangle of branches was beyond me.

"Yeah, sorry, I'm fine," I insisted distractedly. "I should go home and let you get back to, uhhh, catching bad guys."

They laughed and headed for their patrol car.

I waved, trying to act normal. "Thanks for the advice on the cameras. We'll talk to the security company about that." Or then again, maybe we wouldn't. I wasn't so sure I wanted dragons on camera.

The officers got in the patrol car. "Did you feel that warm breeze? That was weird," I overheard the tall one say.

His partner turned to him, mystified. "What?!" Both car doors slammed shut, and the remainder of their conversation was lost to me.

Waiting until the officers were out of sight, I walked down the sidewalk and hung my elbows over the fence, leaned into the neighboring yard, and squinted into the overgrown lilacs and dogwoods. The dragon, so dark she was almost black, disentangled her ivory-colored horns from the branches and peered at me. Her dark eyes would have been invisible to me if it weren't for the soft gleam from the streetlamp mirrored in her pupils. The twin reflections disappeared momentarily as she blinked, then reappeared as she continued her calm gaze.

Resigned and deflated, I stood there, leaning on the fence, watching the dragon. *So here we go again. Unbelievable.* She lumbered across the grass to me and quietly snuffled my arms and face. Even if I could have mistaken the dragon for something else, I could never have mistaken dragon breath. It smelled every bit as pungent as I remembered.

"Except for your horns, you're so dark that you blend in with the shadows. Should I call you Shadow? Or maybe Midnight?" The dragon lightly nuzzled my elbow, clearly indifferent to whatever I called her. Far too spent to brainstorm anything more creative, I settled on Midnight.

She didn't seem distressed or eager to show me some malady. Before I examined her more closely, I decided my husband might as well be introduced to a dragon. If I waited long enough, he was bound to stumble right into this scene anyway.

Bidding Midnight to stay put, I went inside. The lights were out, save for one. I found my husband at his desk in the office, busy with paperwork, because the paperwork was never finished. Quickbooks glared rudely on his computer monitor.

"Hey, Jon? Why don't you shut it down," I implored. "It's a holiday."

"Yeah, well, we're here," he replied tiredly, still staring at the screen. "But I know, I should deal with this tomorrow."

Pulling my chair across the office, I sat next to him. He knew something was amiss and looked up quizzically.

"Jordyn, what's wrong?" Jon frowned as he scrutinized my anxious expression.

Pausing, I shifted awkwardly in my chair. Even though Jon was the only person I had ever been able to talk to about the dragons, this was different.

"So… you know my stories about dragons?" I asked hesitantly. "That you've always thought were a joke?"

"Yeah?"

"Jon, they're not a joke. The dragons are real."

Seconds ticked by as his face evolved from shocked to angry — I must be joking, and it wasn't funny — to confusion, disbelief, then horror and fear. Obviously, I wasn't joking. He knew I had been seriously stressed and worried, but now I was clearly losing my grip on reality. He hadn't a clue how to react or what to do.

Abruptly, I got up and pushed my chair back to its place. "Follow me."

"What?!" Jon protested.

"I'm serious! Come here and see for yourself," I demanded. I was already marching down the hallway, back to the parking lot and the lilac bush with its hidden dragon.

Jon followed several steps behind me as I approached the fence to tell Midnight I was back with a guest. However, the yard was empty. My husband leaned over the fence beside me, staring in bewilderment in turns between me and the bushes as I scrutinized the lilacs, dogwoods, even the shrubby boxwoods that were far too small for concealment. No dragon.

My strange behavior confused and frightened Jon. He fluttered in my wake, speechless from shock. Ignoring him, I stomped through the side yard, crushing the fallen leaves with a forceful *crunch, crunch, crunch,* and surveyed the trees and bushes in front of the clinic. No dragon. Back to the parking lot, I looked up and down the alley. Still no dragon. I scanned the empty lot with its few elm and pine trees next door. No dragon. Marching across the parking lot, I checked the roof of the clinic. Absolutely no dragon to be found.

Turning slowly in a circle, I squinted into the darkness in all directions. Houses surrounded the clinic, and haphazard rows of fences shielded the back yards and sheds that bordered the alley. The dragon could have been hidden anywhere. But continuing to search was pointless; evidently, she didn't want to be found.

I was absolutely livid. A dragon's trickery had disrupted my rare day off from the clinic. I'd somewhat made a fool of myself in front of the police, then really made a fool of myself in front of Jon. Now my husband thought I had lost my mind. Angry in general at the dragons for returning, irritated at this particular dragon for appearing only to disappear, and mad at Jon for disbelieving me, I sat in silent fury on the drive home. My head throbbed with renewed ferocity, and the pain steadily crawled forward toward my temples like lava from a volcano.

Ignoring Jon's puzzled and concerned looks, I went straight to bed, desperate for sleep but dreading the inevitable dreams. However, sleep eluded me. Staring at the ceiling for a while, then in turn at the insides of my eyelids, I acknowledged that while I wanted to indulge in my anger, steeping in my fury until it fizzled out, there was more to it than that.

While dragons were not at all predictable, I never knew one to appear and then merely disappear without treatment of any kind. That night, the dragon stayed so briefly, I hadn't even determined what was wrong with her. Perplexed and anxious, I worried whether she was hurt or sick and needed my help. And, to be honest, I was angry with myself for leaving her for those few minutes, wanting to introduce my husband before I examined her, and she just... left. Perhaps she thought I had abandoned her, and that bothered me most of all.

Whether or not she returned — and though I didn't want to admit it, I truly hoped she would — I strongly suspected there would be others. And a small part of me, the part I didn't want to acknowledge yet, was pleased to have the dragons back.

10

Initiation

The dragons returned in full force before I was quite ready for them. Following the security alarm debacle, I had just started to wrap my brain around the probability of treating dragons again when one showed up for treatment. Then another in less than a week, and yet another only days later.

Once my shock and frustration waned and resignation set in, I realized that as a practice owner, I could become much better equipped to perform dragon medicine. And then I got excited about the possibilities. After all, I could order whatever supplies and medication I wished (within reason, budget permitting), and any of those materials could be documented for "clinic use" without scrutiny.

Perhaps I could even experiment with controlled substances for sedation or anesthesia, which I'd badly wanted to do at my previous clinic, but couldn't accomplish without the whole endeavor crashing down. As long as I documented the use of controlled medications in such a way that met legal requirements, I could think of no reason not to try those drugs on dragons.

I would be able to run laboratory tests, assuming I could collect the samples to do so. I could leverage the x-ray machine, if the dragon in question was small enough for that, or the surgery suite and anesthesia machines. When the building or equipment inevitably got banged up in the process, I had no boss to answer to; I WAS the boss. And when we eventually expanded the clinic into the adjacent vacant lot, which we tentatively planned to do several years later, then I could incorporate a hospital ward for dragons. That, too, was something I'd badly wanted more than once in Arizona. The possibilities were endless, and I would be able to help the dragons so much more. Although, as I schemed of all the ways I could help my winged patients, I did not dream of any way to actually fund my grand ideas. Building a dragon hospital ward sounded great until I thought about the costs involved.

Another complication arose in the form of my office manager, a.k.a. my husband, who didn't believe dragons existed. Not only that, he likely thought I was going insane, as evidenced by the frequent concerned glances and awkward stares when he thought I wasn't paying attention. Jon was responsible for ordering the medical supplies, and he closely monitored the books. He would undoubtedly notice when loads of medications and supplies for "clinic use" disappeared without explanation. Nor would he agree to order equipment or make modifications to the building that didn't make sense to him. Nor would he take it in stride if building repairs had to be undertaken on a regular basis. Unlike my old boss, we took pride in the appearance of our clinic.

And that's why I was bound and determined to introduce my husband to a dragon.

It took months to accomplish, with multiple near misses along the way. Just as they had been in Arizona, the dragons were talented at catching me when I was alone at the clinic. But now, I made every effort to drag Jon to the clinic whenever a dragon was present. I failed time after time. He'd been hiking or biking miles up the trails, cooking dinner, showering, or sleeping. And when I'd finally convinced him to come, sometimes only minutes after a dragon had flown away, he'd been irritated by my lame explanations. "Oh, I'm sorry, I just this moment solved that computer issue myself," I'd fibbed sheepishly. I was running out of excuses to insist that he come down.

Eventually, my persistence paid off. Jon sat with me at the clinic late one evening, having reluctantly agreed to go over some accounting questions after hours. I didn't know for certain a dragon would show up that night, but those days there was a fair chance on any evening, and I hoped one would appear. Sure enough, as I stepped out of the back door into the darkened parking lot to go home, a dragon stretched his great head and neck from behind my Volkswagen. I stopped in my tracks as the dragon regarded me for a few moments with sand dollar-sized brown eyes that gleamed softly in the bit of light that strayed through the doorway. Three pairs of white horns spiraled tightly from his brow and temples, starkly contrasting with his dark face. The dragon flared his nostrils, then brought the rest of his body from behind my car, revealing his dark brown trunk, limbs, and wings adorned with white spikes and claws. Considering how tall and lanky he was, he must have been tightly huddled to have been concealed so well by my little car.

Any moment my husband would walk out the door into

this scene, and I was elated. I stood by to let it happen, and sure enough, Jon soon stepped through the door carrying a thick file folder in one arm. The moment he saw the dragon, he startled and recoiled, flinging the folder of papers to the ground.

"WHAT THE HELL IS THAT?! WHAT IS IT?!" my dear husband yelled, then followed up with some colorful profanity.

Jon was shouting far too loud, and not only was I concerned he would attract the attention of neighbors, I was worried the dragon would get agitated. Adult males could be quick to act defensively, as I had learned the hard way years before. He was already tense, snorting and looking suspiciously at Jon, and the last thing we needed was for him to get blasted by the dragon's breath weapon or fire. Also, our accounting documents were scattered over the sidewalk and in danger of blowing away.

"*Sshhhhhh*," I hissed. "Jon, calm down! You're scaring him. Here, help me pick these up."

Jon stopped shouting long enough to look at me incredulously. "Scaring that?! I'M scaring THAT?" He stabbed his index finger toward the dragon in terrified indignation. "What about—"

"Yes, you are," I interjected calmly. "And if you keep scaring him, he may act dangerously... defensively, I mean. Please lower your voice."

The moment I mentioned danger, Jon froze and stared at me, eyes wide and mouth agape. To his credit, he stopped yelling. After a minute, he broke out of his paralyzed fear and slowly bent down, keeping his eyes fixed on the dragon, fumbling his shaky hands over the sidewalk to gather a few papers. "Jordyn… is that what I think it is?" he asked quietly, his voice tremulous and about an octave higher than normal.

Honestly, I was impressed that my husband, typically quick to panic and slow to calm down, had recovered this rapidly. Well, somewhat recovered, anyway. I don't think anyone ever fully recovers from seeing dragons, maybe not even me. "Jon, look at me." Seconds went by, and he finally tore his gaze away from the dragon and gazed into my eyes.

"I know you've always thought the dragons were a joke," I told him gently. "I know lately, you thought I was going crazy. But I've been telling you the truth. The dragons are real, they actually come to me for treatment, and now you get to meet one. Jon, this is a dragon. Dragon, meet Jon. What do you think we should name him?"

Eyes still wide in shock and disbelief, Jon stared at the dragon as the creature warily scrutinized him back. The dragon's agitation eased once my husband was finished yelling.

"Here, take these." Pressing the file folder into his hands, I looked around for any stray documents. We'd gathered them all, unless some had scattered in the wind. "Okay, let's see what's going on with you, big guy."

Jon stood back cautiously as I examined the dragon. He seemed healthy enough, if perhaps a bit thin. Having saved the oral cavity for last, cautious of possible flame emissions, I carefully inspected his teeth and found no explanation for illness. The dragon needed laboratory testing, but with his thick, mature armor, I wasn't sure how to collect blood. Never mind the fact that no laboratory in the world had normal blood work values for dragons, so any lab results would be open to my interpretation.

Thinking hard, I pondered how to draw blood samples. Most likely I wouldn't be able to access any peripheral veins through his heavy scales. *Can I perhaps convince him to let me snip a talon short to collect blood from the nail quick?* Although I wasn't sure what I might use to cut a dragon talon. I assumed they'd be incredibly tough, and dog nail trimmers weren't strong enough to do the job.

While I continued to deliberate, the dragon shuffled away from me, positioned his lanky body into an awkward squat, and unceremoniously defecated right behind my car. His tail quivered and the spade-shaped tip flicked from side-to-side as he made his deposit. That was a new one for me. The dragons were full of nasty surprises.

Shaking my head, I stepped closer to the offending pile to see if he had diarrhea. *Wow, the smell! And I thought their breath was bad.* Nearly retching from the terrible odor wafting from the dragon's feces, I staggered backward as Jon stood gawking with his face twisted in revulsion. Perhaps this dragon wasn't the perfect one to introduce to my husband, but there we were.

On various occasions I had seen little fecal pellets from hatchling dragons, but I'd never had the "privilege" to observe adult dragon dung. It appeared solid and formed in the dim light of the parking lot, but something about it wasn't quite right.

I fished my smartphone (new and novel back then!) out of my pocket and turned on the flashlight to illuminate the oversized pile of droppings. Instantly, I had the answer. Huge, pale roundworms threaded throughout the feces, so plentiful that the pile resembled a giant ball of tangled string. No wonder the dragon was underweight! I'd diagnosed parasites numerous times in hatchling and juvenile dragons over the years and frequently wondered if adults ever suffered from serious parasitic infections. Apparently, they could. Jon crept a bit closer to see the roundworms, grimacing in disgust and horror.

Now I had the perfect opportunity to perform a simple laboratory test without drawing blood. Having fetched a fecal sample container from inside the clinic, I held my breath and dived into the radius of stench to collect a stool sample. The evening breeze had died down after the last light of dusk, and my eyes began to water from the incredibly rank odor that hung heavily in the warm, spring air.

I'd succeeded in collecting the fecal sample without passing out, but I hadn't yet decided how to medicate my patient before the test results came back from the lab. The appearance of the worms was my only clue. They strongly resembled dog or cat intestinal roundworms, called ascarids, and I hoped that standard deworming medications for pets would work for dragon roundworms. But the creature was sizable, and would need a huge dose of dewormer. *This might be a problem.*

My shell-shocked husband followed me into the clinic, quietly watching as I scowled into cabinets and debated whether I had enough of any dewormer to effectively medicate the dragon. Eventually, Jon broke his reverie to ask what I was looking for, and I explained my dilemma. He reminded me that a few weeks prior, we had mistakenly ordered a giant jug of equine pyrantel instead of the usual quart-sized bottle for small animals. He opened the cabinet beneath the sink, and there it sat, nestled between gallon jugs of antiseptics and disinfectants. I likely wouldn't have found that on my own, and I was grateful he was there.

The dragon downed half a gallon in the parking lot, slurping the jug with his sticky tongue as I poured it into his mouth. He resembled an orphaned calf slurping at a feeder bottle, and I couldn't resist laughing.

"We haven't given you a name yet. What should we call you? I was thinking of Skinny. But that doesn't seem dignified enough. Jon, what do you think?"

Jon's shock had somewhat abated, but he was nowhere near comfortable with the situation. "I have no idea. Well, I guess I'd call him Terrifying."

"Skinny is nicer than Terrifying. Skinny it is."

Since dragons' sense of time was tied to the sun and lunar cycles, I had learned to keep a calendar handy that included the phases of the moon. With instructions to swallow the remainder of the dewormer after fourteen sunsets, at the full moon, I gave the half-full jug of pyrantel to Skinny. Satisfied, he ambled to the far end of the parking lot and flew off.

Jon was frozen in place, staring after the dragon. His face had aged fifteen years in an evening. I could relate to his turmoil, though it had been many years since I had lived it, endured it, and moved past it. I'd done my best to help the dragons ever since I'd accepted they were real, although I couldn't say I was always thrilled about it. And of course Diane, the vet tech in Arizona, had dealt with the dragons in her own way, by choosing to ignore that they existed. What would Jon do?

Certainly, I had done my best to prepare him for this moment. I'd always told the truth about my experiences with dragons despite Jon's conviction that they were imaginary. His confidence in reality was badly shaken, I was sure, having been there myself. What he'd known to be fantasy was now true, and his world had turned upside-down. I could empathize, but I couldn't control how he'd react to his new world. What he chose to do with the revelation remained to be seen.

While Jon was lost in thought, I tracked down a snow shovel and dispatched the horrid dragon dung into garbage bags. Hefting the bags required some strength, and by the time I successfully wrestled them (still warm — *eww*) into the trash cart, both my husband and the file folder he'd been carrying were nowhere to be seen. As I searched inside the clinic for Jon, I found the folder abandoned on one of the treatment tables.

It took me a minute longer to locate my husband. I found him seated at his desk in the office, lights off, staring vacantly at the darkened computer screen.

"Hey, are you okay?" I asked gently.

He lowered his eyes and rubbed his forehead. "I just want to go home."

"All right, you want me to drive?"

Seconds ticked by as he stared at the keyboard. The smell of the dragon feces still lingered in my nostrils, and I knew my clothes, my hair, and even my pores reeked of it. I craved a shower in the worst way. Come to think of it, I needed to stash some spare clothes at the clinic. Even better, maybe we could construct a shower somewhere in the building. The more time I spent around dragons, the more I'd need it.

"Yeah, sure," he finally replied, looking up at me, or rather through me, with haunted eyes. He looked worn out and haggard, with lines etched into his forehead that I'd never seen before. I handed the file folder to him, and he absently placed it onto the keyboard. I had a feeling those papers were not going to make it home that night after all.

Jon remained silent on the way home, lost in thought. Assuredly, his thoughts were much noisier. I remembered the inner cacophony that I'd endured. I didn't miss it one bit.

The next morning, I woke to find him seated on the edge of the bed, staring off into space.

"You okay?" I mumbled. Mornings were never my thing.

He turned to me. "How did you do it?"

"Huh?" Without much success, I tried to shake off some of the sleepiness.

"You've pulled some great pranks before. But I can't figure out how you pulled this one off."

Oh no. You've got to be kidding me. He'd convinced himself that the dragons were an elaborate hoax. I hadn't anticipated that. "It's not a prank, Jon. I don't have the time or energy for that kind of mischief right now."

He wasn't convinced. I rolled over and buried my face in the pillow.

A couple days later, Skinny's fecal test results appeared in my e-mail. The lab forms required species and breed for samples, so I'd sent the feces under the guise of it belonging to a Great Dane. The sample was heavily positive for *Toxacara cati*, the common cat roundworm. *Fascinating! So the pyrantel should work, assuming I correctly estimated the dose.* I wondered how he'd acquired the parasites, and shuddered to think he might have snacked on a few house cats. But then, mountain lions lived in the area. Perhaps those were part of dragons' diets. I wasn't sure whether mountain lions carried *Toxacara*, but I wouldn't have been surprised.

Even though I had double-bagged the dragon dung and tightly tied the sacks closed, the staff bitterly complained about the stench emanating from the trash cart. They weren't exaggerating. The odor grew worse day-by-day until we finally welcomed the garbage collection truck with much relief. Thankfully, the truck was equipped with a mechanical lift for the trash carts. I had been seriously worried about the health of anyone stuck with manually loading our garbage that week. The last thing we needed was to have sanitation workers passed out in the parking lot, overcome by fumes.

Over the coming days and weeks, Jon whipsawed with dizzying frequency between belief and denial and all the associated emotions. One moment he was convinced I was telling the truth. The next moment, he was trying to figure out how I'd borrowed an animatronic dragon. I never knew which Jon I would talk to next, and I found the constant oscillation exhausting. Undoubtedly, it was more exhausting for him.

Finally, he started to come around, I thought, as he recalled past details about dragons and reframed them with the possibility they might have been real. First, he asked me about the burned shoe that I had discarded ages ago. Had a dragon truly sneezed fire onto my foot? Yes, it had, I assured him. The dragon had sneezed scorch lines onto the pavement of the clinic parking lot, too. But my boss had assumed that neighborhood kids had set off fireworks there.

What about that terrible smell that I came home with once? Wasn't that the same time as the burned shoe? Like skunk smell but not quite, also sort of like burning rubber? Yes, I told him, how could I forget? I truly got blasted by a dragon's breath weapon. But that was by Pepé, the blue dragon, not Sneezy, the dragon that burned my shoe. Same week, though, and come to think of it, same set of shoes. And, I added, I sincerely hoped that Jon would never personally experience a breath weapon.

Then he remembered the very first dragon, the one on Humphreys Peak that I originally thought I hallucinated while I was desperately ill with altitude sickness. Had THAT been real? Well yes, I explained. That was Emerald. I had thought I'd hallucinated her, even as vivid and incredible as she was. But later, I had found the unquestionably tangible first aid supplies I'd used on her wing. And then she'd turned up in the flesh at the clinic. But just as I thought Jon was close to accepting the dragons, he was right back to denying their existence. It was infuriating.

For weeks, he wrestled with this. Having once gone through my own dragon-induced near-breakdown, I could sympathize with his turmoil. But I quickly tired of being dragged vicariously and involuntarily through Jon's crisis, and I became increasingly annoyed.

At least Jon was past the point of questioning my sanity. That sentiment had been replaced by him doubting his own sanity. On and on this went, and the days and weeks dragged by laboriously as we snapped at one another about dragons. The only cure for this agonizing impasse, I concluded, was for Jon to meet more dragons. When or how, I didn't know, but I was confident I could make that happen.

11

Treasures and Myths

Multiple dragons came and went during the weeks following Jon's first encounter. At first, I was eager to introduce him to more of the creatures as soon as possible. Then I realized he probably needed some time to come to terms with the first dragon before he encountered another one. So, I reluctantly tried my best to be patient and wait for a good opportunity. Eventually, without any effort on my part, Jon met another dragon.

We had stayed at the clinic until well past dinner time, once again working on accounting and budgeting, this time at Jon's suggestion. He stepped outside before I did, and a small, gregarious dragon walked right up to him, frills and wings flared in excitement.

Depending on the conformation of their faces, horns, and spikes, some dragons looked harsh and imposing, even frightening. Other dragons appeared softer and gentler, far less intimidating and more approachable (to me, anyway). Juvenile dragons, with their immature spikes and broad foreheads, often appeared endearingly cartoonish, although some were cuter than others.

This little guy was as adorable as he could be, slightly shorter than me, with inky, olive-green scales and disproportionately large, bright, lime-green eyes that wouldn't have looked out of place on a stuffed toy. Delicate frills striped with lighter shades of green flared from behind stubby, dark green horn buds on the back of his head. He exuberantly bounced like a puppy, curious, unassuming, and eager to please, considerably less intimidating than Jon's first dragon acquaintance. Less stinky, too, which was a plus. However, thick nasal discharge crusted around both the juvenile's nostrils, which wasn't so cute.

Jon always was and undoubtedly always would be rather jumpy, so unsurprisingly, the dragon startled him. At least that time, he held on to everything in his hands, but he let loose with some loud expletives.

Hearing the commotion, I hurried to the parking lot. Jon quieted down by the time I reached the door, but he backed nervously against the rear of the building, trying to convince the overeager dragon to stay away. "No… no… get back! No, get away from me!"

Chuckling, I headed toward Jon, intending to rescue him. I needn't have bothered; the moment the friendly creature realized I was there, he promptly abandoned my husband and sidled up to greet me, flapping his wings enthusiastically. I was instantly smitten.

"Hey, cutie! You're adorable!" I told him, smiling. "Looks like you're pretty snotty, though."

The dragon pushed his head under my arm, wanting to be petted.

"Nope, let's not do that," I admonished him. "Stay back,

please." Not only would my skin itch from the nasal discharge, I didn't want to risk a point-blank fiery sneeze. The dragon stepped back, drooping his head, frills, and wings in disappointment. *Oh my gosh, you are irresistible.*

Despite his misgivings, Jon was attracted to the puppy-like dragon, too. Abandoning his bag and coffee mug on the sidewalk, he nervously edged closer. I asked him to stay with the dragon while I retrieved exam gloves and a stethoscope from inside. He agreed without much reluctance.

Scratching between the frills on the dragon's head to keep him distracted, I listened to his chest through my stethoscope. He was enthralled with the shiny bell of my scope. Some dragons were especially attracted to metallic objects, and this one was relentless. I persevered and finally managed to auscultate the dragon's heart and lungs without him nosing and mouthing my stethoscope. Fortunately, his lungs sounded normal. The infection appeared to be confined to his upper airways.

Effectively medicating him, however, would be difficult. The juvenile dragon was just old enough to have come on his own, but he was so immature. Was he capable of taking antibiotics consistently for a week? I wasn't so sure.

Bribing him with leftover tacos from a staff meeting, I coaxed him to swallow a dozen capsules of doxycycline. When I made it into a game with a reward, he proved perfectly capable of taking the medication. I only hoped he would keep it up on his own. Imploring him to take another twelve capsules every time the sun rose and set until the pills were gone, I pressed the vial into his small claw and hoped for the best.

The young dragon nuzzled my arm as I pulled off the exam

gloves, asking for more scratches before he flew off. Having wiped the discharge from his nostrils, I didn't mind so much. Plus, he hadn't sneezed the entire time he'd been there, so I let my guard down. As I rubbed and scratched the leathery scales over his head and neck, he sniffed and nibbled at my necklace and earrings, promptly abandoning those to nibble at my rings whenever my hands left his head. "Chewy," I announced. "That's an easy name for you."

Even though his nose was almost dry, my skin started to itch and tingle where the dragon had picked at my jewelry. But he was so charming, I resigned myself to the temporary discomfort. Chewy was worth it.

As he gets older, I bet he'll collect shiny things and build a treasure hoard. Of course, the fantasy trope was that dragons hoarded valuables and guarded them fiercely. In reality, I had learned that only a small minority of dragons were interested in "treasure." And not everything they collected was valuable to humans. While they would indeed acquire coins, precious metals, and gemstones, they also collected things like junk metal, glass bottles, and pretty but "worthless" rocks and the like, sometimes even glittery, plastic things. When it came to hoarding, a dragon could be described as one part pack rat, one part goblin, and one part toddler after visiting the dollar store. Everything they collected was valuable to them, of course, and I'd been fascinated to learn that they would sometimes barter their belongings with other dragons.

The occasional dragon amassed a vast treasure, and the rare dragon became obsessed to the point of violence about protecting their holdings from intruders and thieves, which gave all dragons a bad name (honestly, I believe mental illness plays a role in these situations). However, most dragons lived simply and peaceably and didn't seem at all preoccupied with their belongings.

Closing his eyes in contentment, the inky dragon abandoned my jewelry and leaned into my hand as I scratched behind his jaw. Seizing the opportunity, Jon approached the creature. "Aww, you're just a little guy!" he said in a sing-song voice. Chewy turned to face him and blinked his captivating green eyes, then violently sneezed.

Reflexively yanking my hand away, I skittered backward, removing my feet from the firing range. The dragon shook his head, comically flapping his lips, then sneezed again. Nasal discharge landed on the gravel of the parking lot with a *splat*, but luckily, no fire. A few moments passed before I realized that Jon had disappeared. He had retreated around the side of the building, and was now tentatively peeking around the corner.

"Be careful with the sneezes, okay? You might accidentally start a forest fire. Try to sneeze into your wing. Off with you now, and remember to take your meds." The funny dragon snuffled off to the end of the parking lot and lifted his wings into the sky. At that moment, something huge and dark rose above the bushes of the vacant house next door, and I flinched for the second time that night. "Whoaaa!" Jon exclaimed, as I wheeled around to assess the situation.

The black female dragon flew directly over our heads, visible just long enough for me to recognize her, then she departed into the night behind the juvenile. I was certain it was Midnight, the first dragon I saw in Idaho, the one that had flown off before I was able to introduce Jon to her, before I had even examined her. I'd been so worried that she might have been sick or injured but had left without my help. *What is she doing here now?*

The reason dawned on me. *So the juvenile dragon didn't come on his own after all! Midnight must have been watching through the bushes this whole time, supervising him. Well, then she might oversee his medication too. I hope.*

Midnight's reappearance that night renewed my debate about why she'd come the first time, late on Thanksgiving. *How did she unlock the door, and why? Or maybe the door was mistakenly left unlocked.* At the time, I was certain I'd checked it, but then I wasn't so sure.

She must have been on a reconnaissance mission, I concluded. She'd acted healthy enough during our encounter that night. And she hadn't been back since, until she accompanied the sick juvenile dragon. *Was that perhaps her son? Did word circulate among the dragons to look for me somewhere in Idaho, and then she spread the news once I was located?*

How dragons communicated such complex information to each other across vast distances truly amazed me. The mere thought awed and overwhelmed me.

But why set off the alarm that night? Was she looking for me and happened to find the door unlocked on the rare day the clinic was empty? Did she intentionally set off the alarm, knowing it would draw me to the clinic? Did she unlock the door? And if so, HOW do dragons open locks? One thing dragons taught me over the years: sometimes, you have to be content without knowing all the answers. And you always have the ability to help someone, even if you don't know all their secrets.

The day following the puppy dog dragon's visit, an argument broke out among the clinic staff. The myth of Bigfoot remained prominent and controversial in Idaho, and the nearby university was home to the foremost Bigfoot expert in the United States. Recently we had hired a new veterinary assistant, Kate, who had worked for a year in the laboratory of precisely that professor, and a senior technician, Nicki, started to quiz her on the contents of the lab. "Believe what you will, but the lab does have some compelling Bigfoot evidence," Kate stated. "You should check it out sometime."

Nicki was dismissive and pushed back, then others jumped into the fray. Having no desire to take part in the quarrel, but also no intention to shut it down unless things became heated, I sat nearby, typing records as I passively listened to their debate. "New species are discovered all the time!" Jess interjected. "And some species they thought were extinct for years or decades turned out to have survived, just not seen for all that time." *Excellent points, Jess.*

"There is NO way there could be animals out there of that size, especially in the U.S., that haven't been discovered," Nicki adamantly stated. "A tiny, new species of rodent in some remote part of Asia or Indonesia, maybe, but not some ape-like thing in Idaho. Don't you agree, Doc?"

Turning away from the keyboard, I found all eyes on me. "Well, uhhh…." Everyone stared at me expectantly. "There's… a lot of wilderness out there still with very little contact from humans. Especially in Idaho. Just think how vast the Frank Church Wilderness Area is. The possibility of an undiscovered creature, even one that big… or bigger…." My mind drifted to dragons as the staff gawked and frowned in confusion. "Let's just say there are possibly… *things*… out there that we don't yet know about. Never say never."

Not having received the validation she'd hoped, Nicki sniffed and opened her mouth to resume arguing, then stopped short as a loud guffaw resonated from the clinic office.

We all turned in surprise and stared through the doorway as Jon walked down the hall and out the back door, laughing hysterically the whole way. Apparently, he'd been trying to hold in his laughter during this entire debate, but could no longer keep it together once I was put on the spot.

Jon's amusement was a vast improvement over the agonizing weeks of his wildly fluctuating disbelief and angst over the dragons' existence. I happily took my husband laughing at my predicament over that emotional roller coaster.

12

An Ally

After meeting Chewy, Jon reluctantly became resigned to the fact that dragons would continue to visit the clinic every few nights or weeks. After all, denying the existence of dragons is difficult when you've had to scrub one's snot out of your shirt. So he was convinced, although he was never entirely comfortable around them. When he happened to be there during a dragon visit, he would typically stand well away from sneeze-range, warily observing as I examined, diagnosed, and treated the great flying creatures.

Not long after Jon was initiated, I began to consider introducing our employees to dragons as well. After years of seeing dragons, I was getting bolder and not so desperate to keep them hidden, perhaps a bit cavalier about their possible discovery (in hindsight, perhaps too cavalier). At the same time, I certainly wasn't about to shout, "Hey world, dragons are real!" from the rooftops. But having a veterinary technician, maybe even more than one, to assist with their care would have been a huge relief. Between running the clinic during the day and treating dragons at night, I was perpetually spent and urgently needed help.

Which technician to introduce first? My gut told me Jess was the best choice. Petite, energetic, and hard-working, Jess had been an avid backpacker in her younger days, staying in hostels across the globe and working odd jobs to fund her travels. She'd worked with koalas in Australia, and once back in the States, she'd found work in wildlife rehabilitation before becoming a vet tech. Thanks to her experience with wildlife, she confidently handled exotic animals, even birds (my least favorite patients). After all that Jess had seen and done during her travels, she was perpetually upbeat, adaptable, and practically fearless. Of all my employees, she seemed the most likely to accept and perhaps even enjoy the dragons. After all, if she could handle koalas, surely she could manage giant winged creatures.

Now and then I joked about dragons with my staff. They had all heard the story of my "hallucination" from altitude sickness. Pointedly, I started talking about how interesting it would be to have dragons as patients. Of course, I left out the reality of how dirty, smelly, dangerous, and draining dragon medicine could be. Of all the staff, Jess was most entertained with the "fantasy" of dragon veterinary medicine.

Having made my choice, I waited for the opportunity.

The chance came when Jess was on call with me. We took in a Labrador with marijuana toxicity at about two in the morning, settled him into a hospital kennel, and got him stabilized on intravenous fluids and IV lipid emulsion. We then decided to go home for far too little sleep before our official work day started. Both Jess and I were in our cars when a dragon poked his head from between the building and the fence. I glimpsed his head and horns before he retreated into the shadows, but Jess couldn't have seen him from the other side of my Volkswagen. She started her engine as I hurried out of my car and tapped on her window, startling her. She lowered the window, looking confused and concerned.

"What's up?"

"Hey, I need your wildlife-wrangling skills."

Now she was really perplexed. "For… what?"

"Come here and look at this."

She paused a moment, turned off the engine, and reluctantly got out of her car. I couldn't blame Jess for her reticence at three in the morning.

Leading her toward the side yard and its hidden dragon, I fervently hoped my assessment of Jess's mindset was accurate, sincerely wanting this introduction to go well.

"So these, umm, creatures have been visiting me for treatment for years now. Fair warning, they're big, and you have to be careful around them, but they're… uhh, mostly harmless."

Jess gawked at me in utter bewilderment. "Doc, what are you talking about?"

We reached the corner of the building, and I stopped, facing her. "Jess, you know how we've been talking about dragons, and how fun they would be as patients?"

She frowned at me. "Yes….?"

Turning toward the darkness of the side yard, I quietly called to the dragon. "It's okay, you can come out!" I hoped he was still there, and hadn't pulled a disappearing act like Midnight had several months before.

Nothing happened for a few seconds, then I heard a quiet snort, a heavy footstep, then another. Next to me, Jess tensed, her eyes wide, but she stood her ground. Touching her elbow, I motioned for her to step back and give our patient some room. She shot me a puzzled look but complied, and we both backed into the parking lot. Another footstep, then another. Leaves rustled. Something wasn't quite right about the dragon's footsteps. They were uneven, some falling more heavily than others.

A scaly, tan-colored nose emerged from the shadows, quietly snorting again, followed by the rest of the head, complete with brown spikes and twisted horns. My gaze swiveled between the dragon and Jess's face, closely monitoring her reaction. Her eyes were wide with shock, mouth gaped, but her eyes divulged her excitement, if perhaps some fear as well.

"NO WAY! NO WAY! NO FREAKING WA—"

"Jess, ssshhhhh!" I hissed at her. *"You'll scare him!"*

The rest of the dragon emerged from the shadows, wings, tail, and all, a handsome adult male. He heavily favored his left rear limb, lifting it awkwardly off the ground as he stood uncomfortably on three limbs. He raised his wings away from his body, his right wing positioned higher than his left, and I realized he was using them for balance.

Jess continued to chatter excitedly, but reduced her volume to a frenzied half-whisper. "I can't BELIEVE this! Why didn't you tell me they're real? I can't BELIEVE it. This is the COOLEST FREAKING THING I'VE EVER SEEN!"

So far, my decision to reveal the dragons to Jess was proving to be wise. Smiling, I coaxed the dragon to lie down while Jess retrieved a flashlight from the clinic. She stood nearby, giddy with excitement, as I wrestled through an orthopedic exam on the dragon's swollen and painful leg. A thought struck me: the vast majority of injured dragons I saw were males. I rarely encountered injured female dragons. Apparently, some facts of life were universal, regardless of species.

The dragon's tan scales sparkled in the bright light of the flashlight. Darker brown scales covered his dorsum, or topside. Short, dense, beige feathers cloaked his neck and the upper portion of his chest. I had never seen that coloration and feather pattern before. For that matter, I hadn't met many feathered dragons at all since I'd left Arizona. He would have blended in perfectly with the desert Southwest, but not so much in the green of Idaho. But then, dragons had far more tools for disguise than their hues and patterns.

"Hmm…" I pondered as I gently coaxed the dragon to extend his leg so I could better examine the joints. "It's kind of generic, but I think I'll call this one Khaki. What do you think, Jess?"

"I'd call him Incredible!" she replied. "But why the name? Just because? Or do you keep records for dragons?"

"Well, not really. I write notes on dragon medicine in general, but nothing official. I give most of them names to help keep them straight in my head, I guess. The dragons don't seem to pay any attention to what I call them."

After struggling to move the dragon's tarsus and stifle, or knee, through their ranges of motion, I paused. This was, after all, why I wanted a technician in on this little secret, I reminded myself.

"Jess, can you—"

"Can I TOUCH him?" she asked, practically jumping up and down. Her exuberance made me laugh.

Jess helped support the heavy limb while I resumed my orthopedic exam. Sweat broke out on my forehead from the effort, and the underarms of my scrub top felt damp. The dragon stoically offered no obvious reaction as I methodically manipulated the joints, though he subtly tensed his muscles whenever I flexed the tarsus. However, I felt no crepitus, the crunchy sensation from broken bones or joint damage.

"His scales and feathers are SO COOL," Jess gushed.

"Yeah, I don't see dragons with feathers very often anymore. The scales are cool, until you need to get an injection or a catheter through them."

Her eyebrows shot upward. "Oh, yeah, I guess that could be a problem!"

Mostly satisfied that the leg had no fractures or ligament instability, I indicated to the dragon that he could stand up if he wanted. But he remained lying down, and I began to second-guess my diagnosis. *What a nasty, painful sprain... if it really is only a sprain.* Ideally, he needed x-rays to rule out bone or joint damage, but he was far too large to fit into the clinic, much less the radiology room. In my head, I moved a mobile x-ray generator, like those used for horses and cattle, higher on my wish list.

My tech and I went inside to collect anti-inflammatory pain medication from the clinic pharmacy. The dragon was so huge, he needed two giant bottles of carprofen.

Jess put two-and-two together. "I wondered where all the meds went! I could swear we'd get gigantic bottles of carprofen and stuff, and then they'd just disappear. How many dragons have you seen?"

"Oh, quite a few. These days, probably four to six during any given month. Sometimes more."

"Are you freaking KIDDING me?" she exclaimed. "That many dragons come HERE — that often? How did I not know this?!"

Laughing, I assured Jess I would answer every one of her questions. But at the moment we needed to get a badly sprained dragon out of our parking lot.

As Khaki peered curiously at the bottles clutched in his claws, I instructed him to rest his leg for seven moons, and to immerse the swollen joint into snow or an ice-cold river, as high and cold in the mountains as he could get, at sunrise and at sunset until the sprain healed. Of course, I had no idea if he would actually do as I said. Hoping he'd take me seriously, I encouraged him to return if the limb still hurt after a week. After acknowledging me with a snort, the creature limped to the middle of the gravel lot and took off.

Jess stared wide-eyed in awe. "He understands you?"

"Just you wait. Some of them talk back."

She laughed in delight. "NO WAY!"

Jess's enthusiasm was infectious, and I couldn't help but laugh with her. "Yes way. Khaki might be able to talk but just doesn't want to. That's true for many dragons, I think."

She was incredulous. "How did you... I mean, how did they... how did this dragon thing start?"

"Well, let's talk."

We retreated into the clinic and settled into chairs in the office. It was nearly four in the morning, and I was so tired. However, Jess was wide awake, brimming with wonder, and chattering nonstop.

"Is there like a secret club or something in vet school where you can learn dragon medicine? Did someone write some kind of dragon medicine textbook? Or did you learn from—"

"Hang on, Jess," I interrupted with a smile. "Let me answer one thing at a time."

For the next few hours we sat and discussed dragons. Jess asked endless questions, and I did my best to answer them all, walking her through my tenure in dragon medicine from the first creature on the mountain through the secret patients at my former clinic, and my expectation that moving to Idaho would end the dragon visits (for better or worse). But then they had found me. And now there we were, with dragons visiting the clinic more and more often.

Jess listened with rapt attention. She broke in to quiz me about the illnesses and injuries I had seen in dragons, and I described various details to her. They really did breathe fire, I informed her, and some had a breath weapon. She sat riveted but horrified as I recounted the story of getting blasted by Pepé's horrid breath, then laughed when I told her I'd used skunk odor pet shampoo to remove the odor.

Muted light shone through the office window as dawn approached, and the clinic would open soon. I yawned uncontrollably, eyes gritty with lack of sleep. "Hey, let's go get some caffeine before our day really starts. Okay?"

Still energized by the thrill of discovery, Jess was wide awake but happy to go for coffee if I was willing to continue our conversation. We drove to the nearby diner and I bought breakfast for us both. She was almost too distracted to eat.

Pushing eggs around on her plate, Jess couldn't stop asking questions. "So why don't you talk about them more? I can't wait to tell people about them. They're incredible!"

"Well," I began, "say you're visiting your mom or your sister, and they ask about work, and you tell them you saw a dragon. What would they think?"

Her smile faded. "Oh. Yeah. I see what you mean."

"Then think about the greater world," I went on. "Think about big game hunters. And about the government, and how we manage controversial predators, like wolves. Think about all the idiots out there. And human nature, and how dragons would get blamed for so many things. Like livestock losses, or missing people in the national forests." Inwardly, I winced. Honestly, I didn't know whether dragons played any role in livestock deaths or missing people, and I wasn't sure I wanted to find out.

The technician was crestfallen, subdued for the first time that morning. "Yeah. I get it. Good point." Her mood quickly shifted and she bounced on the diner bench seat. "But they're so COOL!" I couldn't resist smiling at her irresistible exuberance.

Practically dead on my feet, I watched with amusement as Jess remained giddy for the entire day, animated by our shared secret. At various points throughout her shift, she quietly mouthed to me, stealthily pointing toward her coworkers, "Does SHE know?…. What about her?…. Does Jon know?!"

I whispered back to her. "No, she does not…. she doesn't, either…. Jon knows, but no one else."

She wanted to stay after work and continue discussing dragons, but I begged off, desperately needing sleep. But thereafter, Jess often remained behind after the clinic closed, absorbing all I said about dragons, and of course hoping to assist with their care again. Her wish was granted on many occasions.

With time, I gradually introduced more of the staff to the dragons with varying success. A couple were nearly as enthusiastic about the creatures as Jess was. However, more than one employee promptly quit, one leaving so hurriedly that she didn't even collect her things from her locker. Jon had to mail them to her. Another stayed on for a few weeks but was anxious and jumpy the entire time, snappish with her coworkers and the clients. She eventually resigned and later sent me a bill for counseling sessions. We hired more technicians, but then others quit over the dragons.

The rapid staff turnover thoroughly annoyed Jon, and he irritably demanded to know what interview questions he should ask of potential new hires. "Should I ask if they're okay handling imaginary animals? How about if I ask if they're fine with maybe being burnt to a crisp by an angry dragon? You think we'll be able to hire anyone that way?"

He'd made some valid points, and I wasn't sure how to solve our dilemmas in hiring and rapid attrition. "Just…. I don't know. Ask them about handling exotics, okay?"

"Exotics? Yeah, dragons are about as exotic as it gets," he retorted.

I sighed. "Seriously, if someone can handle a macaw, or even a fractious cat, they can handle a dragon. It's only… the BELIEVING part that's so hard. You know how that goes."

Jon did know, having nearly fallen apart himself when he learned about the dragons. To this day, Jess remains the only person I've known to meet the dragons and readily embrace their existence without going through a minor to major crisis. We continued to hire staff, and continued to lose some, but eventually, we built a team that functioned well together, whether on the "normal" day-to-day patients or the unorthodox after-hours patients. Granted, some of our staff were more passionate than others about working with dragons, but we made it work.

What our employees said about the dragons outside of work, I didn't know. I encouraged them to freely discuss dragons and dragon medicine among themselves at the clinic, but not to mention the dragons to clients or anyone outside of work, for all the same reasons I'd cited to Jess for keeping them quiet. Most of our staff took that to heart, including Jess, but I wasn't so sure about some of them. Contemplating the possible consequences of word getting around out made me anxious, but I had to acknowledge that anything my employees did or said outside of work was beyond my control. And whatever became of that was going to happen regardless of my angst about it. I had to let it go and let things unfold as they would.

Talkative employees aside, it was only a matter of time before someone witnessed a dragon lurking around the clinic. The dragons were stealthy and talented at camouflage, but they weren't perfect. That they hadn't been discovered at the clinic in Arizona amazed me. (Well, two random people HAD spied the dragons in Arizona, but both had been too drunk or high to believe their eyes). My old clinic had the advantage of its secluded parking lot, mostly shielded by palm trees and the adjacent warehouse. Now, however, homes surrounded my clinic. At least the house next door sat vacant, and tall privacy fences and trees were everywhere. I rarely saw window blinds or curtains open toward the clinic, but still. Who knew for how long the dragons had survived hidden in the mountains, forests, and shadows. I only hoped they would continue to survive once they were more widely known.

13

Bitten

Finally, the inevitable happened: a dragon bit me, badly. I'd always suspected that might eventually happen, and there I was, sitting in the urgent care clinic's waiting room, wondering how I was going to explain what happened. Cradling my left hand within its temporary bandaging in my lap, trying and failing to ignore the throbbing pain, I furiously brainstormed a story that I hoped they would believe.

In truth, I'd been attempting to perform skin diagnostics on the feistiest hatchling dragon I had ever met. He'd managed to chomp three fingers of my left hand, leaving an array of puncture wounds over both sides of my fingers that immediately swelled and oozed rivulets of blood. Most of the wounds were painful but uncomplicated punctures in the soft tissue. However, my middle finger was bitten right over, and perhaps through, the last joint. That finger screamed in pain.

Animal bites were an unfortunately common hazard in veterinary medicine, and I had experienced my share. Once a ferret latched onto my hand and refused to let go for over

130

a minute. Cat bites were the worst, much more painful and prone to infection. And in fact, the year before, I had visited the same urgent care after a cat buried all four canine teeth in my arm. Most physicians treated such injuries on a regular basis, so they were familiar with the appearance of bite wounds inflicted by various species.

My dragon bite raised a problem: I could not have possibly passed it off as a "normal" dog or cat bite. An individual puncture wound, sure; I could have persuaded someone that the culprit was a cat. But these wounds were arranged in a perfect narrow 'U', which did not at all resemble a cat or dog bite, and I knew better than to try to pass it off as such.

The nurse, a dynamo of a guy in bright blue scrubs, called my name and ushered me to an exam room. He asked me standard history questions as he measured my blood pressure (high from pain), and I informed him I was bitten by a patient and was concerned about my middle finger joint. Notably I didn't specify what KIND of patient.

"Dog or cat?" he inquired, watching the laptop monitor as he tapped away on the keyboard.

Oh boy. Here we go. "Neither... uhhh, caiman, actually," I fibbed. My face instantly warmed, and I could feel my cheeks flushing.

The keyboard tapping promptly ceased as the nurse swiveled his head, blinking at me in disbelief. His vivid blue eyes matched his scrubs. "A caiman?!" he exclaimed. "Like those miniature alligator things?"

"Yes. Exactly," I replied confidently, ignoring the fact that I had never handled a caiman in my life.

"Interesting," he replied, his voice edged with excitement. "A caiman bite isn't something we see every day, that's for sure."

"No, I imagine not," I concurred. *I'm willing to bet you don't see dragon bites every day, either.*

Back to business, the nurse returned his gaze to the laptop and typed my "interesting" presenting complaint into the medical record. "Well, the doctor will be in shortly," he assured me as he bustled efficiently out the door.

My falsehood was now permanently documented in my medical records, I realized, and I gulped. My face achieved a new level of redness as I nervously fidgeted on the exam table, rustling and wrinkling the paper stretched over the padded vinyl.

The physician, a petite woman with grey-streaked hair and glasses, knocked and entered. "Hello! You're our first caiman bite of the day," she teased cheerfully. "How interesting!"

Managing a halfhearted laugh, I informed her that I jokingly told my clients you never wanted to be "interesting" in medicine; boring was much healthier. Well, there I was being "interesting" in urgent care.

She peeled back my temporary bandage, remarking on how much blood had soaked through the multiple layers of gauze. Blood continued to ooze from the puncture wounds as she gently rotated my wrist with her purple-gloved hands, inspecting my swollen fingers with professional intrigue. "I've certainly never seen a caiman bite before," she announced, lifting her head to look at me with inquisitive brown eyes.

Gazing back at her kind face, I tried for a smile that better resembled a grimace. *Great! That makes two of us.*

"Was it a pet caiman? Are those even legal in Idaho?" She peered at me intently through her glasses.

Oh no. I hadn't a clue about the legality of caimans anywhere, and I suspected my story was about to unravel. "Well, uh, the owner was just… passing through," I stammered, dodging the question altogether.

"Passing through?" The doctor frowned in confusion. "Someone's traveling with their pet caiman?"

I shrugged, then wished I hadn't. My hand throbbed worse. "Yeah, well, people do strange things sometimes." *Like wrestle biting baby dragons for the purpose of making them well.*

"Your face is so red," she observed. "Your hand must be so painful."

Nodding, I forced another smile. "Yes, it is." *Also, I want the earth to open up and swallow me.*

The physician sent the nurse to gather saline flush and antiseptic. In his absence, she peeled off her nitrile gloves to type exam notes into the laptop. Gingerly, I propped the back of my wounded hand onto my knee, taking care not to bleed on my good work slacks.

Following a minute or two of silence, save for the quiet *tick tick-tick tick tick-tick-tick* of fingertips on the keyboard, the physician ceased typing and turned back to me. "What was wrong with this traveling pet caiman?" she inquired, genuinely curious.

"Well…" I began hesitantly. Lacking any knowledge of caiman diseases, I considered launching into a description of scale rot in dragons, then thought better of it. "I'm honestly not sure. The complaint was not eating," I explained, fabricating as I went. "But I didn't even get through an exam before he bit me, so I have no idea. And I've never treated a caiman before."

"Please tell me you don't have to go contend with the caiman still. Do you?" she asked with concern. To be fair, I was concerned, too.

"Uhhhhh, no, I told the owner to travel on to Boise and go to the specialty hospital," I invented. "They don't have an exotics specialist there, but they can figure out something for him."

Actually, I do have to handle the biting little beast again, because he certainly isn't going anywhere else. I mused about how the specialists would have reacted if I'd dared send one of my dragon patients to them. *They would never forgive me for inflicting that kind of mayhem on their practice.*

"Can't you tie something around their snout, then they don't have the strength to open their mouth and break the tie?" the physician inquired. "I remember seeing that on TV once."

Oh, lovely. The physician had watched Animal Planet once and knew more about caimans than I did. In fact, I'd attempted countless ways to muzzle baby dragons, and I was rarely successful.

"That's... what we were trying to do," I answered, somewhat truthfully. "Obviously, it backfired."

"I'd say," she wholeheartedly agreed. "This is a nasty wound. You know, the skin is so red, it looks almost burned. Interesting."

Squirming, I thought about the short jet of flame the baby dragon had spat at my hand as I'd removed my fingers from his mouth. *Talk about getting in the last word.* And speaking of words, I felt like the term "interesting" was getting old, and I fought the urge to sigh out loud.

The nurse returned with a syringe, flush, and antiseptic, sparing me the need to explain the burned part. He arranged the supplies onto a metal instrument tray as the physician donned another pair of gloves. Curious, the nurse crossed his arms and stood behind the doctor, peering intently over her shoulder as she cleaned and flushed my "caiman" bite wounds. As the saline briskly streamed onto my fingers and rapidly soaked the absorbent pad beneath my hand, fiery pain radiated through my palm, coursing through my wrist to my elbow and then all the way to my shoulder. Sweat beaded on my forehead as I felt the blood drain from my face, rapidly evolving from its vivid flush to a sickly pallor. The physician hadn't offered pain medication and I hadn't thought to request it. The dragon bite hurt far worse than any dog or cat bite I'd ever sustained.

After what felt like ages but realistically was only minutes, the physician finally dropped the empty flush syringe onto the instrument tray with a jarring *clank*. The show was over, and the nurse uncrossed his arms and proffered a brief wave as he left the room. "Okay," the doctor announced as she peeled off her blood-stained gloves. "That should do it. Let's get this bandaged and get you home, Dr. Blackstone. Or... back to work?"

Sighing, I informed her I would go straight back to work. As a solo practitioner, I didn't have the option to have a colleague cover for me, and a nearly full schedule of appointments awaited. *Not to mention, a feisty dragon hatchling still requires my attention.*

The physician finished swaddling my fingers in thick bandaging, handed a written prescription to me, cheerfully wished me a rapid recovery, and sent me on my way. Holding my heavily bandaged hand aloft, I walked through the waiting room, frowning dubiously at the prescription. I'd debated arguing with her choice of antibiotics, but I honestly had no idea what kinds of bacteria dragons harbored in their mouths. Considering how foul their breath smelled, I had a sinking feeling cephalexin wouldn't be powerful enough.

As I reached the front door, I abruptly froze as a horrified realization washed over me. Physicians were required to report dog bites to animal control. Would they report a "caiman" bite? If so, I would have to field some uncomfortable questions about the animal and its owner. My ruse could not possibly hold up to that degree of scrutiny, and a sense of dread set in. Forcing myself to move, I pushed the door open and headed for my car with apprehension hanging over my head like a thunder cloud.

Having downed a handful of ibuprofen and the cephalexin — I figured I might as well try it — I returned my attention to the day's regular patients as well as the feisty hatchling. Attitude aside, he was truly stunning, displaying deep, glossy black scales tipped with gold. He resembled fine jewelry, and I'd dubbed him Fortune until he bit me. Then I added a nickname: Air Shark. Whether the hatchling would retain the gold coloration as he matured, I didn't know. His mother's scales were shiny black, but lacked the magnificent highlights of her hatchling.

And speaking of his mother, the dragons had developed an aggravating habit when it came to seeking veterinary care for their young. They would show up, clutching a squirmy hatchling in one great claw, hand over their progeny, and promptly fly off.

The first time this happened, I'd been furious, convinced that the mother had abandoned her sick baby to me. Treating dragons every few days or weeks was one thing, but I did not have the time or energy to indulge in raising a fire-breathing "pet" that would eat us out of house and home (or burn it down) and terrorize our pets. Not to mention what our neighbors would think.

The first absentee mother dragon eventually returned to claim her hatching, which by then had fully recovered from its respiratory virus and was rapidly burning through my grocery budget by downing raw chicken thighs every few hours. Thereafter, whenever dragons brought me hatchlings to treat, they disappeared for days, even on one occasion for over a week, and eventually returned to carry off their offspring. Where they went and what they did in the meantime, I've never figured out, and the dragons have never confessed. Sometimes I wondered whether the mothers merely enjoyed the respite away from their young. If so, I could hardly blame them. Raising a baby was hard work.

I thought back to the night before when Fortune's mother had materialized outside the back door. She'd handed him over while I was headed inside to see an emergency, a border collie with cluster seizures. Fumbling my keys and backpack along with the hatchling that was already trying to sink his teeth into me, I'd struggled into the building and asked the veterinary technician to find a kennel for the dragon. A discolored patch blemished his scales, but that seemed to be his only problem. He'd appeared stable enough for the time being. The seizing border collie was to arrive any moment, and I'd figured the mother dragon wouldn't return for a day or two at least, so the little guy could wait until the next morning. Those days I kept chicken in the break room freezer for just such an occasion.

Overnight confinement in a kennel hadn't improved the hatchling's mood one bit, and he had furiously screeched, thrashed, and flapped his wings as we'd tried to restrain him in blankets. Jess had shouted a warning as the dragon's head broke free, but too late. He'd bitten my hand before I could react.

Following my unplanned trip to urgent care, I struggled through the day's appointments as best I could. The ibuprofen dulled the pain a bit, but my hand still screamed, especially the punctured joint. Second thoughts ran through my head about visiting urgent care. Perhaps I should have gone straight to the hand specialist. But for now, I had to finish up with the hatchling.

One patch of scales on the left side of his trunk was discolored. Scale rot was common in new hatchlings, and it usually stemmed from some type of fungal infection that responded well to fluconazole and topical anti-fungal therapy. Sometimes bacterial overgrowth complicated the infection, and topical and/or oral antibiotics were necessary.

However, beyond the typical dull, flaky, peeling scales that I was accustomed to seeing with scale rot, blood oozed from the red, irritated skin beneath the hatchling's black scales. His scale rot was either particularly severe, or it was something else altogether. The affected patch was such an eyesore compared to his beautiful black and gold scales, and it would have been a shame if the condition spread. I hoped I could resolve this quickly.

Over my lunch break, we managed to accomplish a skin scrape test and cytology on the Air Shark. Two vet techs and my husband had to hold him down using the heavy gloves we used for cats, again using thick blankets to restrain his wings and head. He writhed, flailed, and spat fire, burning holes through the fabric. Acrid smoke clouded around the treatment table, irritating everyone's eyes and lungs. We'd removed the smoke alarm from the treatment room long ago for exactly this reason. With one hand incapacitated, I couldn't be of any help restraining the hatchling, and quickly grew exasperated trying to collect the skin and scale samples. But I finally succeeded.

My irritation evaporated once I examined the samples under the microscope, my fascination increasing as I scrolled across the skin scrape slide. Cigar-shaped mites wiggled their minuscule feet under the powerful magnification. They appeared similar to *Demodex* mites in dogs, but they weren't quite the same. Unlike other species of *Demodex*, these mites sported pairs of tiny spikes protruding from their heads, not unlike dragon horns. *How fitting, and how incredible!* I found the resemblance hilariously funny, and I laughed until I cried.

Mopping my tears with my bandages until I thought better of it and grabbed a handful of tissues, I instructed the vet techs to somehow administer a dose of fluralaner. The isoxazoline compounds, including fluralaner, effectively controlled external parasites in multiple species of mammals and birds. Even though I didn't know exactly what Fortune's mites were (they've since been officially dubbed *Demodex draconis*, and I was presumably the first practitioner to observe them), I felt reasonably confident that the medication would resolve the infection.

Most dogs willingly ate the flavored fluralaner chews, but I wasn't counting on Air Shark to cooperate with anything we wanted him to do. As I feared, he adamantly refused to eat it. But Jess wasn't about to give up. She painstakingly tucked bits of the medication deep within the folds of a chicken thigh before she extended her open hand, offering it to the dragon. He ate it like a champ, ravenously lunging for the chicken with such ferocity that I was afraid Jess might become the next urgent care patient.

Fortune's mother returned that evening to collect her ornery offspring. I carried him outside using a heavy cat glove over one hand, unable to fit the other glove over the bandages, nearly dropping the wiggly thing before I got him out the door. The mother scrutinized my left hand, stared hard at her hatchling, then looked back at me and snorted. She'd rightly guessed where the injury came from.

Right before she took flight, I heard Fortune angrily hiss and squawk as he squirmed in her grip. A small burst of flame flashed at the far end of the parking lot, then I heard his mother chastise him with a sharp, fierce snort. Smiling, I found myself grateful to see that the stinker was a handful for his mom too, and not just us.

Two days later, I spent the afternoon at the specialty hand clinic, which was deserted save for the physician and myself. Most of my weekend had been spent in a worsening haze of pain and malaise, and I had to acknowledge that my hand was rapidly deteriorating. Feverish and in excruciating pain, I finally caved and called the emergency number for the specialists.

The doctor expressed his surprise upon hearing a "caiman" inflicted the wound, but luckily he didn't press the issue. Lying about the bite made me extraordinarily uncomfortable, but I was loathe to compromise my reputation by telling the truth.

The state of my injured hand preoccupied him far more. The wounds looked terrible. Even though I'd dutifully swallowed each dose of cephalexin (despite my skepticism), my fingers were badly infected. He radiographed my hand, happy to find no fractures, then injected local anesthetic to numb the fingers. The injections were incredibly unpleasant. Tense and woozy, I gripped the padded exam table tightly as he inserted the needles between my digits. But once the anesthetic took effect, I felt blessed relief. The pain was gone, if only for a few hours.

The specialist incised all the wounds to explore and debride the unhealthy tissue, remarking with academic interest along the way about the degree of tissue damage and infection. Glancing now and then at my mangled fingers, saying hello to my exposed digital nerves and tendons, I pondered whether dragons might have some type of cytotoxic venom. Or instead, maybe they carried particularly aggressive bacteria in their mouths. We were about to find out about that, since the specialist took swabs for culture.

The joint in my middle finger was a horrid septic mess, and the fingertip was a grotesque shade of grey. The specialist talked about leaving it open to drain and hopefully heal, but mentioned possible amputation as a last resort. I shuddered and squirmed. I had sacrificed so much to help the dragons, most of which was absolutely worth it, but sacrificing a finger would have been too much.

About a week after the dragon bite occurred, during which I'd visited the hand clinic daily, the specialist called me, perplexed. The culture results were back. Some of the findings were plausible, such as heavy growth of *Salmonella*. That made perfect sense for an obligate carnivore that commonly ate carrion. However, the report also described heavy growth of gram-negative rod bacteria that the lab could not identify.

"Are you familiar with the oral flora in caimans?" he asked. Not that it would have been any use if I had, considering a caiman had nothing to do with this.

"I know reptiles in general commonly carry *Salmonella*," I answered truthfully. "But other than that, I don't. Oral flora in that species has never been studied to my knowledge." I grimaced at my evasive reply.

"Well, maybe someone should study it, because it looks like they'd make some interesting discoveries," the specialist stated. "It's unusual for the micro lab to fail to identify something, at least as far as genus, if not species. Actually unheard of, so far as I know. But at least they still ran the sensitivity report. Whatever it is, it shows good susceptibility to Augmentin, in vitro anyway."

"Huh. Interesting," I replied, then cringed at my word choice. "Well, I'm glad we appear to be on the right track, then." As quickly as I could politely manage, I ended the call.

Following six weeks of frequent visits to the specialist, several more sessions of debridement, broad-spectrum antibiotics, and pain medications, my wounds managed to heal. First, my ring finger mended well enough to leave unbandaged, and next my index finger, absurdly leaving my middle finger as the sole bandaged digit. My middle fingertip was salvaged, but the joint remained permanently scarred and painful.

Fortunately, I never heard anything from animal control. Apparently, neither urgent care nor the hand clinic ever reported the bite injury. That was a close call.

At the veterinary clinic, we were forced to cancel weeks of upcoming surgical procedures and numerous appointments while I recovered. Most clients understood, but my staff was stressed and frightened by the ordeal. After all, if I were unable to practice, the clinic would have no source of income and therefore no resources to pay wages. We made it through, but I resolved to be extra careful around the dragons going forward. None of us could afford for me to get bitten again.

At least I amused myself and my staff by lifting my bandaged middle finger to jokingly flip off anyone who asked about my injury. The comic relief was absolutely vital.

14

Various Hatchlings

Dragon hatchlings were difficult patients, above and beyond the challenges presented by their older kin. Hatchlings were strong and wily for their size, but they lacked the ability to comprehend and comply with instructions. Therefore, my tenet to always gain a dragon's permission went out the window. They couldn't understand and rarely trusted me. Some were more cantankerous than others, as evidenced by the black and gold hatchling that nearly cost me a fingertip, but all of them could be unpredictable and dangerous. And I'd found that baby dragons gained the ability to breathe fire within mere hours of hatching.

Previously, I've mentioned the difficulty of muzzling hatchling dragons, and this cannot be overstated. I've tried placing soft, nylon dog muzzles. The dragons quickly tore the straps and shredded the muzzles, creating an awful stench when they burned the nylon. Metal basket muzzles prevented biting but not fire breathing. Once a technician tried a plastic basket muzzle, and that melted into an awful, stinky mess. I've tried tying gauze loops around their faces. Those didn't last long, but at least they were more pleasant when they burned. The carbohydrates in the cotton caramelized sweetly as they smoldered. I've experimented with some novel materials to muzzle dragons as well. Once I fashioned a muzzle out of a soup can and a metal chain and tried it on a single hatchling. He furiously snapped the chain and mangled the soup can, and wouldn't permit anyone near him for hours until he calmed down.

Hatchlings had their advantages, though. Their pliable scales and skin made injections much easier, as well as placing intravenous catheters. And their diminutive size made dosing for medications and fluid rates considerably more straightforward (and less expensive). Finding a spot for one to stay in the hospital was easier, too. Which hatchlings inevitably needed, since their mothers invariably left them with me for days, much to my consternation, and despite my pleas to stick around. I took to calling this habit the "baby dump-and-fly." Though to be fair, "baby dump-and-fly-but-eventually-return" was more accurate.

One memorable mother dragon didn't follow the "dump-fly-return" routine, and the story still haunts me. She brought a tiny baby clutched in one claw and crept up to the office window early one evening, not waiting for me to exit the building.

Recognizing her urgency, I rushed down the hallway, out the door, and to the side yard, where the mother dragon placed her undersized, green baby into my outstretched hands with surprising tenderness. The hatchling rested limply on my palms, no larger than a kitten. He was weak and felt terribly feverish (normal body temperature for dragons was relatively high, which made sense for fire-breathing species, but the tiny male felt scorching hot). Right away, I noticed neurologic signs: his head tilted to the left, and his pale blue eyes squinted miserably at me with pupils of different sizes. I bent over and placed him onto the ground, helping him stand so I could assess his gait and balance. He feebly wobbled a few unbalanced paces, then collapsed and curled into a pathetic ball, breathing hard. In short, he was a terrible mess with a grim prognosis. I looked up. I hadn't even noticed as the mother left, but she was gone.

"Oh man," Jess remarked. "I don't know if we should name this one, Doc. I'm not sure he's going to—"

"His name is Jade!" I retorted. "He deserves a name. And don't say that! We're going to try to pull him through."

We worked so hard to save him. We struggled to insert the smallest IV catheter we could find into the dehydrated dragon's minuscule wing vein but finally succeeded. We started intravenous fluids, then ran blood tests, and I read over the results with growing alarm and foreboding. We administered IV antibiotics, glucocorticoid steroids, pain medications, and various drugs to reduce brain swelling, and we syringe-fed chicken broth and canned cat food to the little guy. Jade appeared to rally for a day. He willingly ate a few bites of baby food, and he closed his eyes and squeaked in contentment as I rubbed his miniature head with my fingertip, tracing figures-of-eight around his adorably petite spikes and horn buds.

However Jade worsened by the next day. He laid his head weakly onto my fingers and gazed at me morosely with his uneven, ice-blue eyes through half-closed lids as I held him in my hands. His head lay neatly framed within the "U" of my dragon bite scars, an ironic macabre halo. The baby softly folded one minuscule wing against his body; the other wing was encumbered by the weight of the IV catheter and tape, and he could no longer lift it. The IV line snaked from beneath the tape to the nearby pump that delivered fluids with a quiet *whir* into the hatchling's vein, robotically doing its part to save his life. Or trying, anyway.

The minuscule hatchling focused his eyes on mine for a few seconds, sighed feebly, and then he was gone, abruptly slack and lifeless in my hands. His glassy eyes stared inertly at nothing, their spark extinguished, and his lopsided pupils achieved symmetry at last as they dilated in finality. His jade-green scales were somehow already turning to a dull grey-green, flickering and fading beneath my fingers as the chromatophores and still poorly-understood disguise mechanisms sputtered and shut down.

For a fleeting moment, my mind defaulted to emergency medicine mode. With one shout, I could have brought technicians on the run. They would have placed an endotracheal tube and started oxygen while I did chest compressions. We'd have given him atropine and epinephrine through his IV catheter. We could have tried to bring him back. I was on the verge of yelling for Jess, and then I thought better of it. *No. Bringing him back would only prolong his suffering. I cannot win this battle. Let him go.* I stayed silent, tightly clutching the baby dragon as I started to weep.

Jess found me with tears streaming down my face, cradling Jade's tiny body. "What happened — oh no. No! Doc, I am *so* sorry...."

"We... tried... so hard," I choked out between sobs.

Without another word, Jess donned exam gloves as tears

streaked down her own face. She gently unclasped my fingers and lifted Jade's body from my hands as the tissues started to disintegrate. The corrosive chemicals from the dragon's fire breath organs were breaking down his diminutive body, and soon only a scant handful of glittery ash-like material would remain. By removing his body from my hands, Jess saved me from painful chemical burns.

Losing Jade devastated me, even more so because I was expecting my own "hatchling." My husband and I anticipated the birth of our daughter within a few months. Between the powerful emotions evoked by pregnancy and the connection I felt with my daughter-to-be, and my irrational but powerful fondness for the ill-fated hatchling, I was shattered by his death.

For days, I lingered vigilantly at the clinic after work, expecting the mother dragon to return for her baby that was no more. Before I got into my car to go home, I'd stand still and quiet behind the clinic, wistfully rubbing my growing belly, watching and listening closely for any sign of the dragon descending from the sky or lurking in the shadows of the trees. I'd walk slowly through the side yard where she'd so gently handed her doomed hatchling to me, thinking she might lurk near the same spot when she came back.

Maybe the mother assumed her baby wouldn't make it. Or, maybe she somehow sensed when he passed away.

I never found out, because she never returned.

* * *

Like all varieties of grief, mine has stayed with me always, although my sadness has dimmed with time. All these years later, I'm crying as I write about Jade's final days and death. Of course, other dragons have died in my care, and dogs and cats too. All doctors who treated critically ill patients of any species quickly learned that we could not save them all.

Though death has always been a part of veterinary medicine, and I regularly ended the lives of pets to halt their suffering when no other options remained, I was saddened by some of those events more than others. I felt a special bond with many of my patients and their people, especially pets I'd known for their entire lives; their deaths, however peaceful, were hard for me to endure. Losing a patient I hadn't known for long, but to whom I'd quickly grown attached, was sometimes equally difficult. I felt especially close to the tiny, jade-green dragon, and his death wrecked me.

Life went on. I had a clinic to run, patients to see, and staff to manage. Dragons came and went with varying degrees of injuries and illness. Fortunately, several months passed before I needed to care for another hatchling. Even then, I trembled and teared up, reliving Jade's death all over again as I held a snotty, blue, Chihuahua-sized hatchling while his mother hurriedly disappeared into the clouds.

The dragons, especially females, took note of my growing belly, softly sniffing at my baby bump while I examined them. And once our daughter, Ember, was born, the dragons did something extraordinary: they brought gifts.

Some of our staff stopped by the hospital after our baby's arrival, bearing smiles, cards, and presents, holding and cooing at our daughter in turns. Jess stopped in, casually dropped a gift bag and card onto a chair, and plopped a spherical stone and a polished copper bowl into my hands.

"What's up with these?" I whispered, not wanting to disturb

Ember sleeping in the bassinet next to my bed.

"Presents from the dragons," Jess whispered back to me.

"What?!" I exclaimed too loudly, then both of us held our breath as Ember fidgeted beside me. She finally stilled and went back to sleep, and Jess and I exhaled in unison.

She quietly explained to me that dragons had shown up multiple times so far during my brief absence. I had warned the dragons that I would be unavailable for a month once my own "hatchling" was born, and I had nervously arranged for a relief veterinarian, afraid that the dragons would reveal themselves to her. Our relief doctor had no knowledge of our unusual patients, and I wanted to keep it that way. Fortunately, the technicians had successfully intercepted the dragons so far.

The dragons weren't visiting the clinic in need of treatment. They were bringing gifts for the baby. *A head-start to her treasure hoard, I suppose.* The dragons always had new surprises in store, and I was awestruck. "Unbelievable! So they just handed these things over and then flew off?"

"Yep," Jess confirmed, nodding. "I think the round rock might be a geode."

I turned the spherical stone in my hands. A few sparkles glinted from its rough surface, faintly purple under the hospital lights. "You might be right. Didn't happen to bring a hammer, did you?" I joked.

"Well actually —" Jess pulled a claw hammer out of her shoulder bag — "I did, but I didn't count on your baby being asleep."

I snorted with suppressed laughter. "Jess, you're amazing!" We both stifled our giggles.

Following a short maternity leave, I went back to work,

juggling my daughter's needs with the demands of the clinic and my patients, conventional and otherwise. We squeezed a baby swing into the cramped doctor's office. When the swing was in motion, I had to slalom between it and the filing cabinets to reach my desk, rushing past the contraption as it swung toward the wall. The arrangement was cramped and hectic, but it worked.

Jess and I broke open the geode on the sidewalk behind the clinic to find beautiful spikes of amethyst, truly an amazing gift. Besides the geode and copper bowl, the dragons also brought polished bits of copper piping (their affinity for copper of all kinds never failed to amuse me), blue and green malachite beads, cut and polished garnets, brass decorations, and four chunks of sparkly, smoky quartz. Before then, I had no idea that dragons had any tendency to give gifts, and their generosity amazed me. Somehow, they avoided accosting our relief vet in the process, much to my relief.

The dragons continued their visits much as they had before, although now they brought sick hatchlings much more frequently. Whether this was because they knew me to have a "hatchling" of my own, or because the dragons were experiencing a "baby boom" of sorts (and I sincerely hoped so; I feared their species were endangered), or whether it was sheer coincidence, I had no idea. Regardless, more and more hatchlings arrived, along with all their peculiar challenges.

With time, I was able to handle baby dragons with less sadness and more joy. Difficult as they were, sometimes hatchlings made for amusing patients, and they were undeniably adorable (when they weren't biting and spitting fire, that was). Back in those days, before an emergency clinic was available, I regularly took tiny, critical patients home with me overnight: puppies, kittens, and of course, the occasional dragon hatchling. My bathroom transformed into a temporary hospital ward so I could keep a close eye on the small creatures and better manage their intravenous fluids and medications. On one occasion, while a baby dragon occupied a wire dog crate in my bathroom, our cat inadvertently got shut in the room for a short time. The cat was physically unharmed, but remained absolutely terrified of anything with wings forever after, and bolted across the house to hide beneath the couch whenever he spied so much as a songbird through the window.

The absolute worst ordeal with a hatchling dragon (although in hindsight, it was funny) began when a sick baby arrived the night before I was to leave town. My staff were all itching for some time off over the holiday weekend, and my husband and I wanted to introduce our baby daughter to family out of state. We shared emergency call rotation with two other clinics, and I was off duty that weekend, so we decided to close the clinic for an additional few days and take a short vacation. Only the kennel attendants would continue their regular shifts to care for the boarding patients.

This all sounded like a fine idea, until I was leaving the clinic the night before our trip — late of course, and I still needed to pack for myself and Ember — and a dragon landed right behind my car just as I strapped my daughter into her car seat. Suppressing my annoyance (after all, I'd learned my lesson about talking harshly to dragons with breath weapons), I approached her, hoping she had something straightforward going on that wouldn't occupy my entire evening. My heart sank when I realized she held a hatchling in her claws.

The dragon placed the tiny baby in my hands. Her coloration was similar to the male whose death had devastated me months earlier, and she appeared nearly as sick, though a bit larger and stronger. The hatchling tugged at my heartstrings. She would require intravenous fluids and medications for some time, but how? As I stood there furiously debating what to do with the sick baby, her mother turned and lifted her wings and was gone.

"Wait… WAIT!" I fruitlessly called to her, though I didn't know what I would have told her if she'd come back. *"Sorry, I can't save your baby because I'm going on vacation,"* didn't seem like something I could manage to say. I was both touched and infuriated by the dragon mothers' inherent trust in me to care for their offspring. A sick hatchling sat placidly in my hands, and a fussy human baby sat in the back of my car. *Now what?*

Swearing — my kid would undoubtedly grow up with quite the vocabulary — I retrieved Ember in her car seat and went back inside, struggling with the lock and alarm as I juggled the car seat and the dragon baby in my arms. The staff had all left early that evening, in high spirits about the holiday weekend, and I loathed the idea of calling any of them in. Whatever the hatchling needed, I had to accomplish it on my own.

Fortunately, I supposed, the dragon was so sick that she didn't resist when I restrained her wing and placed an IV catheter. A bolus of fluids ran while I drew up medications to administer. I gave Ember a pacifier (with a dragon design, of course) and positioned her car seat facing the dragon. She watched the creature with wide eyes, mesmerized, kicking her chubby feet in excitement. The dragon weakly lifted her emerald-green head with its miniature spike and horn nubbins and impassively returned my daughter's gaze. The hatchling slowly blinked a few times, then wearily laid her head across her forelimb, drew her free wing over her face, and closed her eyes with a sigh.

The dragon stabilized a bit, but she remained quite ill and needed IV fluids and medications for at least a couple days. No question, she'd have to go along on our trip. Squeezing my eyes shut, I rubbed my forehead, deliberating how to pull this off.

I groaned. Jon was going to kill me.

15

The Road Trip

Early the next morning, Jon and I rushed about, hurriedly packing things into the car as we readied ourselves and Ember for our trip. My eyes were gritty from lack of sleep, and I informed my husband he'd be responsible for driving until I caught up on some rest. As I poured myself a third cup of coffee, Jon materialized at my side.

"Do I want to know what's in the Rubbermaid bin with holes cut in the top?" he demanded.

Before answering, I downed a generous swallow of coffee. "No, you definitely do NOT want to know what's in the bin."

Moments went by as he gawked at me, guessing the truth but not wanting to believe it. "So where did the bin come from?"

"Let's just say some Halloween decorations are lacking a home at the moment," I admitted.

He scoffed and walked away, shaking his head. "Unbelievable. Truly unbelievable."

Thus, we embarked on the oddest road trip ever undertaken,

with an infant human in the back seat and a sick dragon hatchling, nestled in a Halloween bin, stuffed into the hatch alongside a duffel bag filled with IV fluids, syringes, medications, and supplies. Then we drove straight into a late spring snowstorm.

We had to stop frequently for me to administer medications to the hatchling, which fortunately corresponded — mostly, anyway — to Ember's needs to nurse or have her diaper changed. Abandoning all pretense, I hung the IV fluids in the car hatch and started a steady flow of fluids using a pump that I'd nabbed from the clinic, draping the power cord the full length of the car to plug into the twelve-volt outlet using an inverter. Veterinarians were nothing if not resourceful.

I was grateful for the tinted windows in our Volkswagen, but avoiding unwanted attention when we stopped at rest areas was difficult. Once, a young girl spied me fussing with the bin and begged to see what was inside.

"Is that a puppy? Can I see it?" Her shrill voice startled me.

"No, sorry hon, it's not a puppy," I replied.

"But what is it? Can I see? Pleeeeeeeease?" she pleaded. Snowflakes dotted the girl's curly black hair as she looked at me with wide, hopeful eyes.

She was profoundly disappointed when I refused. If her mother hadn't been right there, I might have let her.

We had expected the storm, but the ferocity took everyone by surprise, including the meteorologists. We'd hoped to outrun it, but traveling with an infant was a tedious ordeal. Traveling with an infant AND a sick baby dragon was incredibly time-consuming. So we were running later than we hoped, and the snowstorm devolved into a blizzard. Vehicles began to slide off the road, authorities wisely closed the interstate, and we were promptly stranded in a small town in Wyoming.

Having procured one of the last hotel rooms available in town, Jon lugged our daughter in her car seat into the room as I wrestled with the hatchling's bin, the medical duffel slung over my shoulder. I squinted as snow blew sideways into my eyes, and my face stung from the biting cold. The weather was absolutely ridiculous for May. Despite the protection of the bin and the blankets inside, I was worried the little hatchling would turn into a "dragonsicle" before I got her indoors.

After successfully smuggling a dragon into the hotel, we settled in for an indeterminate wait. Despite intermittent electricity and heat, we were comfortable enough. We sourced a couple meals from the local Thai restaurant that tenaciously remained open, and we bought some groceries for ourselves and the hatchling, which was improving enough to gain an appetite. To be honest, it felt nice to be stuck somewhere, just the three of us, without the demands of the clinic, housework, family, or patients... except for one patient, obviously.

We spent the first couple days of our vacation rotating between the needs of our infant and the hatchling, eating Thai food takeout while watching movies whenever the power was on, and firmly refusing entry to the housekeeping staff. Both our baby human and the baby dragon took baths in the bathroom sink, and the dragon breathed fire for the first time in the soapy water, entertaining herself by sending up jets of steam from her bath. Dragon babies were not for the faint of heart, that was for certain. Three tiny soap bubbles floated upward with the steam and slowly swirled toward the hatchling. She crossed her eyes to watch them as they drifted over her nose, then widened her eyes in surprise when the bubbles settled onto her muzzle and popped.

I chuckled. "Okay, Bubbles. I was thinking of calling you Halloween, since you displaced the spooky decorations from their bin," I explained. "But I think Bubbles is more fitting."

"You should call her Rubbermaid," Jon called from his perch on the bed.

All good things had to end, of course. The storm lifted, the roads opened, and we continued on our trip. By then Bubbles was much improved, although not completely recovered, and she was getting quite vocal in her bin. Squawks and snorts emanated from the hatch of the car when she was feeling restive, and sooty, melted spots mottled the inside of the bin where she'd spat fire.

We arrived at my in-laws' house and I was a bundle of nerves, terrified the hatchling would attract undue attention. Fortunately, Ember kept everyone distracted. None of Jon's side of the family had met her before and they were instantly smitten. My cooperative infant turned on the smiles and charm, and I took advantage of the diversion by sneaking the bin and its contents into our basement bedroom. I opened a closet, dragged out a pile of boxes and some musty clothes and shoved them into a corner, and squeezed the bin into the bottom of the closet. Bubbles sneezed as I closed the door. *Sorry for the dust, small one, and I hope you didn't set your blankets on fire.* I peeked through the door long enough to ensure no smoke was rising from the bin, then shut it and returned to my baby and our family.

My husband's family always found me a bit peculiar, I suppose. Veterinarians were an interesting sort, always immersed in gross and absurd situations and fond of dark and crass humor. As the saying went, we were able to ruin anyone's dinner conversation in thirteen seconds flat. I was never great at censoring myself, which was likely why I possessed few close friends, most of whom were also veterinarians and therefore shared my brand of humor. My own extended family was happy to forgive my ramblings about patients and their sometimes gross conditions. But my husband's family never knew what to make of me.

My reputation was not at all improved by that visit. Whenever Ember was content in the arms of Jon or a relative, I disappeared to the basement, taking bits of leftover lunchmeat with me to feed the progressively hungry dragon. She became increasingly vocal, several times drawing attention upstairs with her squawks. I laughed it off as one of our daughter's noisy toys gone rogue, and Jon grimaced in tense collusion.

Bubbles no longer needed IV fluids or injections. I'd brought some oral medications for her but neglected to bring one particular drug, and had to invent an excuse to visit a local pharmacy, where I talked the pharmacist into filling a prescription for my own "dog." And then I realized that I couldn't keep up with the dragon's appetite by pilfering leftovers. I'd have to make a trip to the grocery store.

The house was crowded with people following a family barbecue. The weather had dramatically improved, but it was still chilly for Memorial Day weekend, so most of the family was milling about inside. I quietly briefed my husband on my mission. Ember was asleep, and most of the family were distracted, so now was the time. After covertly pocketing my keys, I exited the back door and rounded the corner of the house only to nearly plow into Jon's sister, Michelle.

"Oh, hey Jordyn! Where are you headed?" she asked, eyeing the car keys I had just pulled from my pocket.

"Uhhh, just the grocery store. We need, uhh, baby supplies."

I was always a terrible liar.

"Great, I'll come with you! I need to get out of the house for a bit," she said in relief. "It's so crowded in there."

Yes, it sure is, especially with a baby dragon hidden downstairs. Michelle was always unfailingly sweet to me, and better than most about tolerating my quirks, so I was somewhat happy to have her along. Though I wasn't sure how I would explain my purchases to her.

We discussed work, family, and life in general during the drive to the store. "Are you feeling okay?" she probed. "You seem awfully stressed."

"Well, you know, new baby, running a clinic, long hours at work… yeah, it's stressful." Which was entirely true. *Just add dragons for sheer chaos and insanity. And by the way, I'm hiding one in your parents' basement.*

We walked the aisles of the grocery store, still chatting casually about anything that came to mind. I picked up some baby wipes, which we didn't really need, but it was in line with my ruse about baby supplies.

"Do they carry wine?" I asked, in part because I badly wanted a drink, but mostly because I was hoping the wine and beer would be near the meat and poultry section, similar to our grocery store at home.

"Yes, they do! And I should buy some beer, too."

Michelle led the way to the alcohol, and I was in luck. Meat and poultry were across the back aisle from the wine section, sale signs prominently displayed.

"Oooh!" I feigned, veering off into the meat section. "Chicken thighs are on sale. Jon loves these!"

"He does?" Jon's sister stared at me, perplexed.

"I'm going to take some home in our cooler."

I glanced at Michelle. She stared in horror and disbelief as I collected three family-sized packages of chicken thighs. She clearly thought I was mad.

"Poultry is really expensive in Idaho lately," I added, hoping for some credibility. It didn't help much.

We picked up some wine and beer and made our way to the checkout, my poor sister-in-law stunned mostly into silence. The conversation on the way back to our home-away-from-home was considerably more strained. As we carried the grocery bags into the house, I overheard my husband's uncle accosting Jon about the noisy "baby toy" in the basement.

"When are you gonna yank the batteries out of that confounded thing?" he grumbled. "It's gonna wake your little one." Fortunately, our kid could sleep through anything, but Jon's uncle didn't know that.

"Yeah," my husband replied. "I should probably do that — oh, hi."

"Jon, I didn't know you were such a fan of chicken thighs," Michelle remarked.

"I am?" he replied with genuine surprise.

Behind my sister in-law's back, I frantically pantomimed to Jon, holding up a grocery bag and nodding my head toward the basement.

"Oh uhhh, yeah, I love them! Why, did you buy some? Cool." My husband was always a terrible liar, too.

Turning to take the groceries to the squawking baby dragon, I found Jon's uncle eyeing me suspiciously. He'd witnessed my entire pantomime.

"I'll pull the batteries out of Ember's toy while I'm down here," I called behind me as I escaped down the stairs. Sighing, I resigned myself to forever being regarded as an outcast by my husband's family. Oh well, my odd reputation was surely inevitable, dragons or not. *Time for a glass of wine.*

Bubbles enthusiastically ate three chicken thighs. She was much more content following the meal, which was sufficient to "pull her batteries," at least for the time being. I locked the door and pulled the bin out of the closet, then sat on the bed watching the sleeping baby dragon and my sleeping daughter while I drank Malbec straight from the bottle. Luckily, I'd stashed a wine corkscrew in my suitcase, but I didn't have a glass. As both babies settled deeper into sleep, I closed my eyes and pressed my fingers against my forehead, which was beginning to ache.

About six ounces later, I heard Jon's familiar footsteps descending the stairs, then a quiet tap on the door. I let him in and locked the door behind him, then reclaimed my spot on the bed.

"How's she doing?" he asked.

"Which one? Ember or the dragon?" I passed the bottle to him.

"Both, I guess." Jon downed multiple swallows of wine.

"Well, our kid is wiped out from being passed around the family all day. If we don't wake her up soon, she's going to sleep straight through and then wake the whole house at two or three in the morning." I paused to reach for the bottle, but Jon pulled it away from me and took another swig before handing it over. "Bubbles is doing great. She could go home, if only we were home for her mother to collect her. Who knows, maybe she's been back to the clinic by now, probably scaring the hell out of our kennel attendants." The two kennel workers we had at the time weren't all that fond of dragons.

"You think you can keep her quiet until we go home? She

was really noisy this afternoon."

Laughing, I reflected on the fact that most new parents worried about their baby disturbing people by crying, not about a baby dragon squawking in a plastic bin in the closet. The wine had calmed my nerves and loosened my sense of humor, and the more I thought about the absurdity of it all, the harder I laughed, pressing my face into a pillow to stifle my giggles before the entire extended family found cause to investigate. Wiping tears from my face, I reassured my husband (and myself) that surely, we could make it through one more day.

I planned to stay in the basement as much as possible and feed the dragon every time she awoke, in between nursing and changing our daughter, of course. To be honest, the thought of avoiding my husband's family sounded rather appealing. Eyeing the bottle of wine, I wondered whether I should give some of that to the dragon, too.

Turned out, we didn't have an entire day to wait. I kept the increasingly frisky dragon reasonably quiet throughout the morning and afternoon by repeatedly shoving food at her. The few times she squawked, I managed to pass it off as Ember making noises. I'd excused myself from socializing by claiming I had a headache (which was true), but I couldn't camp out in the basement forever.

Much of the extended family had left the night before, and we sat down to dinner with my husband's parents, sister, and brother-in-law. Jon cradled Ember in one arm, and I fervently hoped Bubbles wouldn't make a peep. I had run out of explanations for the noise.

My husband took a drink as he glanced toward the dining room window, momentarily froze, nearly choked, then nervously looked at me while he distractedly *thumped* his glass onto the table. Water sloshed over the tablecloth, and a drop dribbled down his chin.

"Jon, you okay?" Michelle asked between bites of mashed potatoes.

"Ummm, I think baby needs to be changed… can you help me?" he implored, looking meaningfully at me.

Something was amiss, and I doubted Ember's diaper was the culprit. "Yes, of course," I replied, not sure what he was up to. Shoving my napkin next to my plate, I hurriedly stood up and nearly tipped over my chair. Michelle called after us, offering to help so one of us could stay at the dinner table. She was so sweet, and I felt bad for brushing off her offer, but I had a feeling we needed to be alone for this endeavor, whatever it was.

Jon descended to the basement so rapidly, I worried he might trip and tumble down the stairs, infant and all. With the bedroom door hastily shut behind us, my husband informed me in a frenzied whisper, "A DRAGON IS RIGHT OUTSIDE THE DINING ROOM WINDOW, and what the HELL are you going to do about THAT?!"

Amazing. Absolutely amazing. HOW do they find me? I wondered for at least the hundredth time. Rubbing my eyes, I pondered what to do. I'd brought no medical supplies, other than those for the hatchling— *Oh. Bubbles.* Beaming, I told Jon I suspected I knew the dragon currently occupying the back yard, and I had an inkling of why she was there.

As quietly as I could, I carried the baby dragon in her bin up the stairs. *Please don't squawk. Please don't squawk. Please....* I hoped to escape the scrutiny of Jon's family, but when I emerged into the kitchen, they all stared expectantly in my direction.

"I'm going to, just, uhh, put this bin in our car."

They frowned in confusion at me and each other as I carried the bin out the front door without further explanation. *It's definitely time for another glass of wine.*

Rather than going to the car, I crept around the side of the house to the back yard. Sure enough, a dragon crouched in front of the tall hedge that bordered the yard. She sat quite still, nearly indistinguishable from the shadows, and I sensed her more than saw her. It took me a few moments to confirm what I suspected and hoped: it was the hatchling's mother. How she found me to collect her baby, or how dragons found me wherever I was, I had no idea. Countless things about dragons remained complete mysteries to me.

Bubbles was excited to see her mama, and squeaked and squawked happily while I tried to shush her. Hoping this wouldn't be one of those rare times a dragon spoke out loud, I handed the little hatchling over. The mother dragon appraisingly sniffed her wiggling baby and flapped her wings appreciatively. Dragons really were quite expressive creatures if you knew what to look for.

The hatchling needed a few more days of oral medication, and I quietly voiced instructions to the mother as I pressed a small bottle into her claw. She scrutinized the vial and quietly snorted. As I backed away across the lawn, she lifted into the sky and promptly disappeared into the clouds.

Until that moment, I hadn't entirely realized how much hiding the baby dragon had weighed on me. Once I deposited the empty bin into the hatch of our car, I rolled my shoulders and stretched my neck, dissipating some of the knots. Leaning on the Volkswagen, beginning to shiver from the cold and the dregs of tension, I watched the moon peek from behind the clouds. Then, without a single concern, I went back inside to face the confused and worried scrutiny of Jon's family.

Except for one concern, that was. *What on earth am I going to do with all these chicken thighs?*

16

The Plunge

After a rough start in business, the veterinary clinic was doing well. Conversations with Jon about the accounts became less stressful, although truth be known, we didn't love working together. In particular, he was not a fan of the dragon medicine expenses that ate up our profits, and neither of us loved the rumors swirling about my after-hours patients. Jon was especially bothered by how much time Ember spent at the clinic, because invariably, we were both at work.

Our daughter was literally growing up in the clinic, and clients sometimes stopped by without their pets to see her. The baby swing was replaced by a portable crib/playpen, then a standing activity center as Ember grew bigger and more active. The veterinary clinic was her home away from home, our staff and clients her extended family.

Aside from rumors about dragons, other news was circulating about the economy. Word was, the housing market was poised to crash. And when that happened, it would likely drag the rest of the economy down with it. Talk of impending recession became louder.

But at the moment, business was thriving. We took out a few equipment loans, one of which was for a new x-ray generator. Of course, some dragons that ideally should have been x-rayed wouldn't fit in the clinic, so I still needed a mobile x-ray unit, but that would have to wait until we paid down the existing loans. Now that I had plenty of technicians to help, I looked forward to radiographing the next small, injured dragon that came along. A juvenile dragon with a fractured wing was the first to try out the new x-ray machine.

And that's how we discovered that exposure to radiation made dragons glow. We positioned the young dragon, coaxing him to hold still and let us manipulate his injured wing. Jess stepped on the pedal to trigger the generator, and the machine whirred as it radiated through our patient to the digital plate below.

"*Whooooaaaaaaaa!*" we both exclaimed simultaneously as the dragon's wing brightly glowed in the darkened room, demarcated exactly where the x-ray beam radiated through his wing, with a bit of haze along the edges from radiation scatter. Gently, I lifted the wing and examined the opposite side. The underside glowed as well, although not as brightly.

I'm not entirely sure how this happens, and I would love for a radiologist and/or physicist to weigh in, but radiation must excite the molecules of the dragon's disguise mechanisms to the point of fluorescence. However it works, radiation absolutely wrecks dragons' ability to camouflage themselves. Fortunately, this is temporary, as I determined after keeping the juvenile for several hours. This gave me time to splint his fracture following a long string of "normal" emergencies, and I saw with much relief that the wing no longer glowed.

Nonetheless, we named him Glow Wyrm, of course.

How dragons avoid fluorescing from natural radiation is beyond me. Perhaps that's why I rarely see them active and flying in the daytime. Given enough time, maybe exposure to sunlight would make them glow.

A few days after the phosphorescent dragon, Jon plopped a stack of papers in front of me and sat down in the chair next to my desk.

"What's this?"

"A spreadsheet I put together," he explained. "Take a look."

Thumbing through the pages and skimming the titles, I realized Jon had kept track of the medications and supplies I'd used for dragons over the previous six months... make that the past year. I winced as I scanned the sub-totals, then closed my eyes once I saw the grand total. "Ouch."

My dear husband nodded. "Yeah. Jordyn, that could have gone to staff wages, equipment, hell, even our retirement," he said bitterly. "Or Ember's college fund. Or the land you want to buy someday, if that ever happens. I doubt it, and if we keep this up it won't for sure."

Leaning back in my chair, I sighed and crossed my arms. "What do you expect me to do, Jon?" I asked defiantly. "It's not as if I can turn the dragons away. They have nowhere else to go." Plenty of times, I mused why dragons sought veterinary care now, after they'd survived for so long without it. But after some thought, and also a few nuanced comments from verbal dragons, I'd realized that they must have been critically endangered. Seeing the opportunity to obtain veterinary care, they took it, even for relatively minor issues, because it increased the survival odds for their species. Knowing this, I felt committed to provide that care.

"We can't keep this up and cover all the clinic needs, and our personal income needs, especially with a recession coming," Jon retorted. "Isn't there any way you could ask the dragons to reimburse you? Some of them keep treasures, after all."

I snorted. "Like what, geodes and copper piping? I don't think that's going to buy much enrofloxacin."

Jon sighed, defeated. "Look, you can't keep treating dragons for free and still expect to pay for everything else, like my salary." He gave me a pointed look.

After a few moments, I finally realized what he meant. "Are you saying that I have to choose?" I asked incredulously. "Either I refuse to see dragons, or you're quitting?"

"No, you don't have to choose," he replied calmly. "I know you could never turn the dragons away."

"Then what—"

"I've chosen for you. I start my new job a week from Monday."

"WHAT?" I was dumbstruck. "New job? Doing what?"

"Accounting."

Astonished, I stared at him. "Seriously? You're leaving, just like that? To be an accountant?!" I exclaimed, my voice edged with anger and fear.

"Hear me out," Jon implored. "I've got ten days to train you, and maybe a receptionist, to take over the bookkeeping. And I'll still help out in my spare time. I'll be able to spend more time at home with Ember while you work. The benefits at my new job are great, so that takes another expense off the business. And honestly, accounting will pay me much better than the clinic ever could, with or without dragons. If you really want to buy land someday, well, this is the only way it's going to happen."

Admittedly, Jon had brought up several good points. I sat for a moment, letting it all sink in. Accounting sounded awfully dull compared to veterinary medicine. But then, Jon would be good at it. And he was so easily stressed; maybe a dull job with dull coworkers suited him better. *Speaking of coworkers...* "You and I won't—"

"—have to work with each other anymore," Jon finished.

I smiled grimly, tears welling in the corners of my eyes. I couldn't argue with any of his logic, and even though we were both relieved at the idea of no longer being stuck together at work, I was sad for him to leave the business. I didn't love the bookkeeping, accounting, inventory, and hiring or firing parts of things. I wanted to practice medicine and let someone else worry about those details. But owning a practice required adaptability. And if the predictions were accurate about the impending economic collapse, the clinic would have to adapt to a great deal beyond Jon's departure.

Unfortunately, that's precisely what happened. The housing market crashed, the stock market plunged, and the economy sank into a deep recession, bankrupting numerous businesses in the process. People's savings evaporated and caring for their pets became an impossible luxury. The number of appointments dwindled rapidly, until sometimes entire days passed by with almost no patients to be seen and only a handful of phone calls. The situation became truly desperate.

Jon's new job was our lifeline, since I stopped taking home much in the way of salary. I was so fond of our staff and didn't want to let anyone go, although I had to cut everyone's hours. Gradually, some of the staff quit on their own, seeking greener pastures elsewhere or moving to take refuge in their parents' homes, broke and discouraged.

But the core of my staff stayed, including Jess. I felt very fortunate to employ them, since the dragon patients never slowed down. If anything, we were treating more dragons than ever before.

The few dedicated clients who brought their pets often stayed to chat, which was fine with me since I usually didn't have any other appointments waiting. We commiserated about the economy, and they'd tell me about so-and-so who'd lost their house and someone else they knew who'd lost their life savings. The stories were so common and so painful.

Sometimes, the conversation evolved to the rumors circulating around town about my unorthodox patients.

"So what are you up to after hours, Doc?" a client named Daniel asked. "You know there are some funny stories being told about the animals you see." He frowned at me, knitting his bushy eyebrows together. Daniel was a grizzled, weathered old man with an unpredictably cranky German Shepherd that I had treated for years. The unruly dog perfectly complemented his irascible owner. Daniel voiced praise and complaints with equal carelessness, usually at high volume, and frequently intimidated my staff in the process.

"Oh? And what's that?" I replied, feigning ignorance.

Daniel leaned forward and lowered his voice conspiratorially. "You've got a former worker, or maybe more than one, that says you see big winged things in the parking lot," he said.

"Like what, wild turkeys? Or macaws? I don't like to treat birds. Macaws can sever your finger with one bite." I wasn't about to admit to anything I didn't have to. The dragons were safer remaining anonymous. And maybe I could get Daniel talking about birds instead of rumors. But he wasn't easily dissuaded.

"Nah, Doc, they were talking about—" He leaned farther forward for emphasis and raised his eyebrows— "dragons."

"Like bearded dragons? Daniel, I don't see reptiles. Remember when you called about your grandson's boa constrictor? I told you I didn't know the first thing about snakes. There's an exotics vet in town for that."

Daniel sat back in his chair, his face hardening with impatience and irritation. "No, no, you know damn well what I mean. Not snakes or lizards, I'm talking big, winged, fire-breathing dragons." He made flapping motions with his hands, demonstrating the flying part, since I was playing dumb.

"Oh, like FANTASY dragons? Imaginary dragons?" I smiled at Daniel as if he'd made a great joke. "And what do you think about that?"

He scoffed and crossed his arms. "Well, I think it's total BS. But I want to know what you think, Doc. There are some awfully funny rumors going around."

"I think some people have overactive imaginations."

"Could be, Doc, could be," he acquiesced. "But then, I always say, if there's smoke, there's gotta be fire somewhere." Daniel once again leaned forward to drive his point home. His shrewd, deep brown eyes stared at me intently beneath scraggly eyebrows weaved into a frown.

I cringed at Daniel's figure of speech. *Sure, there's fire. Especially whenever a dragon sneezes. That's why the clinic maintains an abundant supply of bandages and burn cream.*

Another client, a tiny, elderly woman with a bunch of cats and likely dementia, brought up the dragons with no preamble whatsoever.

"Dr. Blackstone, I want you to know I think it's wonderful that you take care of the dragons. There aren't as many of them around as there were. I used to find them in my garden all the time. They'd dig up my potatoes, but now I don't see them very often. I know they're in trouble, and it's so good of you to help them. Bless you, Doc."

My technician and I both froze, still holding the woman's skinny black cat on the exam table, my ophthalmoscope directed somewhere near the cat's tail instead of his eye with my attention riveted elsewhere. The tech and I stared at each other, then at the elderly woman, who blinked at us sanguinely from behind thick glasses.

"Uhhh, well, thank you, Ms. Higgins. Let's talk about Junior's eye infection, shall we?"

Our clients that could be described as more "rational," I suppose, never said a word about dragons, and I suspect if they heard any of the gossip, they dismissed it outright. Of course, I suspected the "rational" parts of us were what prevented our eyes and brains from seeing and recognizing impossible things like dragons. But some of our, shall we say, more eccentric clients, those who believed in things like Bigfoot, UFOs, or ghosts, ate up the rumors and mentioned them with increasing frequency in the clinic.

My concern about the dragons grew, since I still felt that they were safest remaining unknown. Now that I had the assistance of my employees, I was better equipped to help the dragons. But the downside of revealing them to my staff was that I had exposed them to a portion of the public, if only the lunatic fringe of public willing to take them seriously. Whenever I left the clinic, I carefully surveyed the parking lot and its surrounding fences, trees, bushes, and the alley behind, looking not just for dragons, but also for spectators looking for dragons. It was only a matter of time, I thought, before someone decided to stake out the area and watch for the impossible to happen.

Keeping a business afloat during a major recession was stressful enough without fretting about dragons, yet I couldn't help worrying about them. But during that time, I worried about everything… the clinic, my staff, our clients, my family, the entire veterinary industry. Back then, I found it hard to fathom how the business would survive, how we'd manage to take care of our remaining staff, or how we'd ever save any money for ourselves or Ember. *What if we go bankrupt? What if Jon loses his job, and the clinic has to close? Will we lose our home?* For the time being, Jon, Ember, and I were housed, clothed, and fed. *But will that change?* The elusive land that I so badly wanted to buy someday seemed an impossible, even farcical, dream as my constant apprehension about our mere survival took over. All we could do was hang on and do our best to pull through.

17

The Gift

If any advantage was to be found in the drastic business downturn, it freed up more time to work with dragons. This meant I had the opportunity, if not the finances, to experiment with things like sedation, anesthesia, and even surgery on the creatures, things I had been itching to do for years. I had dabbled a bit with some of the milder medications on hatchlings and young juveniles, but I hadn't collected any meaningful data, and I'd never sedated an adult. Learning to sedate dragons, I reasoned, would actually save the clinic money, since it would save us time and trouble. Since I had the spare time, I decided to tackle this.

One of the biggest hurdles for sedation or anesthesia in any species was the paperwork. Administering opioids or any controlled substances required additional licensure and record-keeping to satisfy DEA and state requirements. Any patients that received controlled drugs had to be well-documented in the medical records, and the drug logs had to link appropriately to a real patient, an actual visit, and details on the medications they'd received, including dosages, routes administered, and why. Except for lab work, I didn't note my dragon exploits in the clinic records. If we started sedating them, that had to change.

This was tricky with dragons. No veterinary practice management software existed with "species" or "breed" options for fantasy creatures. So we improvised. Most hatchlings were entered into the computer as "bearded dragons." As for the adult dragons, it didn't seem remotely plausible to call them small lizards.

Consequently, we created patient records for the larger dragons using gigantic dog breeds: mastiffs, Great Danes, Pyrenees, Saint Bernards, and the like. The staff or I thought up names for many of our winged patients, but we couldn't possibly come up with names for all of them. Therefore, we ended up with many stray, giant-breed dogs named "Draco" in our computer system, and I typed a few shorthand notes in each record that included descriptions of size and coloration. Even so, it was difficult to keep track of which record was for which dragon. Certainly this was all a bit shady, and likely wouldn't have held up to the DEA's standards if the clinic were audited. But then, even if I kept meticulous records on each and every creature (and what in the world would I have named them all?), would any self-respecting inspector be inclined to believe me? I decided I would do everything I could to help the dragons, keep records to the best of my ability, and hope to stay under the radar.

Carefully planning my strategy for drugs, dosages, and administration, I created charts and logbooks to help me and the staff keep track of our experiments and their results. This was to be a proper, organized, well-documented study.

But after only three months, I fed the remaining charts to the paper shredder in frustration and defeat, having concluded that dragons did not tolerate opioids or benzodiazepines. In fact, "did not tolerate" was an understatement. No matter which drugs I administered, individual or combined, and regardless of dose, minor to major disasters ensued.

Sedation was supposed to make our lives easier by calming the dragons so we could efficiently perform diagnostics and treatments while they were quiet and comfortable. Instead, despite whatever sedation protocol I tried, my patients transformed to volatile, uncoordinated, combative beasts, which was counterproductive to say the least. To my horror, four of my employees sustained burns and cuts, as did I; nothing too serious, but we depleted our first aid supplies with frightening speed, and I sent two of the staff to urgent care for sutures. The powers-that-be at our workers' compensation insurance company were becoming suspicious.

Fortunately, no dragons or other patients were seriously injured in the process. The clinic, however, was a different story. Everything from windows, cabinets, and dog runs, to an overhead light, two computer monitors, the privacy fence, and even the brand new x-ray table were damaged. The list of repairs rapidly ballooned and costs piled up.

"I thought you were looking for ways to save money, not waste it," Jon groused as he nailed new fence boards into place, and I couldn't argue with him. We spent a slew of our evenings and weekends patching up the building and its contents, but we couldn't fix everything ourselves. Windows and specialized equipment were beyond our skills and expertise.

"Oh my!" the x-ray repair technician exclaimed as she surveyed the damage. "You know, you really should sedate the big dogs if they're going to struggle that much—"

Not having the patience to worm my way through that conversation, I walked away, calling over my shoulder. "Thanks for your input! Let me know if you need anything."

The government's administration sent out stimulus checks to shore up the economy, and every cent of ours went toward repairs to the clinic. Jon was livid about the expenses, my employees were downright grouchy about the whole endeavor, and I had to admit that I wasn't having fun, either. I couldn't let this go on.

So, even though I didn't have the opportunity to try every possible dose or combination of drugs, I gave up on controlled medications. I did, however, determine one safe and effective protocol for dragon sedation, so my experiments weren't entirely in vain. First, I would administer an alpha-2-adrenergic drug, such as dexmedetomidine, for pre-medication. Second, I'd administer a dissociative anesthetic to render them completely unconscious for a short while. Dexmedetomidine and propofol became my go-to sedatives for dragons of all ages, and since neither was controlled, the paperwork was much easier. I would need to figure out something more powerful to undertake advanced surgeries in the future, but that would have to wait.

As for pain management, I relied on non-steroidal anti-inflammatory drugs (NSAIDs) and GABA analogue medications, like gabapentin, all of which were well-tolerated by dragons' livers and kidneys. At least, I hadn't yet seen a single dragon with disease or failure of those organs, and by then I'd run laboratory tests for plenty of them.

Although I no longer used controlled substances on the dragons, I still kept copious notes on my observations, but not among our official medical records. Our "bearded dragon" visits declined precipitously, and we stopped seeing so many stray trauma-prone giant breed dogs.

Seeing the dragon patients kept us busy enough, but actual paying clients became more and more scarce. Despite Jon's departure and elimination of his salary as well as the major reduction in my own, the clinic finances were becoming dire, and my ill-advised sedation experiments hadn't helped. I stopped taking home any salary whatsoever and fervently hoped that business would pick up, but it didn't. Instead, dragons arrived with increasing frequency and consumed more and more medications and supplies. I began to panic. Soon I would be faced with a terrible choice: we either had to let a staff member go or start turning away dragons. I couldn't imagine doing either, and I was paralyzed with the prospect of having to make the decision.

Then something wholly unexpected and extraordinary occurred. The clinic phone rang one morning, and the receptionist informed me that someone wished to speak to me personally. Normally, veterinarians were difficult to catch on the phone, but thanks to my wide-open schedule I had nothing better to do. So, I picked up the receiver and commenced an extremely strange conversation.

"Forgive me for contacting you at work, Dr. Blackstone," the caller apologized in a deep, resonant voice. "My staff was unable to find a personal number for you."

"That's by design," I replied unironically. "What may I do for you?"

The caller introduced himself as Thomas Hill, an attorney in Texas, and he was calling to discuss the will of my oldest cousin. My family was vast, and I had first cousins and second, third, fourth, and however-many-times removed cousins scattered over at least a couple generations and multiple states and provinces. I hadn't spoken with this particular cousin in over a decade, and hadn't heard he passed away. I was shocked to hear that I was mentioned in his will.

"I'm sorry, could you please hold on for a few moments?"

"Yes, of course," the attorney replied, without any trace of a southern accent.

The situation seemed too weird, too cliché. This phone call had all the hallmarks of a phenomenal prank. Quickly, I searched for the attorney online, as well as my cousin's obituary. My eyebrows raised in surprise. Both were real, I was sad to see. If this was a joke, the culprits had done their research.

"Okay, I'm back, sorry about that. Please continue."

Mr. Hill explained that my cousin owned a small collection of classic automobiles and bequeathed a car to each of his first cousins upon his death. Knowing what little I did of my cousin, visions of a dusty, dented old pickup arose in my mind. A wheel fell off and the windshield shattered, much like this morbidly comical trick was about to disintegrate.

"I had no idea that Darrell owned any classic cars, or was even interested in them. This is news to me. And why leave one to me, or the rest of us? Not sure about my other relatives, but I haven't seen or talked to Darrell in years. He was always somewhat of a loner. I don't think he stayed in touch with any of us, really."

"Your cousin was estranged from his ex-wife and child, I'm afraid, although he made provisions for his daughter. And there are no other descendants. Whatever his motivation, his will clearly states his intentions to bequeath the vehicles to you and the other four first cousins on his father's side of the family, as well as two first cousins on his mother's side. And you are not the only heir to find this surprising, I assure you. The will may be contested by the estranged spouse, but no such challenge is likely to succeed."

"Yes, I can imagine my cousins are equally surprised," I weakly agreed. The fact that Darrell ever married, much less had a daughter, was news to me as well. I never knew much about him. But then, he was easily twenty years older than I, and we had never interacted much.

"So what kind of car are we talking about, and where is it located? How do I go about picking it up, etcetera?" A motorcade of rusty 1960-something pickups puttered through my imagination, nuts and bolts and bumpers falling off here and there.

"The vehicle specified for you is — one moment—" I heard papers shuffling — "a 1953 Kaiser Dragon. In excellent condition, according to the appraisal."

Now the game was up, and I couldn't help but laugh. *What a great prank! Whoever set this up, they've done well, I have to hand it to them. Are the staff pulling this elaborate joke?* Absurdly, I inspected the office, as if someone could manage to conceal themselves in the tiny room, then glanced suspiciously down the hall. No one appeared to be listening in to enjoy the show. Whomever was behind this, I was seriously impressed, though admittedly quite confused. "I'm sorry," I said between laughter, "could you please repeat that?"

Undeterred by my amusement, the attorney plowed on. "A 1953 Kaiser Dragon. Less than 1300 of these were ever produced, so they're not well known. The vehicle appears to have remained in covered storage in Houston for the past twenty-three years after Mr.— your cousin — purchased it. It remains there still, whatever you wish to do with it."

The guy was persuasive, but I wasn't convinced. "And how do I go about acquiring said dragon car?" I asked, trying to stifle my laughter. "Do I book a flight to Houston and just drive it home?"

"Er, well, I suppose you could do that," he huffed. "The vehicle appears to be mechanically sound, but it's, er, such a valuable car, in pristine condition, and it's such a long distance…." The attorney sounded offended, even pained, at the mere suggestion. He held some appreciation for classic cars himself, I gathered.

"Sorry," I interjected. "You said—'valuable'—how valuable is 'valuable,' if I may ask?"

My jaw dropped at his response, which contained one more zero than I would have guessed. *This has to be a joke! Then again, is it?* Could it have been some kind of karmic reimbursement for my services rendered to dragons?

The attorney was droning on about shipping, and I struggled to focus on what he was saying. "…Could be arranged via a private vehicle transportation company, but the expense would not be covered by your cousin's estate. Or, I am acquainted with a private collector right here in Houston. He is quite interested in your cousin's collection and would be willing to purchase the vehicle at the appraised value. Two of your relatives have already chosen that exact option," he added helpfully. "If you wish to obtain an independent appraisal, my office could help arrange that."

Sure they could. I wondered how much of a kickback the attorney was getting from his private collector friend. If any of this was even authentically happening, of course. And it had to be fake. In real life, inheritances from long-lost relatives didn't come out of nowhere to save the day. *That's the stuff of books and movies.*

"Okay, thanks, but I'm not ready to make a decision just now," I told the attorney, or prankster, or whoever he was. "Could you please send me all the pertinent documents and photos of the Kaiser roll?" I winced at my gaffe. "I mean the Kaiser Dragon, and I'll think about it. All right?"

"Yes, yes of course, I'll have everything sent right away. Call my office with any questions." Confident it was all a joke, I didn't mention a word of the conversation to anyone, and simply waited for someone to reveal their part in it.

A week later, just as I was beginning to wonder if I'd dreamt the whole thing, a thick envelope arrived at the clinic by registered mail. It contained a copy of my cousin's last will and testament, the appraisal, and several photos of a green and white car with a vinyl top the color of lawn grass. Admittedly the car was pretty, and indeed pristine. I had never seen one like it. Some of the photos were close-up enough to reveal rectangular markings in the vinyl that resembled scales. *Was that why they called the car a dragon?* To me, it most resembled alligator hide, although I never saw an alligator that lurid shade of green. Nor a dragon, for that matter. I concluded that whatever company board came up with the Kaiser Dragon model, none of them had ever met an actual dragon.

One of my few appointments that afternoon was for a cat that belonged to a business attorney who had done some legal work for the clinic in the past. As I finished up with his cat's vaccines, I brought up my inheritance dilemma, although I wanted to be mindful of his time away from work.

"If you're willing, Jim, I'll make an appointment sometime soon to have you go over the documents. I realize estate law isn't usually your thing, but I want to make sure this is all legitimate."

"Happy to," he replied. "How about you discount Gertrude's visit today and I'll look over them now."

His offer was more than fair. My exam charge was far lower than his attorney's fees. So we sat down in my office and he reviewed the contents of the envelope.

"Everything appears to be in order to me. Sorry for your loss, but congratulations on the inheritance. So what are you going to do with the car?"

"Why, you want to buy it?" I liked Jim. He was fun to tease.

He snorted. "I'll pass. Not with my current caseload. I'm not looking to invest in old cars. Although this thing—" he tapped a photo of the Kaiser Dragon on my desk — "is possibly a safer bet than the stock market. Maybe you should sell it to the collector in Texas. After you get another appraisal, of course, just to make sure the offer is fair. You could start a charitable medical fund for animals. I imagine many of your clients are struggling to pay for veterinary care?"

Jim's suggestion was spot on, and I was considering exactly that, now that I was beginning to believe the inheritance was real. Although I was certain Jim had dogs and cats in mind. I did, too, but scaly winged creatures were part of my plan as well.

Jon did not agree. "That could go toward Ember's college fund," he fumed. "Or our retirement. Jordyn, you're not bringing home any income at all, and we're struggling to pay for groceries. And you want to buy land. Let's face it, that's never going to happen."

Jon's concerns were valid for the most part. Once things improved, we would have to save up as quickly as possible if we ever expected to pay for our daughter's education, let alone retire someday. As for someday acquiring land, I stubbornly held on to the belief that it would happen, even though it seemed impossibly out of reach. However, those concerns paled in comparison to people we knew who had lost their jobs and homes. I was resolute about helping those who were struggling to care for their pets.

"Yes, but we are managing to pay for groceries and utilities, although barely, I know. But we're able to cover our mortgage, and we're not in danger of losing our house," I insisted. "It could be so much worse. I'll save some of it for us, but, Jon, I see patients all the time that can't be hospitalized or get the surgery or medication they need because their owners can't afford it. Sometimes I do it anyway, but I can't do that for everyone, or we would've had to close the doors long ago."

Jon sighed in exasperation. "That's one reason I left, the write-offs were a nightmare—"

"And you know I can't turn away the dragons," I plowed on. "They're endangered, and they've chosen me to help them. I can't refuse to do that. This money might as well have fallen from the sky. It's not like we were counting on it, and we don't have to keep it to survive. And just think! It's a Kaiser Dragon. DRAGON, Jon. Tell me that's not a sign."

He groaned in annoyance and resignation. "Fine, it's your inheritance. Do whatever you want."

'Your inheritance,' he'd said. The concept felt novel and strange to me. I had never expected an inheritance and was still getting used to the idea. It seemed surreal, and not wholly believable until the very real, tangible check arrived.

Thus, Darrell's Kaiser Dragon Fund was officially established for pets in need of care, as well as our unorthodox winged patients on the side. I had barely known Darrell, but I was sure he would have been pleased to know how many dogs, cats, and small mammals benefitted from his generous gift. I no longer had to face the decision to lay off an employee, and I was able to relax somewhat about the clinic's finances.

And maybe, just maybe, wherever Darrell was in the great beyond, if he was aware of how much his gift was helping "imaginary" dragons survive and thrive…. I pictured him in my mind, laughing uproariously at the cosmic joke. What a great legacy for him.

18

Hiring

Slowly, by tiny, painful increments, we emerged from the recession. The clinic steadily grew busier as time went on. Patients who had missed their regular checkups began coming back, and more and more new clients booked appointments. The schedule progressively filled up, and eventually our days overflowed with "normal" patients, not just dragons. We hired another veterinary technician, then another receptionist. Then another technician.

In due course, I had to admit that I could no longer keep up as a solo practitioner. My workdays became so uncomfortably full, I lost more and more time at home with my family. Ember missed me, and so did Jon. The clinic was doing well enough to support another doctor, and adding another veterinarian would help substantially.

As for the dragons, not only did they frequently visit the clinic, they started turning up at my house. Jon returned from a bike ride one evening and sweatily clopped in his cleats through the garage into the house. "Jordyn, there's a dragon in the side yard," he announced with uncharacteristic nonchalance before putting his bike away.

Our daughter frequently chattered about seeing dragons, which I chalked up to the active imagination of a four-year-old, combined with the fact that she had encountered plenty of my winged patients since she was a baby. I finally realized Ember's dragon sightings were authentic when I found her playing peek-a-boo with a snot-nosed hatchling in our vegetable garden.

She crouched behind a tomato plant, giggling conspiratorially. "Peek-a-boo!" she cried as she popped up, then resumed her crouch.

"Who are you playing peek-a-boo with?" I asked from the far corner of the garden, expecting her to name one of her imaginary friends.

"The dragon," she stage-whispered. "Sssshhhhhhhh." More giggling ensued. "Peek-a-boo!" Ember cried again, raising her arms high as jumped up from behind the tomato plant.

That time, I thought I saw movement in an overgrown patch of purple sage, and I stood up, abandoning the houseplants I was in the process of repotting. Sure enough, lavender-colored blossoms waved to-and-fro in the center of the sage.

"Did you see him, Mom?" Ember whispered from behind the tomatoes.

"Do that again," I prompted her, then watched the corner of the garden intently.

"Peek-a-boo! my daughter shouted. A split second later, a creature briefly raised its head above the flowers, then disappeared into the leaves below. He revealed himself so briefly that I caught only a vague impression of a grey and purple head, but I definitely recognized a snot-crusted nose.

"He was right here," Ember explained, pointing emphatically

at the patch of soil where she stood. "I saw him, and I came over, but he ran away from me."

I frowned in confusion and sniffed as I inspected the garden and the surrounding area, searching for any sign of the hatchling's mother. I wouldn't have necessarily seen a dragon if she were in full camouflage mode, but I thought I would have at least smelled her. The area appeared to be void of any adult dragons. *Why is he here alone? Is he lost? Did his mom drop him off for me? But then why is he hanging out in our garden, and in broad daylight? And why did he run away from Ember?* Regardless of how he got there and why, he was obviously sick. But I was afraid he would flee from me just like he'd fled from my daughter.

"Stay there," I instructed Ember. "I'm going to catch your dragon friend."

"Can we keep him?" She implored, turning on the puppy-dog eyes.

"Absolutely not," I replied. "But you might be able to help me with his treatments. Keep playing peek-a-boo like you were, okay?"

Ember dutifully resumed her game with the hatchling as I crept along the garden's edge, working my way toward the far end, then along the back fence. The hatchling paid me no attention as I sneaked closer to his hiding spot, positioning myself directly behind the sage. Thanks to benign neglect, the herb had grown into a huge patch that overtook the entire corner, so tall that some of the flower stalks nearly reached my waist. No wonder the dragon chose to hide within its jungle of pungent leaves. *I really need to thin this out. It's totally out of control. Pretty, though.*

"PEEK-A-BOO!" Ember cried as she jumped higher than

ever, extending her arms and legs like a starfish.

The hatchling popped his head above the flowers, then instantly retreated to the dense foliage below as the purple blossoms swayed side-to-side. I lunged, but not fast enough to catch him, and I nearly overbalanced and fell into the sage. For a moment I felt as if I were at the arcade, playing whack-a-mole with a grubby rubber mallet. Once my balance recovered, I quickly waded into the sage, and the herb's powerful scent rose with a vengeance as I trampled the plants, pushing the leaves and flowers aside until I was directly over the hatchling. He didn't run away, but instead huddled close to the ground with his undersized wings drawn tightly against his body, curiously peering up at me. A purple-tinged snot bubble clung precariously to one nostril. He was about the size of a cocker spaniel, but the color of a mouse except for the vertical purple stripes on his head and neck. Now that he sat below the flower stalks that coated my clothes and skin in lavender-colored pollen, his purple stripes rapidly faded to a pale, smoky grey.

"Those are some pretty advanced camouflage skills you have, little guy. But let's see what we can do about your snotty nose." I scooped him up.

"Mom! You caught him!" Ember shouted. "Please, can we keep him? Please please please please please…."

Despite my cruelty for quashing my daughter's dreams to own a pet dragon, she willingly helped me wrestle the hatchling into a dog crate. He seemed to sprout extra limbs, wings, and tails in the process. Ember diligently pried the dragon's small but powerful claws loose as I struggled to confine his flapping wings and whipping tail, all the while taking care to aim the fiery part away from my daughter. Between the two of us, all of the hatchling's parts finally slid into the confines of the crate. A feeble flame narrowly missed my fingers as I latched the wire door.

"Your fire breath is awfully weak for as feisty as you are," I remarked. "Are you clogged with sage?"

In response, the hatchling blinked, then sneezed purple pollen-laden snot.

We kenneled and medicated him for two days. The sage odor lingered, disconcertingly reminding me of turkey stuffing. In fact, about half the staff called him Turkey. The other half called him Peek-A-Boo, naturally. The mother finally materialized at the back door to collect her baby. By then he was much less snotty, but he still reeked like sage. Neither the hatchling nor his mother reacted to the odor. Personally, I supposed the smell of sage was better than the dragons' natural skunk odor, but I wasn't sure if I'd be able to tolerate the stuffing when Thanksgiving rolled around.

After Ember's peek-a-boo friend, I paid considerably more attention whenever my daughter mentioned dragons.

My days at the clinic became brutally long, and I grew increasingly protective of my Sundays and rare evenings away from work. Between neighbors who dropped by my house to seek free veterinary advice, or wanted me to remove ticks from their dog or the like, and dragons adopting similar discourtesy (Turkey/Peek-A-Boo was cute, but the novelty grew old as more and more of the creatures appeared in my yard and garden), I acknowledged that I was burned-out and badly needed to establish boundaries. I had to have help from another veterinarian to accomplish that.

However, this presented a quandary. How in the world would I hire an associate to join a practice that regularly saw "fantasy" creatures? I couldn't post an honest advertisement.

'Mostly small-animal practice hiring part-time to full-time DVM. Must be proficient with imaginary animals. May encounter fire-breathing creatures and occasionally get blasted with breath weapons.'

Also, what benefits could I possibly offer to make up for the dangers of dragon medicine? We already kept loads of burn cream and lots of bandaging on hand, free for any of the staff to use as needed. Health insurance, obviously. But what else? Estate planning and life insurance? Unlimited sessions with a therapist? Bulk case of skunk odor pet shampoo? The mere thought of discussing dragons and their pitfalls with a potential hire distressed me.

The dilemma of how to advertise for and choose an associate prevented me from acting on it for months, until my fatigue and frustration reached a degree where I simply had to act. The ads I composed emphasized exotic animals, flexibility, and adaptability. Despite heavily deliberating how I might approach interview questions, I didn't really have any solid strategy, and I decided to improvise.

Attracting veterinarians to Idaho was tough, so applicants weren't exactly beating down my door. Salaries across the state were relatively low, and the student debt load was so incredibly high, veterinarians found it somewhat easier to pay their loans by practicing in more lucrative locales. But a few veterinarians were drawn to the area for the scenery and outdoor recreation, much as Jon and I had been. Within a few months, I conducted the first job interview for an associate vet.

The interview was disastrous. The young, confident, applicant had finished veterinary school that spring. With all the usual enthusiasm of a new grad, she was excited about relocating and starting her career. She arrived dressed in a pretty ivory-colored pantsuit, with carefully coiffed blonde hair and perfect makeup. Not that she would have dressed the same way for a day in clinical practice. However, I couldn't resist imagining her laboriously curled hair singed, mascara smeared, dragon snot on her pantsuit.

A wry grin may have momentarily twitched the corners of my mouth. She noticed. My interviewee had done her research, and she was better-prepared for the interview than I was. She volleyed questions at me, and I didn't have ready answers for most of them. She lost all interest when I hedged my reply on the types of exotics seen in my practice. Last I heard she was practicing in Boise. I wished her all the best.

Six weeks later, a tall and weedy young man sat in my office, dressed in an ill-fitting dark blue suit, incessantly tapping one foot in nervousness. He had worked in another state for a year, didn't love the area or the clinic, and decided to move on. He hadn't gained much proficiency in clinical practice, I gathered. The longer we talked, the foot tapping increased in tempo as his discomfort became palpably noticeable. I found myself distracted in turn by his tapping foot and his tie, which was decorated with a repeating pattern of cat butts.

On a whim, I brought up zoo animal medicine. After all, zoo animals were wild and unpredictable, many of them were rather large, and we didn't know much about the physiology of some of the rarer creatures. That was as close of a "real world" scenario to dragon medicine that I could think of, at least "real" to those who hadn't been initiated to actual, live dragons.

Turned out the nervous young veterinarian was not keen on working with wild animals, in the zoo or otherwise. He quickly stood up, spilling his coffee mug in the process, and self-consciously tugged his too-short pant legs to cover his ankles. He shook my hand with a clammy grip and practically sprinted out the door, the cat-butt tie fluttering over his shoulder. *Oh, well. I suppose I gave him some much needed interview experience.*

A couple more applicants came and went, and I was getting discouraged. This wasn't going well. Finally, a veterinarian named Beth ("Call me Dr. Beth," she'd said) hand-delivered a resume. She happened to stop by right when my lunch hour started, and I invited her to interview right then and there.

She sat across from me, her relaxed posture in stark contrast to the nervous young man who had occupied the same chair months before. She wore grey slacks and a colorful peasant top with multiple, equally-colorful beaded rings in each ear. In addition to the many ear piercings, a small, green gemstone stud glinted from the side of her nose. She sported a high, dark ponytail that revealed a short undercut beneath, a rather uncommon sight in conservative Idaho, and among veterinarians in general for that matter. I liked her already, and I smiled. The haircut, piercings, and tattoos peeking around her neckline and sleeves didn't bother me. If she could provide excellent medicine to our patients, treat our staff and clients well, and maybe, just maybe, learn to handle dragons, then I didn't care even one iota about her appearance.

We discussed the basics. She'd been in practice for three years in the Bay Area and was hoping to move to a smaller town. She was visiting family in Idaho and decided to apply.

The conversation evolved to patients and clientele.

"Tell me about exotics you've seen in practice," I prompted her.

"Like what kind of exotics? Dragons?" she asked, then grinned a moment later, as if she might or might not have been kidding.

I returned the smile. "Well, you tell me. I assume you mean bearded dragons? We see one of those now and then."

"Yes, I'd say two or three percent or so of my patients are reptiles and birds. Maybe another five or six percent small mammals. But I want to know if I'd get to see real dragons." She dropped the smile and crossed one leg over the other, revealing a dragon tattooed over one ankle —a "real" dragon tattoo, not a bearded dragon.

My own smile rapidly faded. Sitting back in my chair, I stared at her, twisting a pen in my hand as I contemplated the young veterinarian across from me. *How interesting.* "Tell me what you know," I prompted her.

"Only rumors." She calmly returned my gaze, perfectly relaxed and seemingly ready for anything. When I didn't immediately reply, she added that her second cousin used to work for me.

The cousin I remembered well. She had worked at the clinic not quite a year. For over a month after finding out about the dragons, she'd grown increasingly anxious and jumpy during her shifts, and eventually quit. Impressed that she'd toughed it out for that long, I had given her a generic but enthusiastic reference letter on her last day, and the last I'd heard, she'd gone to work in one of the administration offices for the local university.

Ironically, she worked in the same department as the Bigfoot professor. From one "imaginary" creature to another. Granted, Bigfoot was unlikely to accost her on the way to her car after work, crouching behind a parking meter or among the marigolds in the campus flower beds.

"And what are your thoughts about the rumors you've heard, Dr. Beth?"

She stared at me intently, her pupils glinting like flames. "I want them to be true. Very much so."

I couldn't help but laugh. There I was, agonizing about initiating an associate to fire-breathing patients, and then Dr. Beth came out of nowhere, already aware of the dragons and eager to work with them. *Well, she might change her mind once she learns what dragon medicine is really like. Definitely not as glamorous as one would think.* But then, her self-assurance gave me hope, and I was optimistic she would do well.

I hired her, of course. The more I got to know Beth, the more I liked her and appreciated her eccentricities. She rapidly became an invaluable part of the practice. The staff loved her, she was great with our dog and cat patients, and most of our clients liked her, too. Although, within the first week of Beth seeing patients, a small handful of our more conservative clientele complained about our new doctor's unconventional appearance. They were invited to take their business elsewhere. Beth's wellbeing mattered far more to me than revenue from crotchety people with outdated ideas.

Beth had made it clear she wanted to learn dragon medicine as quickly as possible. So within weeks after she joined the practice, when I encountered a semi-large wyrm behind the building late one evening, I called her at home and asked if she wanted to come back to the clinic. She arrived within minutes, practically giddy with excitement.

However, the dragon became agitated when Beth and I approached him. I hadn't called a technician since Beth would be there to help, and I was having second thoughts about calling her, particularly considering her inexperience. Besides appearing uncomfortable with our presence, the wyrm acted like he couldn't understand me, and it finally dawned on me that he must have been deaf.

He avoided putting any weight or pressure onto his painful, swollen right forefoot. It may have been fractured, but of course we couldn't x-ray a dragon of that size to find out. Once again, I was reminded that we needed a mobile radiology unit. But that night we had to rely on examination alone. An orthopedic exam on a wyrm's limb required considerable strength, but Beth was up to the task.

Whatever happened to set off the dragon's fire breath, I didn't even know. One moment, I was holding his elbow for Beth to palpate the foot for fluctuant (fluid-filled) pockets or crepitus (the snap-crackle-pop effect that indicated a fracture or joint damage) and check for ligament instability, and the next, disaster struck. Beth had nearly finished her orthopedic exam when the dragon yanked his elbow out of my grip and rose up onto his hind limbs, wings flared ominously to his sides.

"LOOK OUT!" I shouted as I ran toward the building. Beth backed off a few steps but then hesitated, perhaps debating whether to run past the dragon toward the building or toward the alley instead.

Too late. The dragon expelled a short burst of fire, and Beth yelped. Horror and fear squeezed my chest, and my heart pounded. Luckily, the dragon quickly calmed and settled into a wary, uncertain crouch. Watching him closely, I kept a wide berth around him as I quickly scuttled to the darkened end of the parking lot, along the fence that bordered the yard of the vacant house. That's where I thought Beth had gone, although in the confusion I wasn't sure.

"Beth, where are you?" I called into the darkness, my voice shaking from panic. "Are you okay?"

"Yeah, I'm here," Beth replied with a strained and muffled voice from somewhere beneath the elm trees. I panned the beam from my headlamp back and forth until I spotted her. Beth crouched next to the fence, cradling her left arm in her lap.

Light suddenly shone from the house across the alley, and I heard a *thump* and tinny *clatter* of window blinds. I wheeled toward the noise as someone roughly shoved a window open. "I swear that vet clinic— HEY YOU!" the voice's owner shouted, only his silhouette visible to us in the bright light behind him.

I swiveled my head toward the dragon without thinking, but he was nearly invisible, having quickly camouflaged himself. Beth was concealed in the shadows next to me. I turned back to the angry window guy. "Yes?" I replied. I wasn't sure what else to say.

"I'm gonna call the fire department first thing tomorrow! That damned crematorium is DANGEROUS—"

"Sir—"

"—and I'm gonna make sure they shut it down!"

"Sir—"

"—Not the first time I've seen flames come outta that thing, I swear it happens all the time —"

Oh geez, what all has this guy seen? At least he's blaming it on something ordinary.

"Sir!" I broke into his rant. Beth needed my help, and I was getting impatient. "Feel free to call the fire marshal. Our crematory has passed inspection every single time he's visited.

But he's welcome to take another look." I'd told him the truth. The marshal had never once found anything wrong, but he'd routinely expressed his surprise that we had attracted yet another complaint. Luckily, no dragons had been around during the many times he had dropped in… yet.

"I'm gonna call and you're gonna be SHUT DOWN!" the silhouette reiterated, then slammed the window. The blinds swayed across the panes, the light promptly winked out, and the house stood silent and dark once again.

I exhaled in relief and returned my attention to Beth. The headlamp shone over her as she leaned back against the fence, squinting in the bright light. Beth's thin hoodie hung scorched and tattered from her left shoulder to her wrist, blisters already forming on the skin beneath. The colorful koi fish tattooed on her arm leered at me cartoonishly, its eyes and gaping mouth distorted through seared skin. An angry red mark bloomed on Beth's cheek, her ear was blistered, and strands of hair escaped her ponytail and fell over the side of her face in frizzy, scorched coils.

"Oh, Beth, I am SO sorry —"

"Yeah, me, too," she replied through gritted teeth. "But I'll be okay."

"Yes you will, but I'm so sorry this happened. In all my years of dragon medicine I've never seen a grown dragon intentionally breathe fire at me or anyone else. I'm so sorry he did this to you. Let's get you inside… oh, Beth, your tattoo!"

"Yeah, well, what is it they say about scars being like tattoos but with better stories? This will be one hell of a story." She chuckled weakly through her shock and pain as she took my hand to help her up.

Panning my headlamp across the parking lot, I spied the

dragon lurking under the trees. He had dropped most of the camouflage, but was still difficult to see in the shadows. His expression was inscrutable, and I couldn't tell whether he had any regret for injuring my associate. Since he seemed to be deaf, most likely he had reacted out of confusion and fear. But I found it difficult not to hold some ill will toward him for acting as he did. After all, not only should you not bite the hand that feeds you, you shouldn't lash out at the doctor who's trying to help you (I know more than a few "normal" canine and feline patients, and clients, too, who would be wise to take that to heart). I wondered if the wyrm might fly off once Beth and I left him alone in the parking lot, and after he'd behaved so badly, I wouldn't have minded so much if he did. Or at least that's what I told myself. In truth, I didn't want him in pain.

My associate leaned over the treatment tub table as I flushed cold water over her face and arm. She raised her fingers to rake the damp hair out of her face, and several scorched chunks broke free. I swabbed the soggy strands out of her hand with a paper towel and tossed them in the trash on top of her tattered sleeve that I'd cut off.

"Beth, I don't see anything that looks third degree, but you have second degree burns over, well, much of your arm. Your ear, too. I think you should go to urgent care. Or —" I checked the time — "probably the ER since I think urgent care is closed by now."

The young associate, however, adamantly refused to seek medical care. She slathered silver sulfadiazene cream over her injuries with my help, swallowed a handful of ibuprofen, and intended to drive herself home, despite the fact that she was still quite shaky.

"Absolutely not. I'll drive you home in your car and have

Jon pick me up. But let's get this cranky wyrm out of here first. That is, if he hasn't given up and left already."

The dragon was still there, sullenly lurking in the shadow of an overgrown elm tree. How was I going to explain medication instructions, since he apparently couldn't hear me? Could he read lips? That sounded unlikely. Could dragons read written language?

Despite my distress about the whole situation, that concept kicked off a whole cascade of questions I never previously considered. *Do dragons have their own language? I suspect so, but does a written language exist, like actual dragon runes? Some dragons speak English, but can they read it as well? What about the dragons that don't speak to me, can they read? How good is their vision? Can they see well enough to read the tiny print on a drug label?*

I was eager to know more, but Beth was hurting and needed to get home. After I printed a drug label for the anti-inflammatory pain medication, I warily approached the dragon carrying a small whiteboard and a marker. If this idea didn't work, the he would have to figure things out on his own.

The deaf wyrm unceremoniously took the bottle from my hand and held it close to his face, staring at the bottle suspiciously. Slowly gesticulating, trying to get his attention without startling him, I held up the whiteboard, having written "30 TABLETS" in tall block letters. Then, as the dragon stared at my rudimentary sign, I erased it and wrote "ONCE DAILY," then, "TAKE WITH FOOD," and finally, "DO YOU UNDERSTAND?" Notably, I wrote nothing about returning if the swelling didn't resolve. I wasn't sure I wanted him back.

"I'm going to think of you as Fury," I grumbled as the dragon inspected the bottle clutched in his claws. "And that's not intended as a compliment."

Fury gazed at the whiteboard, then peered at me. His head bobbed once, the closest to an affirmative nod I've ever seen from a dragon, then he turned and limped from beneath the elm tree onto the grassy yard where we walked dogs. His wings *whooshed* as he took flight, then as usual, I saw no sign of him.

I tossed the whiteboard and marker onto the treatment table, locked the clinic, set the alarm, and helped Beth into the passenger seat of her Jeep. The ibuprofen hadn't yet kicked in, and she was definitely in pain. It was time to get her home.

19

Recovery

Beth lived in a small brick house a few blocks from the clinic. I hadn't been there since Jon and I had helped her move in, and I was amused to see she'd wired a metal dragon sculpture to the front gate, then delighted to find freshly-potted snapdragons on the porch. The dragon on the gate clutched a small sign in his iron grip. "Beware of Snapdragons," it read, neatly painted in fiery-orange script. Beth was a person after my own heart, and I grinned. But my smile quickly faded, supplanted by worry about my associate and her injury. *Will she still want to work with dragons? For that matter, will she want to keep practicing here, or even continue to work in veterinary medicine at all?* I was too anxious to pay much attention to the decor.

At minimum, Beth would need to take time off to heal. I told her to take as much time as she required, and to call me if she needed anything, and to tell me if she changed her mind about seeing a doctor, and that I would check in with her every day. She jokingly called me "Mom" and waved off my concerns, once again assuring me she would be fine. But I wasn't convinced, and truthfully I was devastated over the whole situation.

Days stretched into a week, then two. Beth's state of mind evolved along with her wounds, which scabbed, sloughed, then scabbed again.

"Look at this," she texted to me, followed by a photo of her koi fish tattoo. The epidermis had sloughed away from most of the surface, revealing the dermis beneath with absolutely brilliant colors of deep-seated tattoo ink. "That's the best it's looked since it was new."

Beth was trying to look at the bright side and laugh this off, but I knew she was struggling. We talked or texted frequently, although I tried to balance my compulsion to check on her with Beth's needs to rest, sleep, and heal. I stopped by her house at least every few days to bring bandaging, burn cream, and groceries. She continued to refuse seeking medical care despite my urging, refused to reach out to her family, and even refused to fill out an injury report for workers' compensation insurance. Granted, we would have had a difficult time explaining to workers' comp how a veterinarian was burned on the job.

"I'm having nightmares," she texted one day. "Maybe dragon medicine isn't for me."

Considering the circumstances, I think nightmares are totally reasonable. I encouraged her to give it time. "Beth, do you want to see a counselor? I could arrange an appointment for—"

"No thanks."

"Okay, do you want to talk to any of your family?"

"Nope."

"Don't you think you ought to see a physician?"

"Doc, the answer is still no, and please quit asking." Beth

retreated into her cave of sorts, determined to ride it out.

"How are you sleeping?" I texted to her a couple days later. "Any more nightmares?"

"Yeah, some," she replied. And then, "I miss San Fran."

My heart sank. *Is she thinking of moving back? Will she resign?* I wasn't sure how much to read into her texts. Honestly, I couldn't blame her if she decided to leave, but I desperately wanted her to stay. Besides the fact that I needed her help, I also really liked her as a person and a vet.

However, Beth didn't leave. Three weeks after she was injured, she was back seeing patients at the clinic, sporting a few scabs on her ear and arm. The koi tattoo looked much less ragged, but scars would no doubt linger on her arm.

"Oh, this?" I overheard her say to clients. "I tripped and fell into a campfire. Yeah, got some nasty burns, but you know, lesson learned." I couldn't help but grin in admiration. Her explanation was much more plausible than my "caiman bite" story.

Beth informed me that she wanted to avoid dragon medicine for the time being, and maybe forever. Saddened, I assured her I would respect her decision, but remained hopeful that she'd change her mind. While Beth recovered, the clinic reverted to its previous routine with me as a solo practitioner, caring for dogs and cats all day and often dragons after hours. And once Beth was back, I continued to see all the dragons, calling a tech into work to help when needed, typically Jess since she was invariably happy to work with them (the extra pay was good incentive, too). Even though I had Beth's help with the clinic's regular business, I was usually wiped out from treating dragons all hours of the night.

The deaf dragon with the swollen foot never reappeared,

much to my relief. He was too volatile and unpredictable for my taste. And admittedly, I harbored some resentment toward him after he'd so badly injured Beth. That said, I hoped he was doing well.

Weeks passed. A month, then more. The mornings and evenings started to feel crisp and cool, and the trees hinted of spectacular colors soon to come. I braced myself for the autumn respiratory infection outbreak in hatchlings, inevitably followed by the annual rash of "popcorn-itis" in adolescent dragons who should have known better. Inconveniently, this seasonal influx of sick dragons usually coincided with the fall parvovirus outbreak in dogs. At times our undersized isolation ward overflowed with miserably ill puppies kenneled across from sneezing baby dragons, with the occasional spurt of flames leaving spots of soot on the kennel walls and doors. Neither the puppies nor dragons were thrilled to be hospitalized so close to each other, but we had nowhere else to put them.

Beth met hatchlings that fall, and despite her trepidation toward dragons, she found the babies adorable — snot, sneezing, and all. But she wanted nothing to do with the mature, less cute (and more dangerous) dragons. And while I was eager to have her help, I was loathe to push her.

At the end of October, six months after Beth joined the practice, I drove us to dinner to conduct her performance review. We indulged in Indian food, Beth's favorite, then went to the nearby brew pub for drinks. Her review was truly the most relaxed one I ever conducted, since I had no complaints about how she treated our patients and interacted with the staff and clients. And she was never one to get anxious about those types of meetings.

As we wrapped up the official review over glasses of dark brown ale, I encouraged Beth to bring up any questions or concerns she had about the practice, her role in it, me as her colleague and boss, our staff, or anything else on her mind. Turned out she had lots of questions, and they were all about dragons and dragon medicine.

"How did you learn to practice on animals that you didn't know anything about, or that anyone knows anything about?" Beth asked, leaning her elbows onto the table and peering at me as if I were a professor lecturing about an enticingly taboo, yet fascinating subject.

Laughing, I responded with a counter-question. "In California, did you ever get stuck with an exotic patient that you weren't familiar with?"

She contemplated this. "Once I neutered a sugar glider."

My eyebrows climbed. "You did?" Sugar gliders were tiny marsupials that resembled flying squirrels. Despite the fact that no one knew much about their physiology or nutritional needs, they were sometimes sold as pets. We did know that they were nightmares to anesthetize, since they had a nasty habit of trying to die under anesthesia. Agreeing to perform that surgery would have required considerable courage. "Had you ever seen or touched one before that?"

Beth grinned ruefully. "Nope."

"And how did the sugar glider do?" I asked, genuinely intrigued.

"Fine," she replied nonchalantly. "He woke up from anesthesia and bit the hell out of my thumb."

We both laughed. The one time I saw a sugar glider in practice, it bit me, too.

"So that's how you learn dragon medicine, Beth," I explained, back to our more serious topic. "By doing, extrapolating knowledge from the species you know to the ones you don't. There are differences, of course, but far more similarities."

Beth considered this. "Do you think there's anything actually magical about dragons?"

My eyes narrowed in thought, and I took a drink of ale. "You mean, magical in the sense that many of us find horses magical, along the lines of dignified and beautiful and photogenic kind of magical? Or do you mean woo-woo, spells, runes, and potions kind of magical?"

"I mean woo-woo kind of magical."

That I could readily answer. "Absolutely not. Dragons have unique physiology, that's for sure, and I don't know much about how fire breathing and breath weapons work, even after years of treating them. But who was it that said — Arthur C. Clarke I think? — that magic is just science we don't yet understand? I believe that is exactly the case with dragons. Does that ruin them for you?" I asked, smiling.

"No, not at all," she replied. "I thought that must be the case, but I wanted your perspective. How did you learn dragon anatomy? By necropsy?" Beth propped her chin onto the back of her hand like The Thinker statue. She was referring to post-mortem examination, like an autopsy.

"Yes, exactly. Usually hatchlings, unfortunately. The younger they are when they get sick, the worse my chances are of saving them. But then by necropsy I learn things that help me save the next dragon."

Beth leaned farther forward. "Doc, what do you do when a big dragon dies?" she asked in a hushed voice. "How do you dispose of the remains?"

"Nothing," I replied, equally hushed. I glanced across the pub to make sure no one could hear us. "Their bodies disintegrate before decomposition even starts. It's the most amazing thing I've ever seen. Sometimes the sicker or older the dragon, the faster it happens. I think it has to do with autolysis from the substances they use for breath weapons and fire-breathing, although I don't know for sure."

"Get out. Seriously?" Beth was riveted.

"Seriously. After a few hours, overnight at most, there's nothing left but dust. Maybe a few sparkles from their scales. Looks almost like someone sprinkled glitter over some cremains." In other words cremated remains, or ashes.

"So a necropsy has to happen right away then... but is it hazardous? With the autolysis and all?"

"Well, I've ruined a few instruments that way," I admitted. "The metal corrodes. Anymore, I always grab the most janky instruments for dragon necropsies, not the nice German stainless ones. And I use triple layers of palpation sleeves with a couple layers of nitrile gloves over top. Haven't burned myself yet. Knock on wood." I lightly rapped on the pub table. "I'm convinced that's why there's no evidence of dragons in the fossil record. They disintegrate so fast, there's nothing left to fossilize."

We continued to discuss dragon anatomy and physiology for quite some time. I had long drained my beer and then ordered a house-made cream soda, then another. As Beth's inquires became more specific, I dug a pen out of my bag and drew some crude anatomy diagrams onto a napkin, which attracted some odd looks from our server when she stopped by our table, especially once I drew wings.

Beth sat back in the booth, looking thoughtfully toward the ceiling. "So tell me this. You always intended to do small animal medicine, right?"

"Right. I love horses, and livestock are great and all — I mean, baby goats are adorable — but after a couple rotations through the barn in vet school, I knew I didn't want to work with them in practice."

Beth blinked at me. "But dragons are as large as it gets."

"In other words, what the hell was I thinking getting into dragon medicine?"

We both laughed. "Something like that."

"Well, I have to say I didn't choose to practice on dragons," I explained. "They chose me." Beth already knew about Emerald, the dragon I'd thought was a hallucination. "I don't think I would have seen the first dragon if I hadn't had cerebral edema. And by sheer coincidence, she happened to be injured, so I defaulted to 'oh, must treat the wounded animal.' Because of that, I guess, she and the other dragons decided I would be their doctor. So I do what I can to help them." Pausing, I took a drink. "You've got to admit, they're so incredibly — magical —" Beth smirked at that — "who could resist them?"

"Oh, I agree, they are incredible. And the babies! Oh my God, the hatchlings are so cute." She paused, thinking. "I never really minded large animal medicine. It just happened that I went into small animal med because I wanted to live in the city. Not many cattle and goats in San Fran. But I tracked mixed animal in school. Did I tell you that?"

"Yes, I remember that. Dragons really aren't that different from working with livestock. I mean, you can get hurt working with cattle, horses, hogs, camelids, whatever. Once I saw a horse charge in reverse out of a treatment chute, and a resident nearly lost her finger when it got caught in a loop of the lead rope. Of course, you won't see breath weapons and fire breathing on a dairy farm. But every species has their potential to harm. Maybe cats most of all."

We both laughed. The night was getting late, so we headed back to the clinic for Beth to collect her Jeep, and then we both planned to go straight home. She had the next day off, but I had a full schedule of surgeries starting at eight in the morning. However, life, as the saying went, was what happened while you were making other plans. As I pulled into the parking lot, a shadowy shape darted along the periphery of the beam from my headlights. Whatever it was disappeared between the clinic and the fence. Beth and I looked sideways at each other.

"I'm going to check that out," I announced.

Beth got out of the car and walked with me to the side yard, lingering a pace or two behind me. Illuminating the dark, leafy corridor using my smartphone flashlight, we found an adolescent dragon, hunched and miserable in the classic "popcorn-itis" posture. Sighing, I reflected for the hundredth time that for such incredibly intelligent creatures, adolescent dragons could be insufferably dumb.

The dragon peered dejectedly back at us as I shined the light over her face. She had velvety, deep brown eyes, the pupils dilated from pain. Her scales were a similar shade of brown, shiny under the glare of the flashlight. The beauty of dragons, and the copious variations in coloration, patterns, spikes, and even feathers, have always captivated me. And I've always held a soft spot in my heart for brown dragons, since the first two dragons I met were brown. This one, hunched and breathing hard from abdominal pain, tugged at my heartstrings despite her idiocy for making herself sick.

"You going to call in a tech?" Beth asked, her voice shaky.

"Yeah. This one is pretty painful, so IV fluids and analgesics are in order. You tracked mixed animal, so I'm sure you encountered more than a few cases of colic in horses. This is similar. Treatment will go way easier with help. But I'm trying to remember which tech is off tomorrow. Do you know?" I was hoping to call someone who would have the opportunity to sleep in the next day, because it was going to be a long night.

"Nah, I don't remember. It's okay, I'll help you."

Surprised, I turned and stared at Beth in the fringe of light from my phone. I couldn't see her expression clearly. "Beth, are you sure? You are in no way obligated to ever touch a dragon again if you don't want to."

"I'm one-hundred percent sure." She pushed her jacket sleeves up and shook her hands and arms, flexing her fingers and wrists, as if she were warming up for a piano recital. "Let's do this, Doc!"

Ecstatic, I grinned at her in the dark. "Okay then, let's do this!"

20

Choices

D r. Beth lifted her stethoscope from the dragon's chest. "Ninety beats per minute. That doesn't seem terrible."

The velvety brown dragon lay recumbent on the ground, wedged in the narrow corridor between the clinic and the privacy fence. The boards periodically groaned in complaint. Cautiously, I lifted the dragon's lips to find telltale bits of popcorn kernels around her teeth, and her mucous membrane color, I noted, was a bit pale. Her breath smelled like a movie theater invaded by a family of skunks.

"Actually, that's awful. Resting heart rate for a dragon, even adolescent, is usually no more than twenty beats per minute. I suspect it's much higher during flight; it would have to be, but I haven't been able to test that theory."

"Yeah, I suppose they are bigger than horses and just as athletic, so that makes sense. Okay then, this girl is in serious shock. I think she needs fluids overnight. Do you agree, Doc?"

"Absolutely," I concurred. "She's by far the worst case of popcorn-itis I've ever seen. We'll have to squeeze her through the back door into the dog ward. But first we'll move those two boarding dogs to the hospital kennels so we won't thoroughly traumatize them."

"Oh my God, that poor nervous doodle in there would faint," Beth replied, laughing, then immediately switched gears. "Where do you find a vein on these guys? Seems like the scales would be a problem."

"Rather problematic. We should be able to access the wing vein on a dragon this size. Once they're older, even wing veins are difficult. Then you have to get fancy and remove a scale."

Beth stared at me in horror. "Wait, REMOVE a scale? Doesn't that compromise their… like give them a weak spot in their armor? You know, like Smaug in *The Hobbit*?"

Guiltily, I gazed back at her. I had removed a scale from a dragon on several occasions, but I'd never felt great about it. It was truly a last resort, and I vividly remembered each instance I'd done it. "Well, yes," I admitted. "You are exactly right to question the ethics of that. I've only ever done that for critically ill dragons when I couldn't get a catheter placed any other way. If they're coherent enough to make the decision, I give them the choice: to risk death or let me remove a scale to treat them."

Beth was still frowning. "Have you ever had a dragon refuse?"

"Nope. Not once. And all of them lived."

Beth's frown lifted. "Huh. Wild. So how do you remove a scale?" Considering her former reluctance to ever touch a dragon again, she was really getting into this.

"Dremel. With a diamond wheel."

"Seriously? Doesn't it ruin the blade, though? How many blades does it take?"

"Well, that depends on how old and large the dragon is."

"But the most blades you've ever used is….?"

I winced. "Five." That IV catheter had been rather expensive to place. Diamond-edged Dremel blades were not cheap.

After injecting the dragon with pain medication in the side yard, we relocated the nervous doodle and his stoic Labrador neighbor to the treatment area. Gently but insistently coaxing the sickly dragon to her feet, we led her through the back door, down the hallway, and into the now-empty dog ward, encouraging her to keep moving as she morosely plodded, still hunched in pain despite the medication. Her wings and body scraped the door frames and walls with a *screech* as she squeezed through the small corridor. She wouldn't fit into any of the kennels, but she would remain overnight on the floor in front of them. I made a mental note to text the next morning's kennel attendant and warn her about our patient. Otherwise, she might have walked into the clinic at seven a.m. and died from shock.

"This is a good-sized vein, but her blood pressure is low. Want me to place the catheter, or you want to give it a try?"

Beth hesitated for a fraction of a second. "You place this one and I'll watch. I'll do the next one."

So there will be a next one. Apparently, Beth had truly come around about dragons in a hurry. Concealing my surprise at her change of heart, I inwardly smiled in gratitude and admiration for her tenacity while I prepared the dragon's wing for intravenous catheterization. If I'd had the time and energy, and wasn't busy with the sick dragon, I would have done a little happy dance.

Verbalizing the process along the way, I placed the catheter while Dr. Beth observed with rapt attention, eagerly absorbing knowledge. The adolescent was too miserable to even flinch when the ten-gauge metal stylet pierced her wing membrane. Once a shock dose of fluids was running — I kept five liter livestock bags of IV electrolytes on hand specifically for dragons — we injected anti-nausea and antacid medications, as well as drugs to stimulate intestinal motility (or normal movement), through the catheter into the wing vein. Then I walked Beth through the finer points of assessing a dragon.

"Right here." I indicated a spot on the wing. "See where these lines of fascia intersect? It's pretty subtle, but you'll always be able to find this junction in the muscle layers. Now press right there. You'll have to press kind of hard."

"Okay, yeah, I can feel that." Beth counted seconds on her watch. "So her pulse is about seventy beats per minute now. We're getting somewhere."

"Yes, and if you can palpate the pulse there, her systolic blood pressure has to be at least eighty. At least that's true for hatchlings and juveniles, and I assume it's the same for adolescents and adults, though I haven't found a large enough cuff to verify that. Ten minutes ago I couldn't palpate her wing pulse. So I agree, we're getting somewhere."

The dragon lay on her side on the cool floor, less hunched now that the IV fluids and medications were taking effect. She wouldn't feel great for a while, but at least she was more stable and comfortable, her head resting on a giant, fluffy dog bed, eyes closed.

"In other words, the wing pulse in dragons is equivalent to the dorsal pedal pulse in dogs," Beth added.

"Precisely. You've got this."

"Oh, I've SO got this!" Beth exclaimed, raising her face and fists in a victory pose. "I love this!" She lowered her hands and laughed.

Beth could be so impulsive, expressive, and funny, and I laughed along with her. The dragon opened her eyes at the commotion and turned to look at us. Her pupils were closer to normal, I saw. Then she closed her deep, brown eyes, turned back to the dog bed, and casually belched a spurt of flame through the door of a cage as she rested her chin back onto the cushion. Black soot instantly coated the metal bars and much of the cage interior.

"Dammit!" I sighed. Though admittedly, it could have been worse. At least the cage wasn't flammable, or worse, occupied by a pet.

"Oh, that stinks," Beth remarked, wrinkling her nose.

"Yeah, nothing about dragons smells great. Just wait until you smell their gas."

As Beth snickered, I carefully moved stacks of bedding and towels well away from the dragon's mouth. Next time she lifted her head, I planned to take away her pillow. I wanted her comfortable, but I also couldn't have her burning down the clinic.

Speaking of the clinic, I wondered how much we'd damaged the building by squeezing our patient inside, so I went to inspect the doors and hallway. The molding was still intact, and the doors still swung on their hinges fine, but she had carved fresh scratches and grooves into the walls. Looking closely at the marks, I counted six different colors of paint layered throughout the years, all the way back to the garish orange of the original clinic. *The 1970s were certainly interesting times when it came to design and color.*

As I walked back toward Beth and the dragon, my shoe caught on a deep gouge in the epoxy flooring, no doubt from the dragon's claws. Epoxy was more difficult to repair than paint, and I winced. The dragon's body and wings were streaked with old paint that perfectly mirrored the layers of colors from the walls, giving her a psychedelic effect.

Not for the first time, I ruminated over the logistical difficulties of performing dragon medicine out of our undersized building. Now the clinic was getting cramped with just our regular caseload, more so with two doctors practicing. We would only get busier, I figured, and we needed more room. Following the recession, I'd begun to perform anesthesia and surgery on dragons, and I'd saved more than a few lives. However, I was limited by the size of our small animal equipment, not to mention the sheer space constraints of the building. I shared my ideas for expansion with Beth.

"Just imagine a surgery suite and recovery room, like the big, padded rooms for horses, with sliding lift mechanisms, except with concrete and sheet metal instead of padding." Horses waking up from anesthesia were at high risk of hurting themselves, thus the heavy padding. Dragons were more likely to damage the clinic than themselves. "And a huge hospital ward with an overhead door, so even a wyrm would fit inside. Everything fire-resistant, of course. Just think what we could accomplish!"

"That would be amazing," Beth replied, though she seemed unsure.

"Plus," I continued, nearly as an afterthought, "we can add more exam rooms and expand the treatment area and the lobby, for, you know, the 'real' patients. We desperately need that, too."

Beth frowned dubiously. "I don't know if we can do all that with the empty lot. What about parking? Will there be anywhere left to walk dogs?"

Mulling this over, I had to admit she had a point. I'd always planned to expand the clinic into the grassy lot where we walked the hospitalized or boarded dogs (not to mention, dragons sometimes hid there beneath the trees). However, we couldn't fill the whole lot with a building addition. We'd have to dedicate a portion of it to additional parking spots to satisfy the city's planning and zoning requirements. Building an addition for small animals wouldn't leave us with enough room for a dedicated dragon facility, especially of the size and grandeur I had in mind.

"We should build a whole new building!" Beth exclaimed as her face lit up.

I glanced at the time. It was past midnight, and I was too tired for that much excitement. "You know I've thought about that, but not seriously," I hesitantly replied as I reached for the dragon's wing to take her pulse. "Tell me your ideas. You think we should stay in this location? Maybe build a two-story clinic with the space we have? Maybe we can add another story onto the existing building."

"No, no, think about it! — I'll daisy-chain more fluids." Beth continued chattering enthusiastically as she spiked another bag of IV electrolytes and attached it to an existing one, so they would all flow by gravity into the primary bag, through the pump, and into the dragon's veins.

"This building is old and dumpy — sorry, Doc, but it is —" Beth had taken note of my pained, almost offended expression. "It was built in the seventies, right? It's going to be loaded with asbestos and a pain to build on. And it's pretty much surrounded by houses. Plus the counter tops are orange. Orange!" Her face twisted in distaste.

Despite my attachment to the antiquated building, Beth's unflattering description made me grin, and I was intrigued. "Okay," I replied, smiling. "So, if you were going to build a clinic and continue to serve the same clientele, but make room for dragons, where would you put it?"

Beth tilted her head thoughtfully. "By the train tracks."

"What? Are you serious?"

"Yeah, think about it!" Beth voice grew louder and more animated, and I watched our patient to see her reaction. The creature didn't move from her freshly singed cushion, though she eyed Beth cautiously.

"There are some empty lots available close to the tracks not far from here, near the rail yard. I drove past them; big, flat commercial lots with plenty of space. There are no houses nearby, and best of all, the trains make lots of noise, right? Noise at all hours, and lights, too."

I hadn't thought of that at all. In our current location, although lots of high fences and closed window blinds shielded the clinic from nearby houses, I constantly worried that the dragons would attract undue attention. The rail yard several blocks away generated some noise that helped disguise our clandestine activities. Nonetheless, we had fielded quite a few noise complaints over the years thanks to dragons.

Also, the fire marshal had become a regular guest, dropping in frequently to check our crematory due to complaints about "flame emissions." He never found anything wrong. Owning and operating a crematory entailed some morbid challenges and required a macabre sense of humor, but I was happy to have it. Otherwise, I didn't know how we would have explained the occasional fiery sneeze or belch. *If we were right next to the rail yard, and a dragon were to create a commotion or even breathe flames, well, it probably wouldn't attract any attention at all.*

Despite the late hour and my fatigue, I found myself getting as excited as my associate. "Beth, that's brilliant."

She raised her fists again. "YES! Let's do it!"

The dragon raised her head to stare intently at us, but luckily didn't belch any more flames. Once she lost interest in Beth's antics, she shifted her feet and wings and curled into a more natural relaxed pose, chin rested near her knee, wings folded neatly along her trunk, eyes again closed. She sighed in contentment, finally comfortable, although still fatigued and weak. I seized the opportunity to slide the burnt dog bed away from her, then stuffed it into the laundry basket where it shed bits of blackened fuzz onto the towels below.

As I quietly stole the dragon's pillow, my mind chattered at a much louder volume, and my pulse quickened. *I never intended to take on a partner. And not once did I consider building an entirely new clinic.* But, as I thought over Beth's words, her passion for veterinary medicine, the practice, and especially her newfound (or renewed) passion for dragons, my vision for the future shifted, heaved, and clicked into a much more sensible place. I blurted the offer before I could second-guess myself. "Okay, who's this 'let's'? You want to buy in and become my partner?"

Beth contemplated this for several moments, frowning. "You know what, I think I do. This feels like home. It feels like I was always meant to work with dragons. Even though the first one scared the hell out of me."

My mood sobered at the memory of Beth's injury. "Understandable, considering how badly you were hurt." Now, months later, under the harsh buzzing fluorescent lights in the dog ward, I could still see marks on her arm. However to my relief, the scars had faded substantially.

"Hey, Doc, lighten up," Beth chided. "I'm okay. BBQ didn't do that much damage."

I gaped at her. "BBQ?! You named that ungrateful beast BBQ?!"

"Well, yeah. He did try to barbecue me, so it fits. Why, what do you call him?"

"I've been thinking of him as Fury—"

"HA! So serious! I like BBQ better. And I'm the one who was grilled, so I get to pick."

We both laughed. "Okay, okay, your choice," I relented. "We shall call the dangerously fear-aggressive dragon BBQ."

"Yes! Let's hope he doesn't bring condiments next time."

Both of us shook with laughter as the dragon warily watched us with one eye. Tears began to run down my face, and I could barely draw a breath.

"Seriously, there better not be a next time!" I gasped, mopping my face with my sleeve. "And speaking of names, what should we call this girl?"

"I was thinking Orville Redenbacher," Beth deadpanned. "Orville for short, or maybe Orvie if we're going for informality."

Once again, I was completely incapacitated by laughter.

Eventually, we returned to more sober subjects. "Beth, I can't imagine anyone else I'd rather have as a partner. So we'll make it happen. But first, let's get some sleep." I smiled. If I even could sleep after the excitement of that night. "One more dose of metoclopramide, and we should give her more pantoprazole, too. And hang more fluids, although let's reduce the rate, and then let's go home. Sound good to you?"

"Sounds great!" Beth practically leapt up from her cross-legged position on the floor. I wished I had half her energy at one in the morning. However, I was enlivened by the anticipation of a partnership with Beth and a new facility, too. All it took was for her to believe it could happen, and then I was convinced it would, too.

* * *

A scant few hours later, I arrived back at the clinic. The dragon had rolled onto her opposite side during the early morning hours. It was best for her muscles, joints, and lungs to change position, but in the process she'd bent one of the kennel doors and tangled her intravenous fluid line around her wing. Despite the abundance of extension sets Beth and I had added to provide plenty of slack, Jess had arrived to find the fluid line taut, the pump beeping in protest. Fortunately, the flow appeared to have stopped only for a short time. Jess had untangled the dragon's wing and restarted the fluids before I arrived.

Sipping coffee from a mug in one hand, I offered a bucket of raw chicken to Orville with the other. She sniffed at her breakfast disinterestedly but eventually mouthed the chicken and tentatively swallowed a few bites. Then she paused, emitted a small belch — no flames — and curled her head to rest under her wing.

Satisfied that Orville was stable and comfortable, I left the bucket of chicken within her reach and headed into the treatment area to start my "real" day. Unless any complications arose, the dragon would be well enough to leave the hospital by nightfall.

My exhaustion was so profound, I almost couldn't recall what being well-rested felt like. And yet, I felt happier and more content than I had in a very long while.

21

Adrenaline

If I'd thought life was flying by at maximum speed before, the next few months would prove me wrong. The clinic grew ever busier, especially after Dr. Beth's addition to the practice. Dragons routinely visited the clinic multiple times per week. Sometimes we even managed more than one during a single night.

I'd hoped that hiring an associate (and soon to be partner) would have freed up spare time for me. In reality, my "spare" time overflowed with all the things required by my house and family, managerial tasks for the clinic, scouting property for the new building, and dragons, always dragons. I mentored Beth on the nuances of dragon medicine, and as time went on, she saw more and more of them without my help. To my increasing frustration, sometimes the creatures still showed up at my house even when Beth was on duty.

"Off with you! Go to the clinic," I scolded one adolescent that slunk in the bushes next to my garage late one night. With a *thud*, I deposited a bag of garbage into the trash cart, the sixth or seventh "one last thing" I'd found to do before finally collapsing in bed. "You're not that badly hurt, and I don't have any suture at home anyway. Go see Dr. Beth. She's a perfectly competent dragon doc, and she's at the clinic right now." Beth was on call and had reported to me that she'd already seen two dogs and one dragon on emergency, and I knew for a fact she was still at the clinic. She was going to have a long night.

The dragon reluctantly retreated and disappeared into my back yard, presumably to take off from the ravine. I lifted my phone to text Beth and warn her about the adolescent with a lacerated neck frill that was headed her way. "I'm on it," she replied. Better her than me, although my turn would come soon enough.

As I pocketed my phone, I forced myself to stop doing all-the-things for a few moments and simply be. Most of the houses in my neighborhood stood dark and quiet, their occupants long asleep. Wispy clouds slowly scudded across a smattering of stars and the moon, which had waned to a mere fingernail clipping of vivid white light. The chirping of countless crickets merged together into a chorus, their buzzing harmony an essential component of any summer night. I breathed in the smell of suburban summer, grass clippings and a cacophony of flowers mixed with hot asphalt, car exhaust, and gossip.

A weak reflection flashed from diagonally across the street. I squinted at the spot, identified the source as an aluminum can, then realized the can was held by my neighbor, who sat in a lawn chair in his front yard. With his dark t-shirt and even darker beard he was nearly invisible, and I never would have seen him if not for the beer can. From his vantage point he couldn't possibly have seen the dragon, but he would have seen the bushes moving and surely had heard what I'd said.

"Pretty night," I called as I waved to my lawn chair witness, feigning nonchalance.

Ten or fifteen awkward seconds passed. Finally, without a word, he stiffly raised his beer in acknowledgement, then lowered it to rest on the arm of his chair. Though I assumed he had parked himself outside to relax, he appeared to be rather tense. I turned and went inside. *I wonder what new rumors will swirl through the neighborhood tomorrow? Then again, if he drinks enough alcohol tonight, maybe he won't remember anything.* Shrugging with indifference (or so I told myself), I closed the door and went to bed.

Dr. Beth had been up most of the night seeing patients but had the following day off, fortunately for her... but unfortunately for me. Some moments in veterinary medicine demanded superhuman abilities, or in other words, didn't allow us to be human. Instances like these filled my day, giving my adrenal glands a serious workout.

First, a Good Samaritan rushed a blue heeler into the clinic directly after witnessing a car hit the poor dog. Unluckily, I was in the middle of a surgery at the time and couldn't abandon my patient under anesthesia. My techs tried to stabilize the dog while I shouted instructions for pain medications and IV fluid rates as I finished surgery, then immediately pulled off my gloves and rushed to the heeler's side.

Jess's grave expression gave me an instant summary. The dog was in bad shape. "I don't like this," she said, nodding her head toward the ECG monitor. Strings of ventricular premature contractions, a dangerously abnormal heart rhythm, marched across the screen between a few feeble stretches of normal beats.

"Get the lidocaine—"

"It's already drawn up." Of course, Jess was a step ahead of me.

"Perfect, start with a bolus," I instructed, then raced through the mental gymnastics to calculate the dose in my head as Jess turned to show the syringe to me. "Yep, that's about right." We hadn't even yet had the chance to weigh the dog, but the dose was accurate enough, and hopefully effective enough, to save his life.

The dog, an intact male (undoubtedly why he was roaming in traffic), stared straight ahead with glassy eyes as I examined him, though he seemed to be aware of me. His eyes and teeth revealed his age as no more than two years, and he was cute in spite of the bloodstained coat. A hand with papers materialized in front of my face. With dismay, I reviewed the blood work results and shook my head.

"Has anyone scanned for a microchip?" I asked.

"Yes, none," two of the staff replied at once. If he'd had one, we probably could have quickly located his owners.

"Anyone call animal control yet?" I added.

"Yeah, they said to go ahead and treat, but to call them when you know his prognosis."

"It's terrible," I replied sadly. "I'll call them now."

In the end, the dog didn't make it. Despite efforts by animal control and our staff, his owner was never found.

The day was not done with my adrenal glands yet. Next, a patient went into a seizure while I was in the bathroom, then again while I was in the middle of informing a sweet elderly couple that their cat had cancer.

Then, a client yelled at the poor receptionist and stomped out because he'd had to wait fifteen minutes for his appointment, despite being informed that the only doctor in the clinic was juggling emergencies and would see his pet as quickly as possible. I would have liked to have said this was a rare event, but unfortunately I could not. One of the techs temporarily took over the front desk so the receptionist could take a break, and I made a mental note to call the offending client.

To cap this nightmare of a day, I euthanized a cat I'd known for years and whose owners I considered friends. The staff and I had seen the cat quite frequently over the past ten months as we'd supported him through kidney failure, and thanks to his unshakably sweet personality, he was one of our favorite patients. Sadly, his disease had advanced to the point where we could do nothing more. We all cried.

After closing, I sat in my office with puffy, red eyes shut tight, elbows propped on my desk, fingertips pressed to my throbbing temples. The wall clock ticked three or four minutes away in relative peace. Someone walked in, and I opened my eyes to discover Jess plopping a cold soda in front of me. A beer would have been even better, but I was on call for emergencies for the rest of the night. I didn't dare drink alcohol.

"Hey thanks, Jess."

"Sure. You okay?" She sat down and opened her own soda with a *crack* and *fizz*.

"Good enough," I answered. *Not really, but what can I do?* "What about you?"

"About the same," Jess replied. "Looks like we have matching headaches."

"There's still plenty of ibuprofen in the break room cabinet. Are you on call with me tonight?" I should have known the schedule, but my brain was too fried to remember.

"Yep. That's why we're both drinking soda. I think we need the caffeine," she explained.

As I cracked open my own drink, I tiredly nodded my agreement. We sat for a while, quietly sipping the cold, bubbly, caffeinated sweetness in solidarity. Carefully, I pressed the chilled can to each of my temples in turn, attempting to calm the throbbing pain without spilling high fructose corn syrup onto my lap. The unusually loud *buzz* from the fluorescent lights, the *tick tick tick* of the wall clock, and the *fizz* of our sodas all grated on my nerves and jarred my ear drums, which was an ominous sign. *That's all I need tonight, a full-blown migraine.*

"You think we'll see any dragons tonight?" Jess asked. Despite being as tired as I was, if not more, her eyes still lit up at the thought.

"Maybe. Probably. Who knows?" I replied, not answering her question at all.

"Your hair is sticking up so bad, you look like a punk rocker," she observed, grinning over her soda can.

I couldn't resist laughing. "After today, I'm lucky I haven't pulled all of it out. Man, what a day."

"No kidding," Jess agreed. "Well, I'm going to get some dinner before the emergencies start coming in, if I can." She dropped her drink can in the recycle bin, and I winced at the *clank*. "Are you leaving soon?"

I sighed. "No, I don't think I finished a single record today. I'll stay awhile."

"Well, try not to stay too long," Jess admonished as she rose from her chair. "See you, hopefully not until tomorrow."

"Yeah, right," I snorted. "Go eat, and try to get some rest."

My cell phone stayed blessedly silent for over three hours. I spent most of that time plodding through records, struggling to remember case details through my haze of exhaustion. I'd switched off the overhead lights to stop the *bzzzzz* from annoying me as I arduously typed, squinting at my computer screen. The clock sustained its hypnotic *tick, tick, tick, tick.* With my head aching in protest at the effort, I finally folded my arms across the desk and rested my forehead onto them. *Only for a few moments, then I'll finish up.*

Within seconds, I sank into a deep and dreamless sleep.

22

The Sentinel

The phone jabbered, vibrating the desk beneath my folded arms. And vexingly jabbered again, and again. I eventually woke, stiff, painful, and confused. Grabbing for the phone, I fumbled and somehow flung it to the floor three feet away, where it continued to incessantly babble its aggravating ring tone. Swearing, I reached for it and nearly fell. My arms and legs were numb and tingling after sleeping so awkwardly slumped on my desk for… how long? I had no idea, but no daylight shone through the window. Finally, I successfully retrieved the phone and answered the call, still not entirely awake.

Fortunately the caller didn't notice my disorientation, or at least didn't seem to mind. Her Maltese had vomited, just once, and she was worried. We chatted for a minute, and since the dog otherwise sounded fine, I advised the woman to keep an eye on him for the night and call me if he developed other signs of illness.

The call ended and I sat for a few moments, trying to get my bearings. Except for my desk lamp, the office was dark.

The wall clock *ticked, ticked, ticked,* begging my attention, and I finally checked the time. A quarter past ten! I must have slept for over an hour. No wonder my limbs had fallen asleep. Stretching my neck painfully, I touched my face with tingling fingers, feeling the indents in my forehead and cheek from the pressure of my forearm.

What was I doing before I fell asleep? Records, of course. The bane of my existence. Nudging the mouse to wake the computer monitor, I discovered that my elbow had mashed the keyboard during my slumber and typed over a page of gibberish. "Great," I sighed. Taking care not to highlight any vital part of the record in my sleepiness, I deleted the offending string of characters. However, I wasn't careful enough. The entire plan section I'd typed for a patient — I was certain I'd typed it, unless I'd merely dreamt it — disappeared. Unfortunately, the software developers had never seen any reason to add an "undo" function, so my progress was gone. Granted, only a small portion of it, but the loss infuriated me nonetheless.

"Oh, that's just fabulous," I groaned as I sat back in my chair. I'd finished only half of the day's records, but the remainder would have to wait. I was far too sleepy to keep going and too cranky to even try. Violently clicking the mouse, as if that would help, I shut down the computer. In every sense of the word, I was done.

Testing my still-tingling legs and feet as I stood up, I irritably snatched my phone, keys, and bag and headed for the back door. Two-thirds of the way down the darkened hallway, I realized I hadn't taken off my lab coat, nor had I emptied the pockets that annoyingly bumped into my hips with every step. Pausing, I glanced in each pocket to take inventory: three pens (one of which had leaked ink), the controlled drug safe key, one syringe, four capped syringe needles, a stack of gauze squares (thankfully clean), one empty drug vial, and at least two dog toenail clippings. *Ah, the glamorous life of a veterinarian.*

Turning around, I took one step toward the office to hang up my lab coat, then abruptly about-faced, nearly upsetting my balance. "Nope," I told myself as I resumed marching down the hall. All that could go home with me. The lab coat needed washing anyway, and I was loathe to spend one minute longer in the clinic.

With relief, I pulled the door open.

"AAAAHH!" I shrieked. "WHAT THE —" Bashing my shoulder on the crematory as I reeled backward, I fled from the menacing, orange head that hovered immediately through the doorway. The creature stood on the sidewalk just left of the door, his body out of my view, his neck nearly obscured by shadows. Consequently, the seemingly disembodied head with its short, pearly-white horns floated before me like a sinister, spiky orb. He stared at me inquisitively with bright green eyes as I backpedaled in fright. Finally, I halted and stood there panting, heart pounding, as my eyes worked through the visual calisthenics required to recognize the dragon's neck. Since he had one, my panicked brain finally reasoned, the dragon must also have had a body.

Forcing my shoulders away from my earlobes, I sagged in relief and gave myself a few moments to recover. "Holy crap, you scared the hell out of me!" I breathlessly reproached. "You were… you looked… I mean you were just your head! I couldn't see the rest of you at all. You looked like a floating head!"

The dragon continued to stare at me, tilting his not-disembodied head in curiosity. Floppy, tangerine-hued frills draped loosely behind his horns and jowls as he shuffled the rest of his formidably spiked body into view. Brown stripes rippled across his sides, shoulders, and haunches. He brought to mind a regal Bengal tiger, although I had to admit the likeness made him seem terrifyingly predatory. Wincing, I thought of the Amur tiger I'd read about that hunted and ate poachers in Russia.

I sighed. With especially poor timing, the dragon had positioned himself in a bad place when I was in a particularly rotten mood, but he obviously hadn't intended to frighten me. In fact, much to my relief, he remained impressively serene despite my theatrical overreaction. The whole dragon appeared intimidating enough (to the uninitiated, anyway), but something about only seeing his head, or what seemed like only a head, terrified me. Regardless of body or head, he behaved far more docile than his imposing appearance suggested.

"Okay," I told the orange creature. "Just… give me a minute, then I'll come help you." Leaning against the wall that still sported gouges from the popcorn-itis patient, I took several deep breaths to quiet my pounding heart and jangling nerves. The dragon slowly withdrew his spiky head from the doorway, ambled halfway across the parking lot, casually turned three circles, and sat down. He comfortably arranged his limbs, wings, and tail around him, settling onto the gravel much like a dog nestling into a cozy bed for a nap. In spite of my annoyance with him, I grinned. For their ferocious and ruthless reputations, dragons could be delightfully endearing.

Laboriously peeling myself away from the wall, I trudged outside to join the dragon in the parking lot. He watched me attentively as I closed the door and dumped my backpack onto the sidewalk. I held my phone for a moment, debating. *Should I call Jess to help? She ran her butt off today, and she works tomorrow... I'm not going to call her unless I have to.* Rather than drop my phone into one of my overfilled pockets, I propped it on top of the bag and increased the volume so I would be sure to hear any emergency calls. Turning toward the dragon, I stopped short as I saw fresh blood spattered on the concrete. Shiny, red droplets arrayed in a crooked pathway that led directly toward my orange friend. Blood had splashed the parking lot, too, but it was tricky to spot among the gravel.

"All right, big guy, you're bleeding from somewhere," I told him as I walked to his side. "Where are you injured?"

Without rising, the dragon helpfully lifted his left wing, exposing the underside of the vast membrane that stretched between the bones. Multiple scarlet droplets rained down, streaking his forelimb along the way. A laceration gaped from the lightly scaled hide over the main wing bone, the margins irregularly torn. Ominously, something stuck out of the wound. Blood completely coated whatever it was, and it certainly wasn't part of the dragon.

"How did you....?" I frowned. I wished the dragon would speak. As laid back as he was, I hoped he would confess what happened, and especially how something got embedded within the wound. With a sense of dread, I realized he might have been intentionally wounded by... a human? *Could a person have done this?*

But no such luck. The dragon slowly blinked as he held his bleeding appendage aloft. He never said a word as he gazed in turn from me to the lot and alley behind.

"All right, I'll go inside to get—"

With a muffled *thuuup*, the dragon suddenly camouflaged himself, leaving me staring at the fence through him rather than at him. The boards wobbled sideways for a moment, distorted by the transparent creature in front of them, then abruptly returned to normal. He was gone, and I couldn't even tell which way he went. Dazed, I stood silent, my exhausted brain trying to work out what happened. Right at the moment I realized the dragon must have seen someone, I heard the crunch of footsteps on gravel, and I spun around to find a man approaching from the shadows of the alley. He strode up to me before I could even think of how to react.

"What the f— was that... thing?" he demanded as he pocketed something, freeing his hands — *A vape, maybe? Or a weapon?* The hood of his green camo jacket cloaked his face in darkness, and I couldn't read his expression.

"What do you... what thing?" I stammered.

The guy advanced close enough for the light to shine beneath his hood, illuminating his face as it hardened, jutting his scraggly goatee forward as he clenched his jaw. He came uncomfortably near me as I backed toward the safety of the clinic. The powerful smell of cheap vodka filled my nostrils, quickly followed by the unmistakable odor of cannabis. *Huh. I've never thought of it before, but cannabis smells a bit like breath weapon.*

"Where'd it go? That... *thing* you were talking to, lady. What the f— was it?!" he demanded. Coming closer, he stared at me with deranged eyes, the pupils mere pinpoints within eerie, steel-grey irises. *What would make his pupils constrict? Not alcohol or cannabis... maybe meth? Or heroin?!*

Raising my arms defensively, I accelerated my retreat toward the building. "Nothing — I mean, I don't know what you're talking about! Sir, you need to keep your distance—"

"Why, am I scaring you?" the guy mocked in a singsong voice. He glanced over my shoulder to the door that offered me tantalizing safety, its overhead light shining like a beacon. His ghostly eyes shifted to my bag on the sidewalk. My phone rested on top, its screen reflecting the beam overhead, too far away to be of any use. He quickly moved to cut me off from reaching it.

My anger ballooned even larger than my fear. "No, because it's rude. Stay away from me! What do you want, anyway?"

"I seen somethin' big, somethin' I ain't never seen before, and I wanna know what the f— it was. And I don't like liars."

"I think you're seeing things. What are you on, anyw—"

"Ain't that an animal clinic? You must be the animal doctor. You even got a fancy doctor coat."

My white lab coat stood out like a sore thumb in the darkness, I had to admit, and I regretted my choice to wear it home. I furiously thought through my earlier inventory of the pockets. *Is there anything I can use as a weapon?* Sadly, a half-inch-long syringe needle, let alone dog toenails, wouldn't do much damage. *Should I yell?* Knowing how effectively the clinic's neighbors ignored all manner of noise and disturbance from our parking lot, I couldn't count on anyone to help, or even pay the least attention if I shouted.

"Sir, you need to leave right now! I'm going to—"

"You're gonna what? Make me?" he mocked again. "Hey fancy animal doc, I think you're gonna get me some animal drugs. Yeah, you got the good stuff." He lunged to grab my arm, and I smacked his hand away. "Nuh uh uh, you're gonna be a good girl and give—"

Drawing in a deep breath as I dodged my assailant, I

prepared to shout as loud as I could muster. *Surely someone will eventually pay attention and call the police... I hope.* However, I never got around to yelling, because the guy froze mid-lunge, his hand outstretched but its target forgotten, his face caricatured into a mask of shock and terror. His mouth gaped wide open in a crooked "O" for so long that two of his premolars, blackened with cavities, repulsively leered at me like auxiliary eyeballs. His pinpoint pupils remained fixed on something just over my right shoulder. A dark stain bloomed across the front of his grubby jeans. The powerful smell of urine mingled with the cloud of mind-altering substances along with the tangy, metallic scent of blood and the bitter odor of my own panic.

Confused by his abrupt paralysis, I also froze, my shout dying in my throat. Finally, my exhausted synapses fired and told me to run while the guy was distracted. However, before my body caught up to my brain's commands, I realized why he had frozen. I heard it before I saw it: something fiercely snorted directly above my shoulder. The dragon stood over me, transparent except for his head, which steadily brightened to vivid orange as the camouflage faded. If I had thought the dragon seemed intimidating earlier, that was nothing to how he glared with sheer malice, his mouth open in a savage sneer, his plentiful sharp teeth prominently displayed. Benevolence and tranquility evaporated and pure wrath took their place, his rage directed with laser focus on the motionless man in front of me. I stood my ground. Blood dripped down the front of my lab coat, and my heart glowed with gratitude as I realized the dragon held his camouflaged, wounded wing protectively over me.

The guy remained immobile and silent until the dragon

arched his neck and inhaled. *Dude, if I were you, I'd move. Now.* Breaking out of his paralysis, he choked out a terrified squeak and lurched backward, turning to run toward the alley. The dragon expelled a burst of flame across the gravel toward the idiot's heels, and my face warmed as though I'd leaned over an overzealous barbecue grill.

"WHAT THE F—!" the guy yelled, finally finding his voice again. He slipped and skidded across the parking lot, fell in a flailing tangle of arms and legs, clawed at the gravel to propel himself upright, and fled to the alley. The dragon fired another short burst for good measure. "F—IN' LEAVE ME ALONE!" our villain shouted as he reached the alleyway, one pant leg on fire. He paused to extinguish the flames, nearly tumbling over as he spun in chaotic circles while he desperately slapped at his calf. Regaining his balance, he ran, trailing wisps of smoke from his blackened jeans.

Only then, I realized I was hyperventilating. Now I wasn't sure whether to laugh, cry, or break down and curl into a quivering ball of shock. If I hadn't had a patient to treat, I might have chosen the latter. Taking several deep breaths, I extracted myself from underneath the protective cover of the dragon's head and wing and turned to look at him. He stared at the alley, green eyes narrowed in furor, vigilantly watching for the guy to return. The rest of his body gradually faded its camouflage until the whole dragon stood clearly in front of me, his body tensed, wings raised in readiness.

"Thanks," I panted, "for coming to my defense. And for… well… not actually hurting him." *Beyond minor burns and singed leg hairs, anyway.* I wouldn't have wanted to explain to the police how the jerk got badly injured or — *gulp* — died in my parking lot.

Softness gradually crept back into the dragon's face and eyes as he relaxed a little. He had appeared so placid before he transformed into the remarkably fearsome creature that scared off my attacker. I concluded I never, ever wanted to be on his bad side. For that matter, crossing any dragon was undoubtedly a terrible idea, and I did not intend to ever try. I wondered, after I'd reacted so dramatically to what looked like his disembodied head, had he opted to try the same effect on our unhinged visitor? Intended or not, I had to admit the ploy had done the trick.

Collecting my thoughts and trying to steady my shaking hands, I returned to my original task of patching up the dragon's wing. *Where were we? Supplies.* In spite of the reassuring presence of my scaly guardian, I nervously locked the door behind me when I went inside to gather a tray of antiseptic, instruments, suture, and bandaging with shaking hands. Though I'd calmed my nerves considerably by the time I headed back outside, I still jumped at the shadow of an anesthesia machine, then rolled my eyes at my own unease.

Maintaining his watch on the alley, the dragon reluctantly lay down in the parking lot so I could reach the wound. Flushing with saline solution washed much of the blood out of the laceration, but it continued to steadily ooze from around the foreign material, which I identified as wood. After local anesthetic injections, a snack laden with powerful pain pills (for the dragon, not me), and profuse apologies, I yanked the wood out of the depths of the wound, nearly toppling over backward when it finally gave way.

The beam from my headlamp shone over the blood-soaked chunk in my hand. I had feared that it was part of an oversized arrow, a small spear, or some other type of weapon. However, on closer inspection it most resembled a simple, broken tree branch. A dead tree, from the looks of it.

"Did you somehow crash into a tree? Or... fall out of one?" My questions were intended to be rhetorical, merely thoughts I'd voiced out loud. But the dragon turned to look at me, his fierce eyes shifting into something that resembled shame, then he sheepishly lowered his gaze to the ground before returning to his guarded watch toward the alley. "I was just curious. I'm not here to judge. No matter how it happened, we'll get it patched up, don't worry." He didn't seem to be as concerned about his wing as he was about drug-addled intruders. "Besides, no matter what happened with the tree, you've done a great service tonight. I should call you Knight. Not with shining armor though; more like knight in bloody armor."

The branch had torn a rough V-shaped laceration into the wing membrane, and the jaggedly broken wood had shredded numerous blood vessels on its route through the deeper tissues. Swearing under my breath as I struggled with the height and angle of the wound, I ligated vessel after vessel to stop the bleeding. Even with the creature lying down, the dragon's wing stood much taller than my head, and my shoulders ached from the effort of performing surgery at about the height of my chin. I had considered using a step stool, but I'd feared the dragon might have knocked me off my perch if he leapt up to confront anyone. As it was, he kept distractedly lifting his wing, far more focused on his self-imposed guard duty than on me. Over and over, I gently coaxed him to lower his wing, placed a few more sutures as it gradually climbed, then coaxed him to drop it again.

Eventually, although blood still angrily oozed from countless tiny, torn vessels, I gave up trying to ligate them all. I could have tied knots for another hour and stopped the hemorrhage altogether, but I didn't think my arms and shoulders would have held out that long. Suturing the incision closed should have further staunched the bleeding, but to my frustration, blood continued to seep through. I stepped back and pondered the persistent hemorrhage while I awkwardly rubbed my arm over my eyes. Worrisome thoughts about clotting disorders ran through my mind. I'd discovered such conditions more than once in canine patients that bled excessively from wounds, but I had yet to encounter this in dragons. Although more likely, his blood pressure remained elevated in response to our unwelcome visitor, and the bleeding would resolve once his agitation subsided and his blood pressure dropped.

Mumbling further profanity as I raised my aching arms once again, I scrubbed the scales and membrane surrounding the laceration, dried the area, covered it with stacks of gauze, and stuck a huge self-adhesive bandage over the whole thing. The bandage wouldn't last long, but it would provide enough pressure to help stop the bleeding.

"Okay, Knight, let's figure out meds for you to take, then you're all finished." He quickly rose from the gravel and stood facing the alley, clearly still on guard duty. "I don't think that idiot would dare come back," I assured the dragon as I piled instruments, soiled gauze, and bits of suture into the tray. "He's probably home changing his pants."

With a twinge of guilt, I thought about belatedly calling the police. They would question why I hadn't called them right away, which would be awkward to explain, and of course I couldn't tell the truth. Reports about drug-seeking idiots didn't hold much weight coming from a delusional veterinarian seeing fantasy creatures late at night, but perhaps I should have called anyway. On the other hand, considering how thoroughly Knight had frightened the guy, maybe he'd think twice before accosting people ever again. I grinned at the thought.

Ignoring me, the dragon remained standing at his post while I went inside for medications. The anesthesia machine's shadow didn't seem nearly so spooky after my adrenaline had dissipated. Maybe my adrenal glands didn't have any more stress hormones to give. *Pain medications, antibiotics, and... why not?* I added a couple doses of yunnan baiyao, a Chinese herb that helped control bleeding, though what the dragon's laceration primarily needed was pressure and time.

Weary beyond weary, I returned to the orange sentinel. "Keep this clean and dry, please," I instructed as I pointed to the bandage, "and remove it after three suns." As I passed the medications to him, I noticed he held the blood-soaked broken branch in one claw. It had dried to an ugly, dark, crusty thing that was barely identifiable as wood. *Why on earth does he want to keep it? Is that... a souvenir? How strange!* I shook my head. All these years of treating dragons and they still amazed me. So much remained an enigma, and I had a great deal yet to learn.

But not right away. It was time for me to go home and try to recover from my miserable day... well, night, also. Fervently, I hoped that I wouldn't be needed for a single emergency for the rest of the night. I wasn't sure I could tolerate much more, but if an emergency happened, I would have to find a way.

"You're free to go," I told the dragon, who showed no signs of departing. He glimpsed at me, then returned to scrutinizing the alley and the perimeters of the parking lot. After half a minute, he settled onto the gravel in a wary crouch and refused to leave. "Thanks, but you don't need to stand guard for me. I'm leaving." Another brief glance, then back to his surveillance. "Well, okay then. I'm going home. Please don't… I don't know… set anyone or anything on fire?" The dragon ignored me entirely, and I shrugged. *Another surprise.* My unconventional patients had always promptly flown away, and I'd never met a dragon who had felt compelled to stay. *But then, I've never been assaulted in the parking lot before. I'm lucky Knight was here when it happened.*

After quickly locking the clinic and gathering my things – this time, I wadded my blood-stained "fancy doctor coat" into my bag – I got into my car. A hint of skunk odor wafted from the upholstery, and I shook my head. My little Volkswagen was far from new and sported many dents and scratches, though the engine ran just fine. However, it still smelled like breath weapon, and I'd long resigned myself to the fact that it always would.

Bleary-eyed and focusing hard to keep from falling asleep, I drove home and stole into the house as quietly as I could. Too tired to change out of my stained and hairy scrubs or even brush my teeth, I collapsed onto the couch. Sleep took over in an instant, but this time I dreamt vividly of dragons, monsters with eerie, pinpoint eyes, blood, fear, fire, and gratitude.

23

The Promised Land

The engine complained as my old Volkswagen pushed through tall grass and a bit of brush, bumped over rocks and gopher mounds, and came to rest in a small clearing. GPS assured me I was in the right place. I turned off the ignition.

Getting out of the car, I turned in a slow circle to scan my surroundings, a broad canyon bisected by a gravel road. A creek paralleled the south side of the road, bursting with maples, birches, aspens, willows, dogwoods, firs, and countless other trees along the banks, all dewy and dripping from the previous night's rain. Chokecherry and service berry bushes, sagebrush, grasses, and shrubs covered the slopes of the ridges, the sage growing thicker toward the hill tops. Water rushed and rippled in the creek. Clouds shaded the canyon as far as I could see. Even with the heavy cloud cover, a multitude of birds called and sang from the trees, at least four or five different kinds that I could hear.

Wow. Just wow. "NO SERVICE," my phone proclaimed. *Even better.* I tossed it onto the passenger seat, shut the door, and headed straight for the creek, inexorably drawn by the rushing water. The stream was swollen from the influx of rain. A little fish — *Cutthroat trout, maybe?* — swished quickly away from the bank, and a chorus frog hopped under the refuge of a willow leaf. Now I was absolutely enchanted.

If only I could convince the landowner to sell this acreage to me. Jon and I had been talking about buying land for years. We wanted to build a modest house away from the mild but incessant clamor of our small city, and this was absolutely perfect. For so long, buying land seemed an impossible dream. But maybe, just maybe, that dream was close to reality.

The owner was a friend, an older veterinarian nearing retirement who owned a practice in the next city up the highway. He'd called to ask if I wanted to buy his practice. I didn't.

"No, Carl, thanks, but I've got enough on my hands with one clinic, especially since we're going to start construction on the new building soon. You don't happen to have a mobile x-ray machine you'd sell me, do you?"

"What do you need that for?" he'd exclaimed. "Don't you have a fancy, new digital system?"

"Yes, but I want something for backup." *For dragons.*

"Nope, sorry, mine is a stationary one. It's probably older than you are." From what I had seen of Carl's clinic, I believed him.

Then Carl mentioned offhand that he owned land he might want to sell, too. THAT got my interest, and I'd peppered him with questions, growing more and more excited as he described his property. So there I was, on this cloudy but hot June day, exploring the canyon. Jon and our daughter were out of town visiting his family (grinning, I remembered our stressful visit there with the hatchling in the plastic bin), and they had no idea I was there. No need to get their hopes up until I was confident the land met our wants and needs.

Jon would be ecstatic about the creek and wildlife, I was certain. Ember was ambivalent about moving away from the home she had always known, but the fish and frogs would easily win her over. I'd been there less than ten minutes and already knew I loved it. I had hours to spare, and now that I'd met this land, I was determined to spend every possible moment exploring it.

Hiking wasn't my original plan, but fortunately, I had taken a small day pack and a water bottle, and I set off with those. My intent was to cross the creek and climb the ridge to take in the view from above. From the canyon bottom, I couldn't see anywhere near the boundaries of the property. I wanted to look around from higher up, to "get my bearings," as it were, so I could describe everything to Jon in detail. *I'm sure he will have lots of questions.*

Finding a place to cross the water without soaking my feet, however, proved challenging. No matter, the riparian area along the creek was fascinating, and I continued on and on along the stream, pushing through the jungle of branches, brush, and wild clematis vines, drawn deeper and deeper into its secrets. I had worked so hard for so long that I'd rarely found the time to backpack or even hike in years. I relished the rare and wonderful opportunity to explore this rugged patch of nature.

Each time I pushed through the vegetation into an open area along the water, I discovered a whole new story as though it were depicted in a shadow box. Within minutes I came across a doe and fawn, chins still wet from their drink in the creek, the fawn spindly-legged and adorable. I froze, they froze, and we stared at each other until the doe sensibly and urgently led her baby away from me into an aspen grove.

Continuing on, I entered the next shadow box, then the next, like stumbling onstage into the middle of a play in first one theater, then another. Sometimes the play was languid, in intermission perhaps, featuring butterflies, mosquitoes, and stately globe mallow blooms offering their finest imitation of hollyhocks. Sometimes the play was more interesting, starring fish, frogs, and scampering rodents.

Farther up the creek, I emerged into a broad, dark clearing beneath firs and junipers, the thick canopy of branches shading everything beneath into muted sepia-tones. Four steps in, as I squinted in the half-light, a dozen velociraptors exploded in frantic flight into the branches. Let me correct that. Wild turkeys, actually, but close enough to dinosaurs. I felt as though someone had chucked feathered bowling balls past my head. Once my panic somewhat subsided, I realized I'd crashed into some kind of plant with burrs. At least my rapid heart rate subsided during the three or four minutes I needed to pull all the cursed, prickly spheres from my clothes.

In my head, I was already naming these unique spots along the creek. The small, pretty clearing gently canopied with birches and maples, where a flat spot invited a yoga mat and two tree trunks begged for a hammock, I dubbed The Cathedral. Standing there for several minutes, I'd imagined how it might look on a sunny day, the light filtered into shifting dapples on the grass.

The wide spot in the creek where the water pooled in a languorous shallow spot, where I spied three chorus frogs, was the Frog Pond. This expansive, yet closed-in and darkened grove, with its low-hanging branches and exploding wild turkeys, would be known as Spooky Hollow, and the—

WHAT HAVE I DONE? Freezing in place, chest hammering far worse than it had from the turkeys, I quickly looked behind me, up, to the sides, panning through the branches, frantically searching for a dragon, as the unmistakable smell of a breath weapon assaulted my nostrils. I hadn't been directly hit, but I must have done something to spook the creature. It had to have been somewhere, but the grove was so dark. *WHERE is it? And what could I have possibly done to provoke one? Will fire come next?*

Oh. My panic deflated into embarrassed relief as I spotted the black and white tail of a skunk scuttling into the bushes thirty feet away. Apparently, after all my experiences with dragons, I found them everywhere, whether or not they were actually there. The skunk hadn't even seriously sprayed; he'd only spritzed a little warning.

Rattled but still captivated, I continued with more caution along the creek, in no hurry to find a crossing. The brush and branches tore at my clothes and pack, and criss-crossed my arms with scratches as I pushed through the overgrown flora.

Pausing for a water break, I swiped my arm over my face, pushing damp strands of hair off my forehead. My sweating skin felt gritty after slogging through the bushes and trees, and my clothes were damp and sticky from the sultry air along the creek. But then, our normally arid region had been strangely muggy and hot lately. I was accustomed to the heat. But having lived for years in a dry climate, the humidity felt very peculiar to me.

Snorting, I remembered the laughable refrain about Arizona. "But it's a dry heat!" Which was true, until monsoon season came along, then insufferable damp settled in for months. And that's what Idaho had felt like for weeks. At least the cloud cover helped keep the temperature down, but by that point, I was so soggy I might as well have waded through the creek, except I didn't feel like climbing the ridge with sloshing boots.

Multiple fish, frogs, small waterfalls, rabbits, two pheasants, and ten wild turkeys later, plus one startled raccoon (but thankfully, no more skunks), I had lost track of how far I'd gone. The canopy overhead disoriented my senses, though I knew which direction I faced thanks to the creek that flowed more-or-less straight west. Eventually, I found a fir log fallen across the stream and crossed to the other side, squeezing through the unyielding branches of a toppled juniper.

Emerging from the trees, I scrutinized the terrain to reorient myself. The clouds remained low and heavy. I couldn't see where I'd parked, but based on the contour of the ridges, I must have traveled about half a mile. That didn't seem like much, but scrambling through heavy undergrowth was tedious and slow. I'd already had quite the journey, and I wasn't yet anywhere near my goal of climbing the ridge.

I inhaled deeply. Breathing was easier away from stifling mugginess of the jungle by the creek. Thanks to the clouds, the air felt slightly cooler in the open. Though the temperature felt like it had climbed a few degrees since I'd left my car. Of course, the humidity made it seem even warmer, and I wiped the sweat off my forehead.

After traversing a short distance through a grassy meadow studded with chokecherry bushes and elderberry trees, I discovered a game trail. Two sets of fresh deer tracks were imprinted into the firm black mud, one set delightfully tiny. *This must be where the doe and fawn came down the ridge for a drink.* The trail led more or less toward the ridge top, at a reasonably navigable angle from what I could see.

Best for me to climb the slope before my water runs out. I reached for my water bottle… but it was gone. Shrugging out of the straps and unzipping the pack, I searched the interior, hoping I'd absently put the bottle inside the main compartment. I hadn't. My water had disappeared. It must have been torn from its pocket on the outside of my pack as I pushed through the brush and branches.

Backtracking toward the creek, I searched for the yellow bottle, but it was nowhere to be found. I thought back to the last spot I'd drank from it. The bottle could have been anywhere along a quarter-mile section of the creek, most likely tangled in branches and difficult to spot. I swore, contemplating the creek water. Even if I had a spare bottle (I didn't), I was loathe to drink from the stream. I'd treated countless dogs for *Giardia* after they'd drank from similar water sources, and I didn't have time to be sick for weeks.

Years later, I would find that bright yellow bottle wedged between rocks and half-buried in mud along the water bank. It would invoke vivid and disquieting memories of this day.

Pausing to assess the sky and the distance to the ridge top, I debated the conditions. Thanks to the clouds, it was warm but not miserably hot. I felt hydrated for the time being. But then I had no water. Hiking straight back to my car would have been the most sensible thing to do.

Gazing up the slope, I admitted I wasn't in the mood to be sensible. The land already held me captive. And I badly wanted to see it from high upon the hill. I wanted to dream, plan, and figure out how we could make this our own. I wasn't ready to leave.

My years of hiking and backpacking had taught me how to calculate risks, but they hadn't quashed my stubbornness. I checked the time, checked the sky once more, estimated how long I would need to climb and descend the ridge, and made my decision. *Surely, I can make it.* I would be thirsty when I was done, but a convenience store sat literally minutes down the road, no doubt offering every imaginable variety of beverages. *I'll be okay.*

Snapping a dead branch from a scraggly elderberry tree to use as a walking pole, I set off up the game trail. The going was reasonably easy for some time. But hiking became more difficult when the trail meandered into steeper terrain farther up the ridge, and my balance was not nearly as refined as that of the deer. The elderberry pole became more and more vital as I went.

My first serious miscalculation was the elevation of the ridge. In the clarity of the rain-cleansed sky under the low clouds, the top seemed much closer than it actually was. As I scrambled up the steep, narrow trail, reaching false summit after false summit, I finally admitted I wouldn't make all the way. *Not today, at least.* I was already thirsty and nowhere near the crest of the ridge. An outcropping of cream-colored boulders sat about 200 feet to the west, perched on the hillside like an abstract gargoyle, nearly level with where I stood. Abandoning the deer trail, I headed for the boulders, winding a circuitous path through mounds of sagebrush until I eventually reached the rocks.

Panting, I climbed the boulders hand-over-hand to reach a flat spot where I gratefully sat, then took in the view. My thirst quickly forgotten, I gazed far up and down the canyon, to the opposite ridge, and the mountains beyond. The clouds were higher and not quite as heavy as they had been earlier, the light a bit brighter. My Volkswagen looked like a toy far below, abandoned near the road by a careless child, waiting to be rediscovered. The roof of a barn peeked through the trees toward the west end of the canyon, barely visible in the distance. In the other direction, I spied solar panels mounted next to the road. But I couldn't see a single house from where I rested. Long lines of game trails crossed the opposite ridge, and three deer ambled along one of them, barely visible to me. Though I had climbed too high to hear the running water, I could clearly hear a hawk screeching from a stand of firs near the creek. *Too bad I didn't bring binoculars.*

Despite my failure to reach the top, I could see well enough to make out what I thought were some of the property lines. Vague hints of old fences crowned the hilltop to the north, and I spotted a few fence posts along an interrupted line to the west. Based on what Carl had told me, the property line to the south was well behind me, on the back side of the ridge. Some kind of fence presumably sat to the east, somewhere this side of the neighbors' solar panels, but I couldn't see it. I was too far away. At the thought, I felt small, insignificant, and overwhelmed, sitting there on my small perch on the vast acreage. Dreaming of owning land was one thing. Could we truly manage to buy this huge property, build a house there, and properly take care of everything? *We honestly have no business owning this much land.* Not to mention, we undoubtedly couldn't afford it, despite the fact that land in Idaho was shockingly cheap. Nevertheless, I was thoroughly infatuated with it.

In spite of my doubts and misgivings, I commenced scheming. For the time being, my colleague wasn't decided on selling the property, debating whether to bequeath it to his three children or sell it and pass on the money to them. If he decided to sell it, the timing was awful for us. Despite some help from Darrell's Kaiser Dragon Fund, the mortgage and construction loans for the new clinic were straining our finances as far as they'd go, and we hadn't even started building yet. But with some time, perhaps we could afford to buy Carl's acreage, or at least a portion of it. *Maybe I can convince him to subdivide.* If he were to split up the acreage into smaller, more manageable parcels, we could buy one of those in a few years. That made the most sense to me.

If I could talk Carl into subdividing, I wanted this part, exactly where I sat. I could imagine a small house just down the hill, solar panels atop the roof. A wind generator above me, harvesting the currents that swept across the hilltop. *A bridge there, or maybe there. A small shop. Chickens, a garden, and goats! We would have plenty of room for goats. Ember could have a horse.* I began to piece together an aerial map of sorts in my head, imagining where I would put a small barn, a corral, a chicken coop, a greenhouse....

As I sat there dreaming, absently rubbing the bits of plant material and grit from my pants, my fingers happened upon a hamster-sized flap torn over the side pocket. Alarmed that I might have lost more than my water bottle, I promptly took inventory. No, the pocket itself was intact, my car key and lip balm nested safely inside. Losing my key as well as my water would have been catastrophic. If that had happened, I would have been forced to risk catching *Giardia* from the creek.

Briefly, I felt a moment of panic over the absence of my phone, quickly followed by a pang of guilt for my reliance on it. Then I remembered the device was waiting for me in my car. I regretted not carrying it along. There might have been cell reception that far up the ridge, and I could have checked in with Jon and Ember. I was dying to tell them about the property. Plus, I'd seen a multitude of things I would have loved to have photographed.

Relieved to have lost no more than my water, I returned to observing the canyon, looking for the hawk that I could still hear but hadn't yet spotted. Noticing shifting shadows across the sage, I turned my attention skyward. The clouds were moving, fast.

The air where I sat was completely still. But the thick blanket of clouds steadily moved toward the northeast at a dizzying pace, driven by winds high in the sky. And like a fluffy, grey comforter pulled off a bed, the clouds swiftly rolled away, their shadows keeping pace below them, and bright sunshine abruptly illuminated the canyon.

The effect was exhilarating, thanks to the privilege of seeing the grandeur of the canyon in bright light for the first time. However, with the sudden influx of sun and heat in the abnormal humidity, the air pressure climbed multiple points within seconds, pressing on my eardrums as though I were in a descending airplane. Now I wasn't only warm and thirsty, but miserably hot and parched. A weak breeze reached the ground, briefly swaying the trees and brush, not strong enough to offer any meaningful relief.

The first hints of a painful drumbeat thrummed at the base of my skull. Groaning in fierce regret and genuine alarm, I recognized the predicament into which my stubbornness had led me. Now I was exposed in hot, full sun with no water, high on the ridge, with a headache that would surely worsen in the heat. My family had no idea where I was, and I was alone. Carl knew I would be there, but he didn't know when, nor would he have thought to check in if I didn't call. My failure to notify anyone of my whereabouts and plans was a blatantly rookie mistake. Of all the stupid situations in which to put myself, this was thoroughly asinine.

Counting on the clouds to stay put was my second serious miscalculation. I should have been prepared for any weather. While I'd anticipated the possibility of thunderstorms and sensibly stashed a rain jacket in my pack, I hadn't considered the opposite scenario. I didn't even have a sun hat.

Climbing the ridge without water, my last, monumental miscalculation, was an idiotic decision even if I'd had the continued protection of the clouds. I'd allowed my judgment to be clouded by the allure of the land, the intoxicating possibility that it might be ours one day, and my fervent desire to explore it.

So, there I sat, already dehydrated, risking heatstroke, with a fledgling migraine to boot. My obstinacy might prove to… what this time? Would I end up with a harrowing story, a precautionary tale for others? *Or will I succumb to my own idiotic bullheadedness?*

I had to get down from there, back to hydration and shelter. Immediately.

The game trail I'd commandeered for my ascent would have taken me back to the deer tracks a half mile east from my car, approximately doubling the distance I needed to cover. *Too far.* Bushwhacking through the sage and bushes directly down the hill would be the shortest route, and with luck I would happen upon another game trail.

Armed with the elderberry pole, my sunglasses shielding my throbbing eyeballs from the unforgiving sun as best they could, I set out directly down the slope, hiking as swiftly as I could, squeezing a crooked pathway through sagebrush. Without the benefit of a trail, the descent was hard going, and more than once I had to double back to find a passable route through the heavy brush.

As I descended, relying heavily on the pole to keep my balance on the steep terrain, the sagebrush thinned out and gave way to chokecherries and service berry bushes. Pretty, diminutive shrubs densely crowded the ground between them. These seemingly innocuous plants promptly became my worst nemesis.

Let me introduce you to snowberry bushes. These fibrous, low shrubs with their petite leaves display clusters of pink and purple bell-shaped flowers during the spring that turn into waxy, white berries by late summer. The dainty blooms starkly contrast with the murderous tangle of branches and roots below. Snowberry spreads by firmly rooting itself into the soil every foot or so, seemingly all the way into the earth's mantle, resulting in a chaotic warren of trip hazards. Snowberry is pleasant to look at, but hellish to hike through.

Once I reached the stands of verdant berry bushes, the snowberry quickly and unmercifully initiated me to its murderous trap. Mere feet into the thicket, I stumbled and nearly fell, my boot snarled on a root sucker. I couldn't move my feet through the tangle at all; I could only step over the shrubs, burying my boots into the maze with each cumbersome step, then laboriously yank them out for the next step. And snowberry was everywhere. Looking to the east and west, my heart sank as I saw the cursed shrubs extending along the slope as far as I could see. The game trail I'd ascended was now 350, maybe 400 feet to the east. Truly miserable from the heat and the pounding headache, which steadily worsened with exertion and thirst, I cursed as the root suckers repeatedly ensnared my feet, untied my boot laces, and attempted to trip me. I stopped to double-tie my laces, then forged on, grasping chokecherry branches in addition to the elderberry pole for balance as I fought through the quagmire.

Open meadows lay tantalizingly below, and I only had to get through the miserable shrubbery to reach them. However, between the precipitous terrain and the labyrinthine tangle of plants, not to mention my aching head, I made pathetically slow progress. I hadn't found a single game trail in this mess. Apparently, the deer knew better than I, and were clever enough to route around it.

Finally, I reached a small clearing. A cottontail rabbit scampered into the brush as I crashed through the shrubs toward the tall grass. I still had a fair distance to cover, and plenty more snowberry to fight through, but the clearing offered a welcome brief respite.

Or it would have been a respite had I not tripped on a root sucker, falling headlong into the grass. I wasn't hurt, per se, but I hit my head firmly on the ground, and my pounding skull didn't appreciate the impact at all. As I lay there, allowing myself a few moments to recover, I felt the first vestiges of nausea. Whether I had heatstroke or a full-blown migraine, I didn't know, but I was in trouble. I couldn't stay there.

Forcing myself up, I battled through the next array of snowberry, growing progressively weaker as the headache and nausea began to claim victory. Right as I reached the next small expanse of grass, still too far from the creek, a wave of nausea washed over me, rapidly followed by dizziness. I staggered forward a few steps, then sank to the ground, face pushed into the meager shade provided by the grass. If this was a migraine, it was the worst I'd ever had. The meadow swirled sickeningly beneath me as I clung to the ground.

Just a few minutes. Then I'll get up. Just a few.... I had to keep moving. The dizziness would surely abate soon.

A cedar waxwing squawked from a nearby chokecherry bush, and I winced as the raucous call pierced my eardrums. "*Up,*" the bird cried. "*Get up!*" This untamed land would never belong to me. *I've become its property.*

My senses contracted until pain, nausea, and relentless, cruel heat were the only things I knew. Within minutes, or possibly eons, merely the pain remained. Then nothing at all.

24

The Guardian

Something gigantic loomed over me, blotting out the sun. My tongue felt sticky and thick. My head hammered a painful rapid staccato, and my eyes refused to open, boycotting my consciousness. But I insisted, laboriously forcing my eyelids open into narrow slits to see what blocked the light.

The gigantic something was a dragon, or rather the massive head of a dragon, an ancient wyrm, unlike any I had ever seen. He stood directly over me, staring at my face. I struggled to focus on his broad head with its flattened forehead, crowded with bumps, spikes, and whorls of rough, tan scales, with a more orderly array of menacing horns in row after row that coursed somewhere beyond my vision. The scales over his face were wholly unique, amorphous, sand-colored plates with irregular margins, like the cracked bark of an ancient tree, or a mud flat baked and cracked in the desert.

The wyrm's gigantic eyes gazed into mine, each of his globes larger than my fist, the irises the exact same sandy hue as his scales. His irises were tattered and lacy, abstract renderings of ancient doilies, belying the creature's incredibly advanced age. I couldn't fathom how old he must have been.

To be fair, I couldn't fathom anything without tremendous and painful effort. Beyond the dragon's massive head, his body was a vague blur to me. *Africa. You should be in Africa.* He would have fit in well there, among the parched mud flats between the grasses of the savanna, dotted with acacia trees beneath unrelenting sun.

I had passed out lying face down, but now I looked upward at the wyrm's lacy eyes through the smudged lenses of my sunglasses. Tall grasses gently waved along the margins of my vision, framing his face. My brain refused to wonder how I'd turned over. Refused to wonder why the dragon stood over me. Refused to stay awake.

Closing my eyes, I returned to nothingness.

* * *

A ceaseless rushing noise slowly but persistently needled me back to dim awareness. I lay in a snow cave, cocooned in my sleeping bag but still chilled, moving my limbs to warm them. Except that I wasn't actually moving, nothing would move. *I have no limbs.* The rushing sound wouldn't stop, and I was irritated by the noise and my inability to move. But snow caves were supposed to be quiet; I shouldn't have heard anything but the sound of my own breath, and I couldn't hear that at all. *Maybe I'm not breathing. Am I dead?*

The snow suddenly faded, promptly replaced by the thin, nylon walls of my tiny backpacking tent. I'd camped too close to a river, and the sound of the running water annoyed me. *It was a good idea, wasn't it, to camp right by the river?* The flowing water seemed so peaceful. But the noise was relentless. I'd awoken on top of my sleeping bag late on a summer's night. I was cold, so cold, and sodden from dew. My tent was colder than the snow cave, and I needed the warmth of my sleeping bag. All I had to do was move, pull the nylon-covered baffles of down over top, and nestle into their refuge. *Move. Get into the sleeping bag. Move! Why can't I move?*

The perpetual sound of rushing water — *It is water, isn't it?* — steadily grew in volume, rippling and flowing and refusing to yield. Now I drifted in the water, floating in the current toward a waterfall. The waterfall had to be close, that's why the water was getting louder, and I would go over the falls and die. *Move, swim! Get out of the sleeping bag, out of the snow cave. Now!*

My head abruptly snapped up, and my disjointed thoughts swam to the surface of consciousness as water trickled from my ears. Water was everywhere, but there was no waterfall. *I'm not moving. I am not going to die.*

As I shifted painfully on the rocks and sat up, dragging my heavy, waterlogged pack with me, I took in my surroundings with the confusion of a toddler waking up in an unfamiliar bed. Dots of water on my sunglasses distorted my vision, and I pulled them from my face with numb, muddy fingers. Water dripped from my chin and hair into the creek, which still flowed over my legs, the torn fabric of my pants flapping in the current.

Lush, green plants that resembled miniature lilies lined the bank to my left with tiny, white, star-shaped blooms reaching toward the sky from their spindly tops. An iridescent blue dragonfly rested on a nightshade leaf, the vine yielding gently to the insect's weight. *Why is it always dragons?* Staring at the dragonfly as the leaf slowly wobbled, blinking away the water that beaded on my eyelashes, I fought through my disorientation. The canyon, the creek, the ridge, the clouds, the sun, the cursed snowberry shrubs, all came flooding back. I'd fallen and passed out in the tall grass, baking in the unforgiving heat. *The wyrm. Was that real?* Had I conjured him, just as I had the breath weapon that turned out to be skunk spray? The creature looked so odd. He couldn't be real. *But the dragon has to be real. Otherwise, how did I get to the creek?*

My head throbbed, although not with the intensity it had previously, and the base of my skull felt tight and painful, chilled from the cold water. My head had been under water. *How did I not drown?* Wobbly and slow, I twisted to examine the water behind me, exploring the creek bed with one hand. A marmot-sized rock had been my pillow, with only part of my face exposed above the water. My sodden pack, still strapped over my shoulders, had helped to elevate me from the creek bed as well.

Gripping the rocks and branches for balance, taking care to avoid the toxic nightshade vines, I stumbled and sloshed unsteadily upright, then clambered hand-over-hand up the tall bank, slipping in the mud. I'd been immersed in a portion of the creek that flowed through a deep channel, and the climb to the top was steep. Flopping myself onto the grass above, drizzling rivulets of water onto the ground, I looked around for any sign of the wyrm, or anyone, anything. Trees lazily swayed in the breeze that finally relieved some of the incessant heat. Songbirds called out while they flitted across the meadow. That was all.

While I squirmed out of my soaked backpack straps, I thought to look for tracks. My own awkward imprints in the mud of the creek bank were the only obvious marks I saw. I crawled to a depression in the grass, the tall blades bent and mashed into the thick thatch of dead growth below. The imprint was huge. *The wyrm's footprint, perhaps?* Squinting across the meadow, I could discern other similar impressions in the grass. *Maybe. Then again, maybe not.* The entire canyon was so overgrown, the tangle of grasses and brush undulating in the stiff breeze, I couldn't detect any definitive trace of the gigantic creature.

Without doubt, no human had helped me to the creek. Had I reached the water on my own without remembering? No, I would have seen my own tracks sliding down the bank, not just the ones from where I'd climbed out of it. Amazing as it seemed, the wyrm must have carried me from where I'd passed out — I thought I could make that out, a trampled area in the grass about fifty feet away — and dunked the silly, overheated human into the cool water of the creek.

Exhausted, weak, muddy, dripping, and chilled despite the heat, I sat there for ages, reflecting. My own stupidity, with hefty doses of luck and coincidence, had led to my first encounter with a dragon. If I hadn't stubbornly kept climbing and made myself so ill, I wouldn't have discovered her, and I never would have known these amazing creatures existed. I'd helped her, and the dragons had chosen to continue seeking my help. *I've saved a number of their lives over the years. Now we've come full circle.* Already, I owed my gratitude to the striped orange dragon that came to my defense at the clinic. But scaring off a criminal when the dragon was already there was one thing. Appearing out of nowhere to rescue me from heatstroke was different. Once again, I'd endangered my life with a misadventure of my own making. But this time, I hadn't come to the aid of a dragon; instead, a dragon assisted me. *And most likely, he saved my life.*

Small clouds scudded across the sky, chasing the thick blanket of clouds that earlier abandoned me to the sun. Now they shaded the mountains far in the distance. I saw no sign of the dragon. The hawk screeched again, this time very close to me, and craning my aching neck, I spied her perched near the top of a fir tree. She eyed me suspiciously.

"Thank you," I whispered, my throat sore and raspy. *I should have drank from the creek while I was down there,* Giardia *be damned.* "Thank you," I repeated louder, to the wyrm if he could hear me, and to nothing and everything in the canyon, for dazzling me, then humbling me, then rescuing me.

It's time to go home. Pushing myself upright and weakly slinging my pack over one shoulder, I took a few shaky steps, my feet squishing and squelching in my boots, the pack dribbling water down my hip. My head throbbed, and my sodden clothes clung to me uncomfortably. Regaining my sense of balance as I focused on putting one sloshing boot in front of the other, I headed back toward my car, toward home. Toward Jon and Ember, and the clinic, Dr. Beth, Jess, and all the staff, clients, and patients I loved.

And the dragons, of course. *Always the dragons.* Admittedly, they consumed enormous amounts of time, money, and patience. More than once, they had aggravated me to tears, and sometimes they'd generated downright mayhem. Dragons had infuriated, delighted, and devastated me. They'd brought me immeasurable joy and crushing heartache. By pushing me, challenging me to my limits and beyond, the creatures had gifted me with a wealth of knowledge unlike any other. In my wildest dreams, I'd never imagined I would learn dragon medicine. I had never meant to become the Dragon Doc. But there I was, rewarded with an extraordinary career rife with adventure and mystique. And now, I'd been rewarded with the ultimate gift of my salvation. The enigmatic but endlessly colorful, beautiful creatures had become the magnificent jewels that crowned my complicated, chaotic, fantastic world.

I couldn't envision life without them.

***

TO BE CONTINUED

Acknowledgments

To *The Dragon Doc Tales* editing, web design, graphic design, and illustration team, Stacey, Sofia, Elena, Nick, GetCovers team, and Mar: you are all so creative, talented, and a joy to work with. Thank you for your skills, hard work, and encouragement.

To my family, Joshua, Mar, and Marilynn, who are my biggest fans and most ardent supporters: thank you for tolerating my frenzied writing jags and endless pleas for opinions and ideas.

To my friends, Lucia, NJ, Dina, Mark, Angel, Greg, and Theresa, thanks for always being there with support, kindness, bad puns, and terrible jokes.

Nikki, Danielle, Carol, and Tara, many thanks for your feedback and suggestions.

To my colleagues and coworkers in veterinary medicine, including the Alta Team and the Moms with DVMs group, you are all amazing. Never forget it. Thank you for your feedback and cheerleading.

Especially to Mar: I love you so much, and I'm so very proud of you. Thank you for being you.

About the Illustrator

J. "Marcel" Burkman is the teenage artist for *The Dragon Doc Tales* series. At about the age of ten, Mar started working hard toward improving his artistic abilities. "I hate it when people compliment my work, saying, 'Oh, what natural talent.' Incorrect. It's nothing but hard work." (Although Mom swears Mar has always been incredibly talented AND hard-working.) Illustrating for his mom's book, brainstorming ideas, and comparing and combining perspectives, was a wonderful bonding experience for them both.

More of Marcel's work may be found on Instagram (re-fined_lobotomy).

About the Author

On a summer day long ago, Dr. S. K. Burkman climbed a mountain, got sick, and hallucinated a dragon. Thus began a lifelong fascination with dragons, and many exhaustion-fueled musings on what they might be like as patients.

Originally from Colorado and British Columbia, Dr. Burkman earned her doctorate in veterinary medicine at Colorado State University. As a busy veterinarian, Dr. Burkman keeps her sanity by writing about dragons. Many of her own adventures and misadventures are woven into her novels.

Outside of work and writing, she enjoys hiking, backpacking, travel, cake baking and decorating, tile setting, power tools, and looking for dragons. She has been married to Joshua for over twenty years, and they have one child. Dr. Burkman and her family reside in Idaho with their motley assortment of pets, and maybe, just maybe, a dragon or two.

Connect with me on:

Facebook, Instagram, or X/Twitter: @iamthedragondoc
Amazon Author Page or Goodreads: Dr. S. K. Burkman

Subscribe to my newsletter:

✉ https://thedragondoc.com

Also by Dr. S. K. Burkman

Now that you are acquainted with The Dragon Doc's introduction to her rather unusual patients in *Wings and Wounds*, read about Doc's next misadventure in *Squeaky Hatchling*, a novelette. Released in 2022, *Squeaky Hatchling* is the immediate sequel to *Wings and Wounds*. Subscribers to The Dragon Doc newsletter may download *Squeaky Hatchling* for free. Additional sequels are to follow, as well as *Common Disorders of Dragons*, a veterinary textbook on dragon medicine.

"Do dragons squeak? They're not supposed to... time to call The Dragon Doc! Read this adorable tale and prepare to laugh yourself silly. Dr. S. K. Burkman has a way with words and wyrms."
— N. J. Gallegos, Author of *The Broken Heart*

"A cute story that made me want to read more about this awesome veterinarian who helps dragons. I love the family feel to the story, the scientific spin, and the portrayal of dragons as intelligent and considerate creatures rather than rampaging brutes." — A. R. Grimes, Author of *The Wyldling Dream* series

Squeaky Hatchling: The Dragon Doc Tales Novelette
https://thedragondoc.com/all_books/squeaky-hatchling
A protective mother dragon, a sick hatchling, and a noisy medical mystery. Just another day at the clinic for the Dragon Doc.

Veterinarian Jordyn Blackstone doesn't just treat your average pets — her patients come with scales, wings, and a habit of scorching her eyebrows. But when a distressed hatchling arrives squeaking like a creaky door, Doc knows she's in for a special kind of headache.

Doc has never encountered a dragon malady like this before, but whatever it is, it can't be good. With the baby's life on the line and his overbearing mother lurking in the shadows, Doc has to unravel the mystery quickly — before things get too heated. Literally.

To make matters worse, Doc's eight-year-old daughter, Ember, insists on helping with a risky procedure. Now, Doc's got a sick hatchling to heal, a grumpy dragon mom to appease, and a pint-sized assistant with a knack for complicating things.

But hey, what's a little danger when you're a doctor for dragons?

www.ingramcontent.com/pod-product-compliance
Lightning Source LLC
Chambersburg PA
CBHW010741310726
48971CB00010B/2894